CATWAD

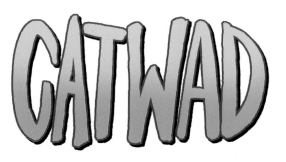

IT'S ME.

Library of Congress Control Number available

ISBN 978-1-338-32602-4 (Trade)
ISBN 978-1-338-50778-2 (Fairs)

10 9 8 7 6 5 4 3   19 20 21 22 23

Printed in China   38

First edition, April 2019

Edited by Michael Petranek
Book design by Suzanne LaGasa

IT'S ME.

JIM BENTON

AN IMPRINT OF
SCHOLASTIC

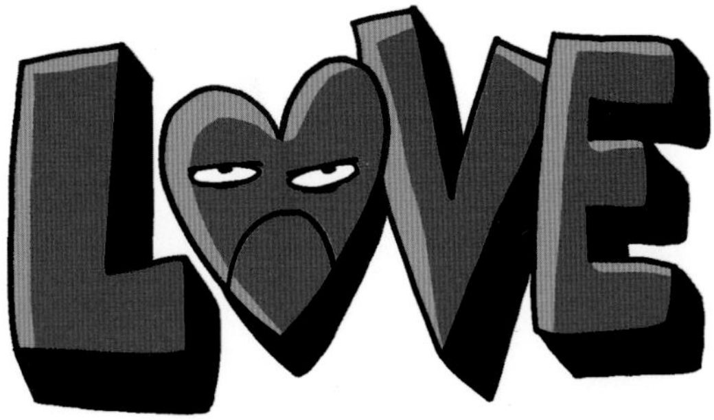
LOVE

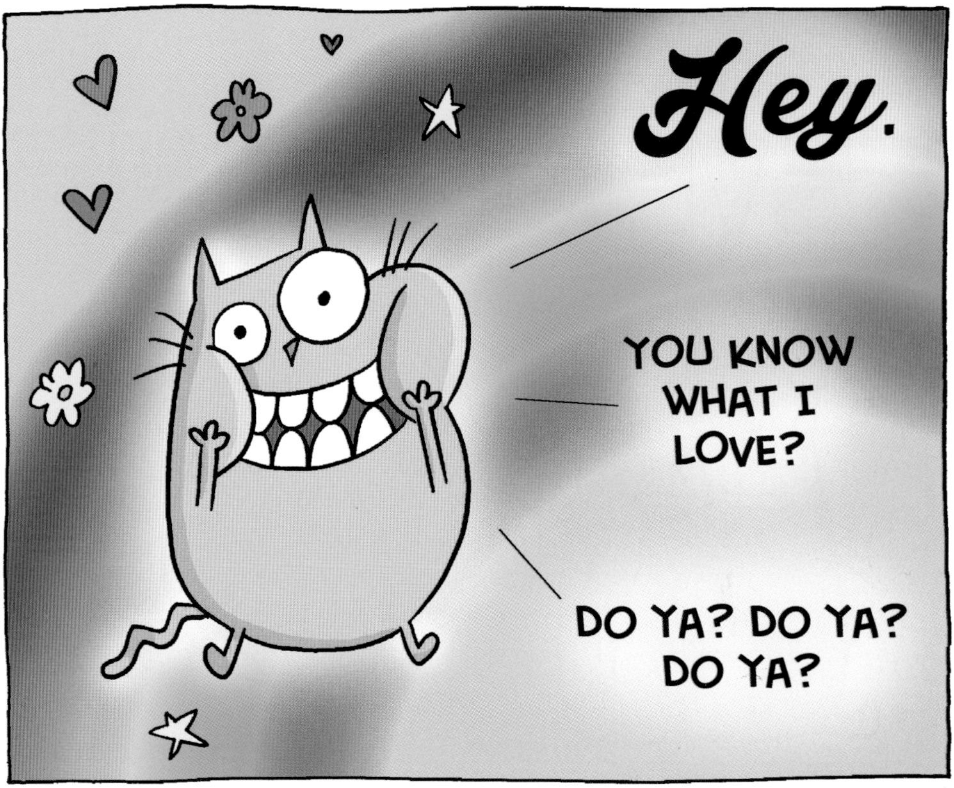
Hey.
YOU KNOW WHAT I LOVE?
DO YA? DO YA? DO YA?

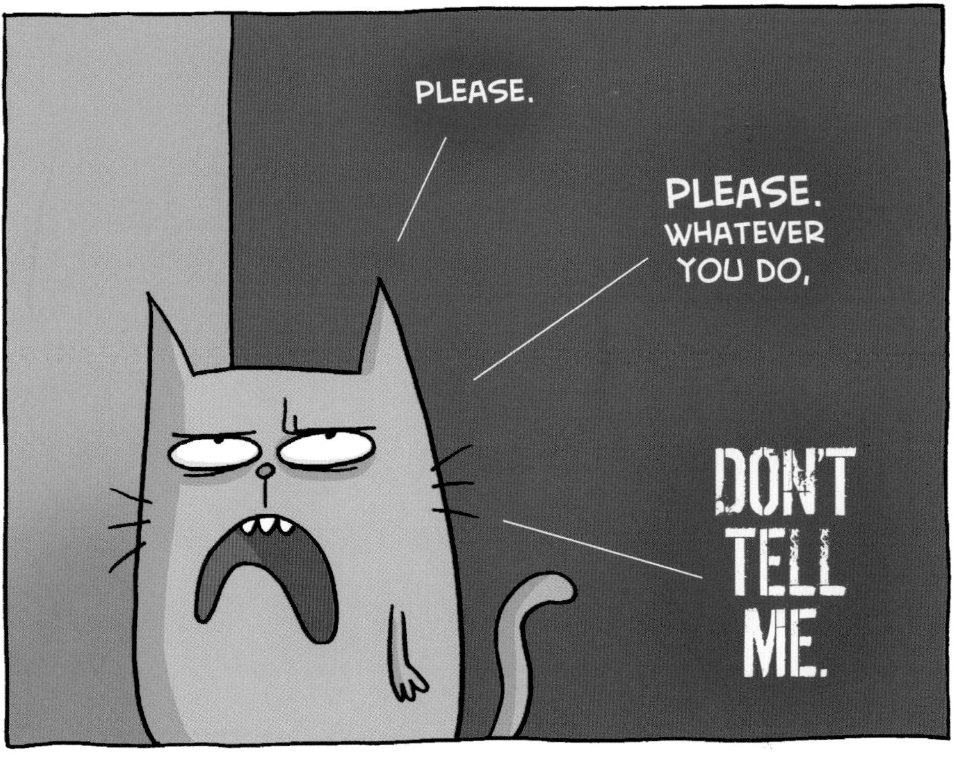
PLEASE.
PLEASE. WHATEVER YOU DO,
DON'T TELL ME.

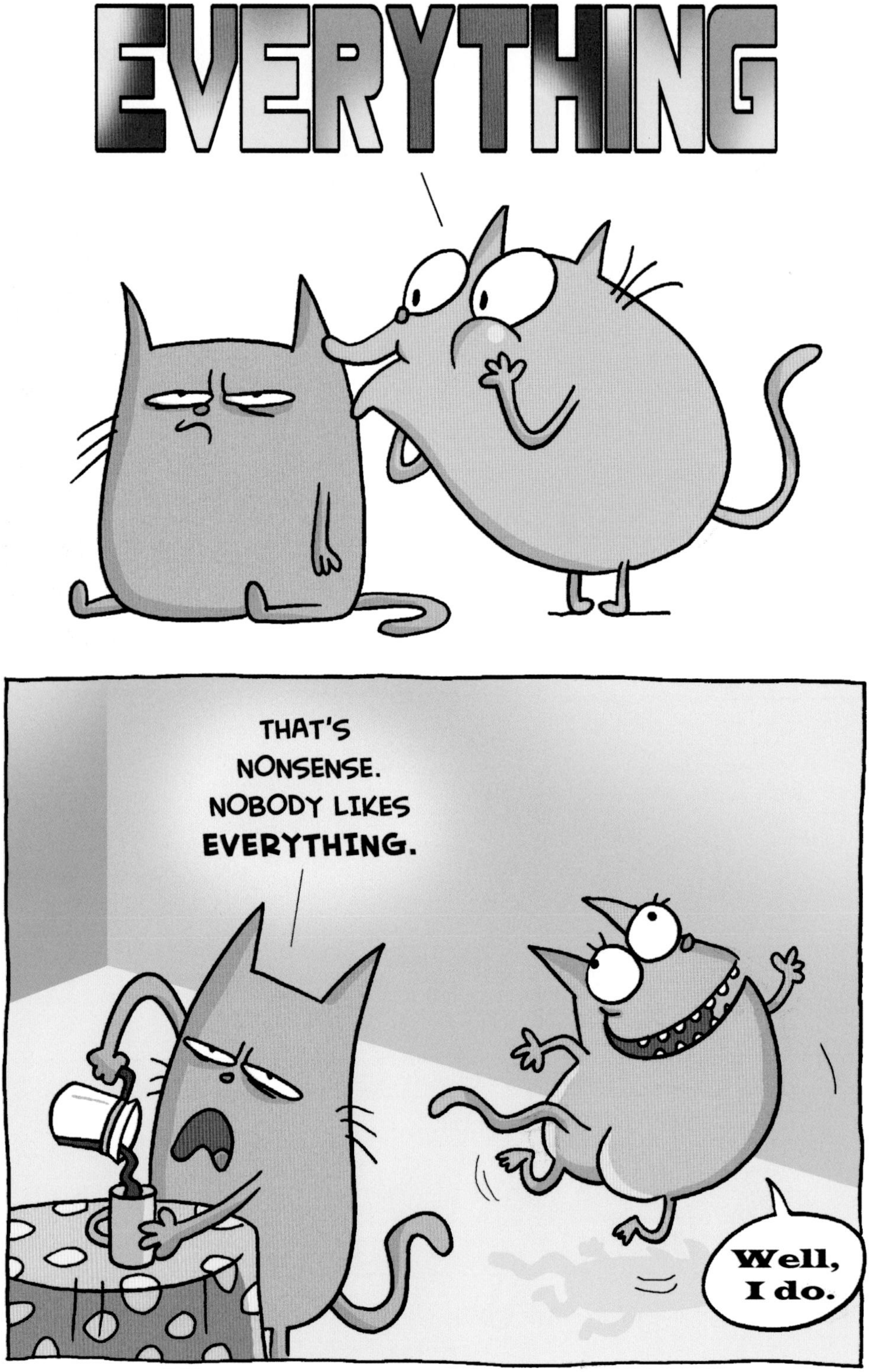
EVERYTHING
THAT'S NONSENSE. NOBODY LIKES EVERYTHING.
Well, I do.

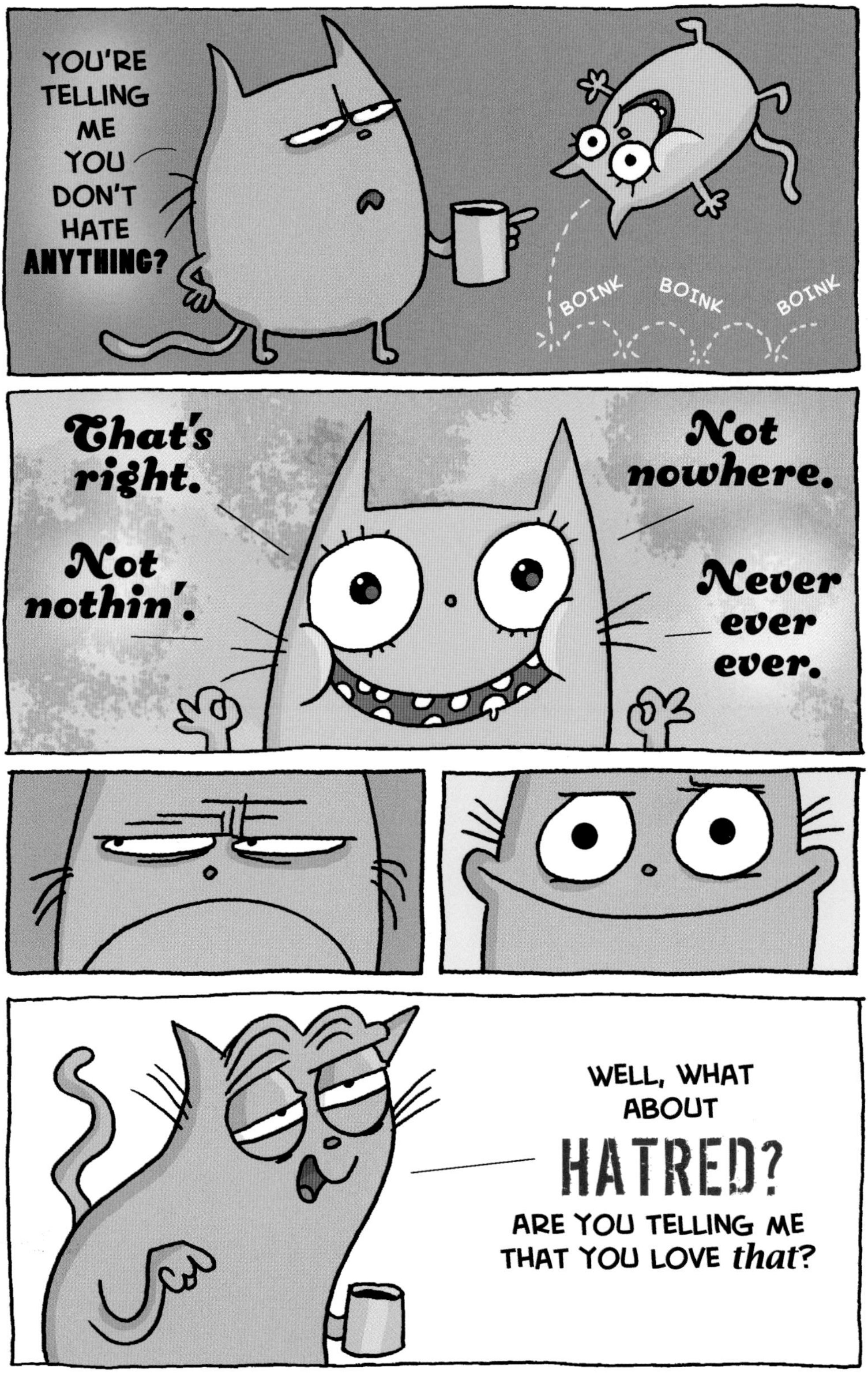
YOU'RE TELLING ME YOU DON'T HATE **ANYTHING?**
BOINK BOINK BOINK
That's right.
Not nothin'.
Not nowhere.
Never ever ever.
WELL, WHAT ABOUT HATRED? ARE YOU TELLING ME THAT YOU LOVE *that*?

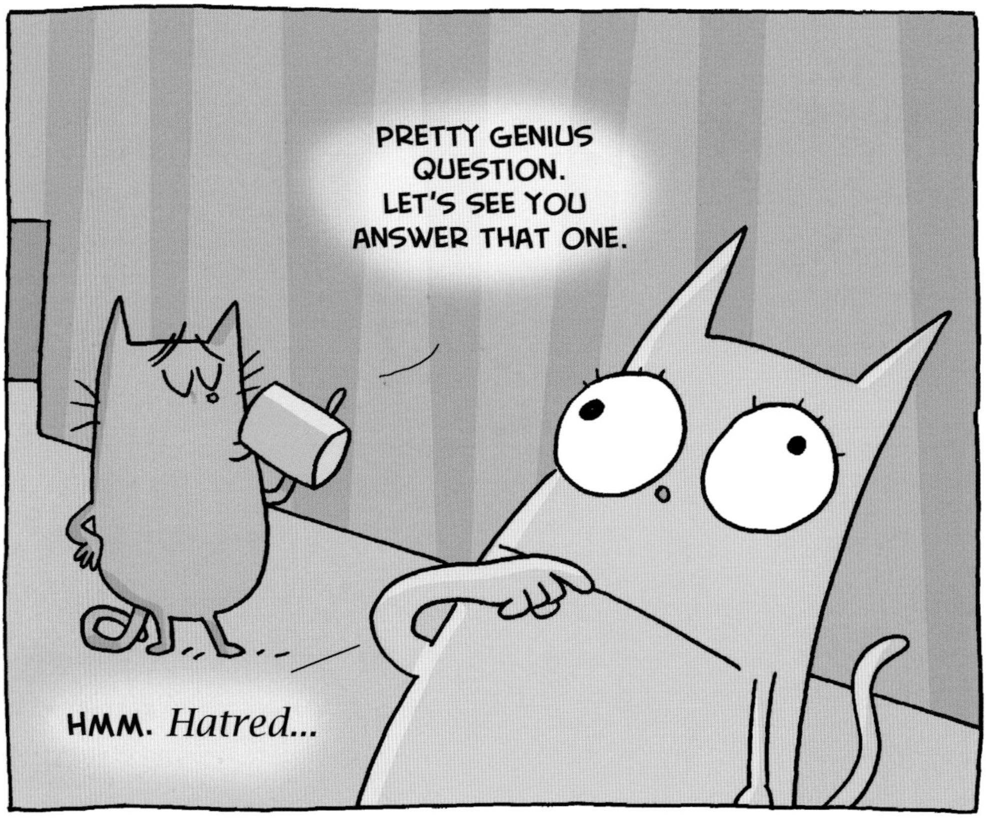
PRETTY GENIUS QUESTION. LET'S SEE YOU ANSWER THAT ONE.
HMM. *Hatred...*

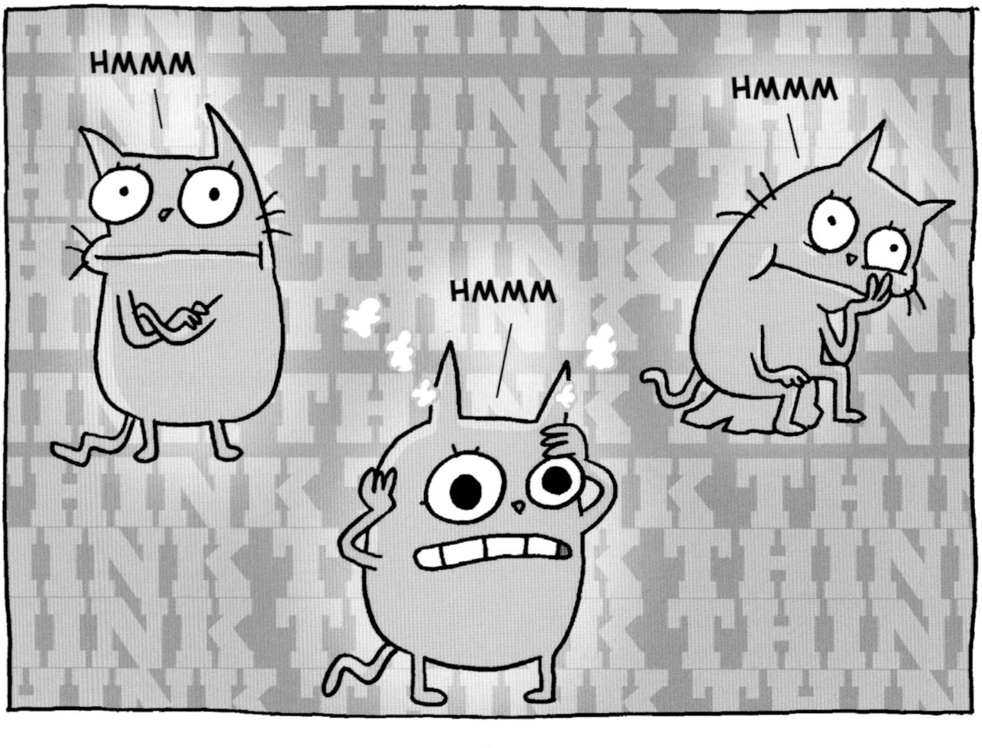
HMMM
HMMM
HMMM

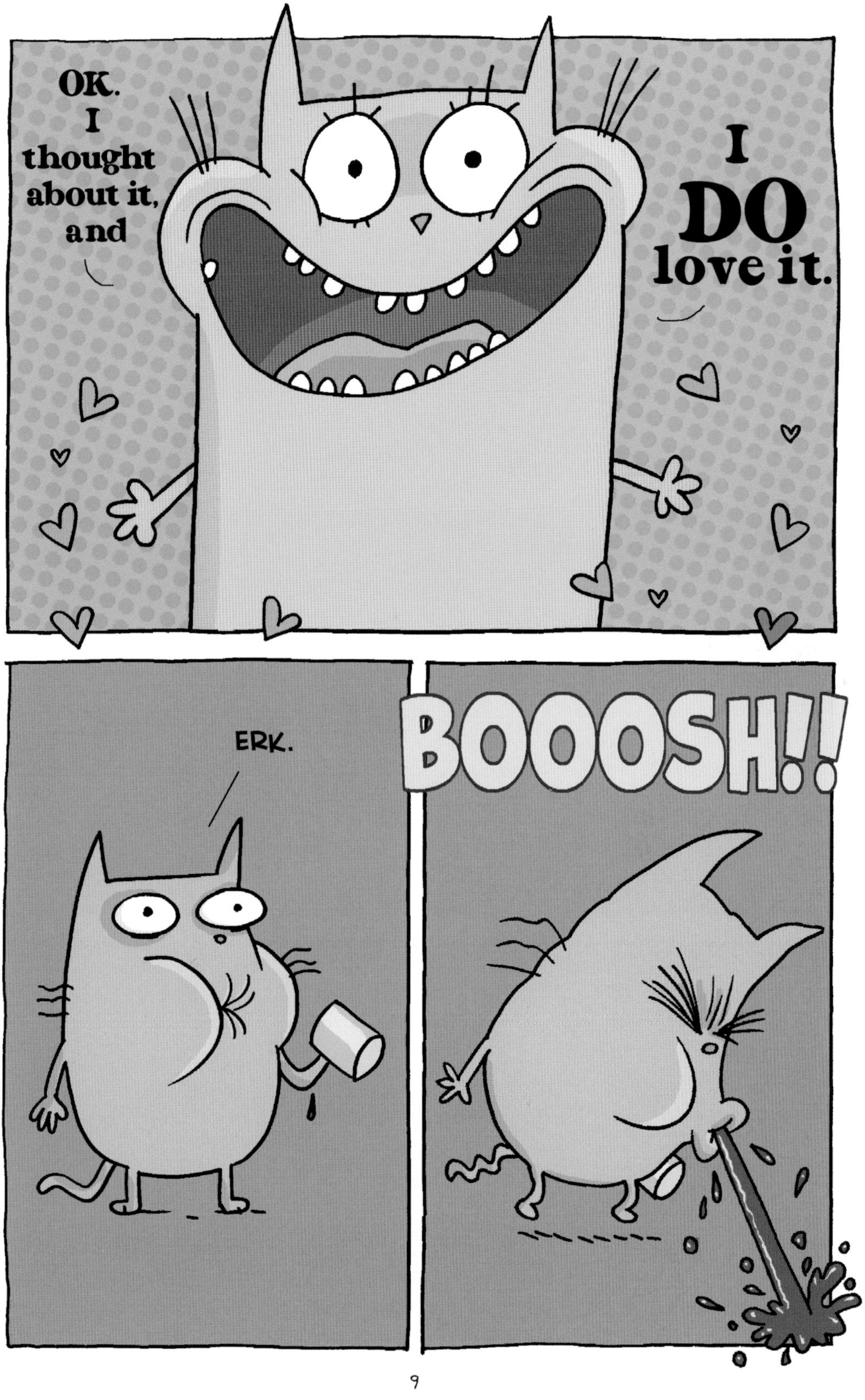
OK. I thought about it, and
I DO love it.
ERK.
BOOOSH!!

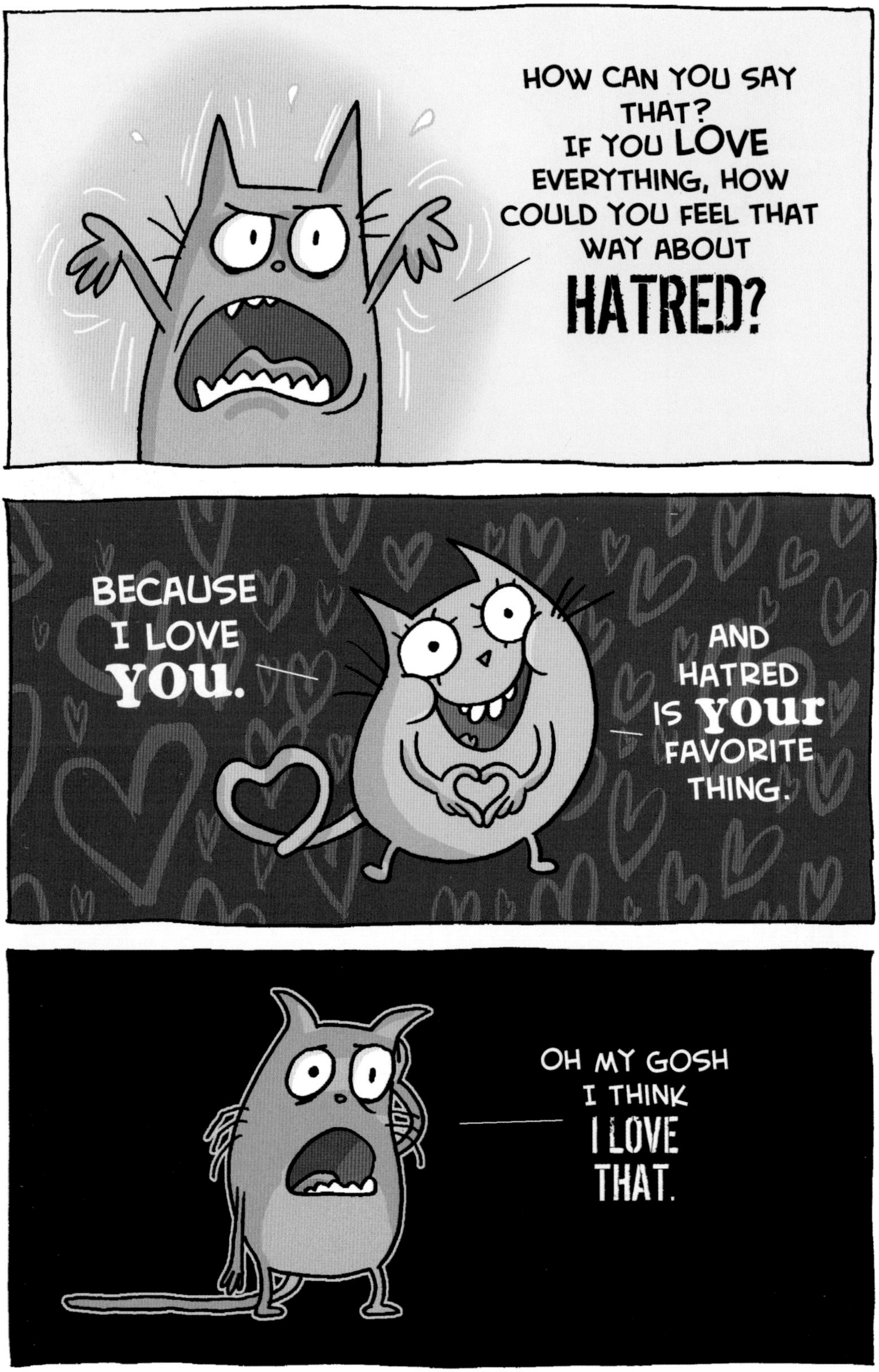
HOW CAN YOU SAY THAT? IF YOU LOVE EVERYTHING, HOW COULD YOU FEEL THAT WAY ABOUT HATRED?
BECAUSE I LOVE YOU.
AND HATRED IS YOUR FAVORITE THING.
OH MY GOSH I THINK I LOVE THAT.

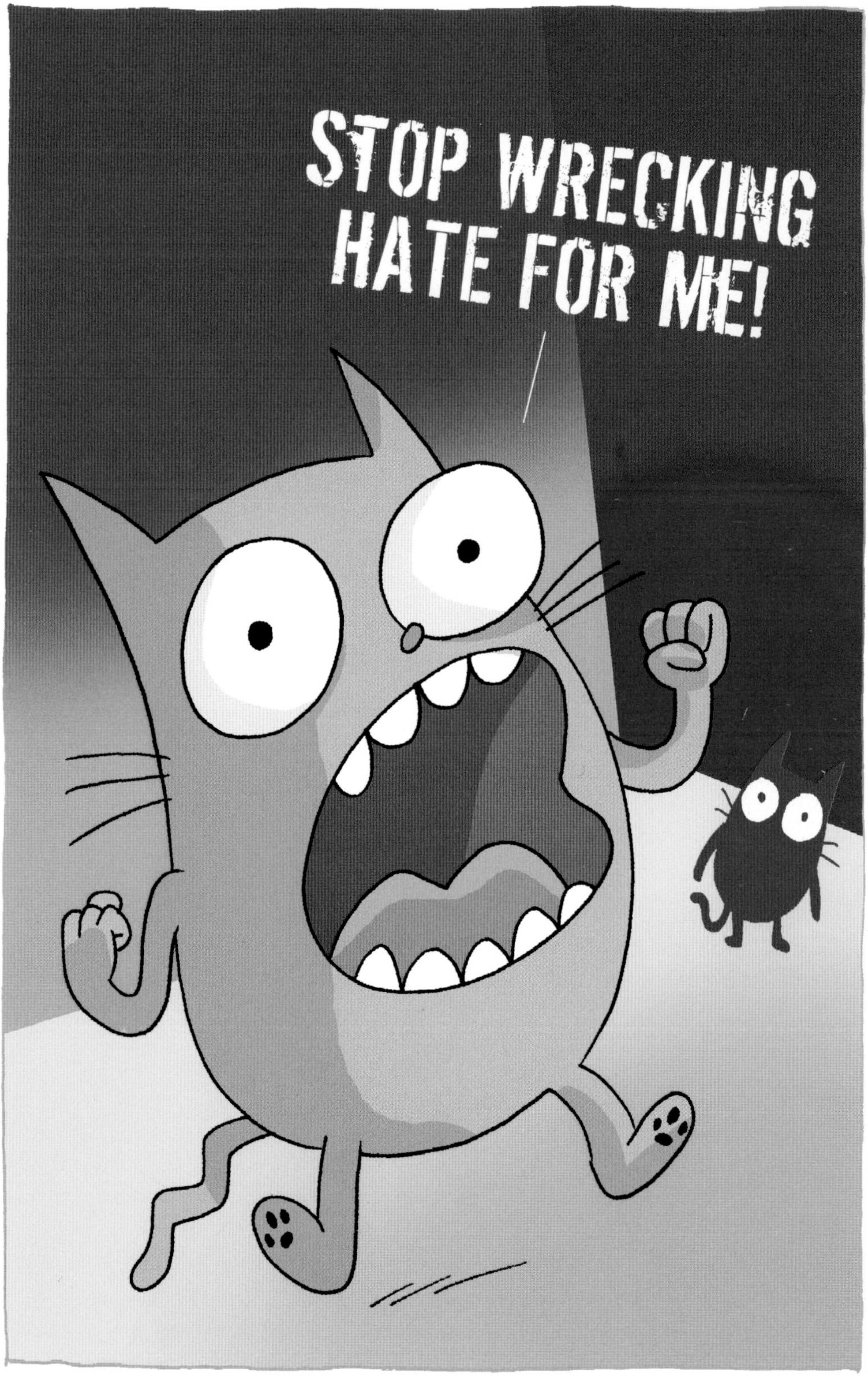
STOP WRECKING HATE FOR ME!

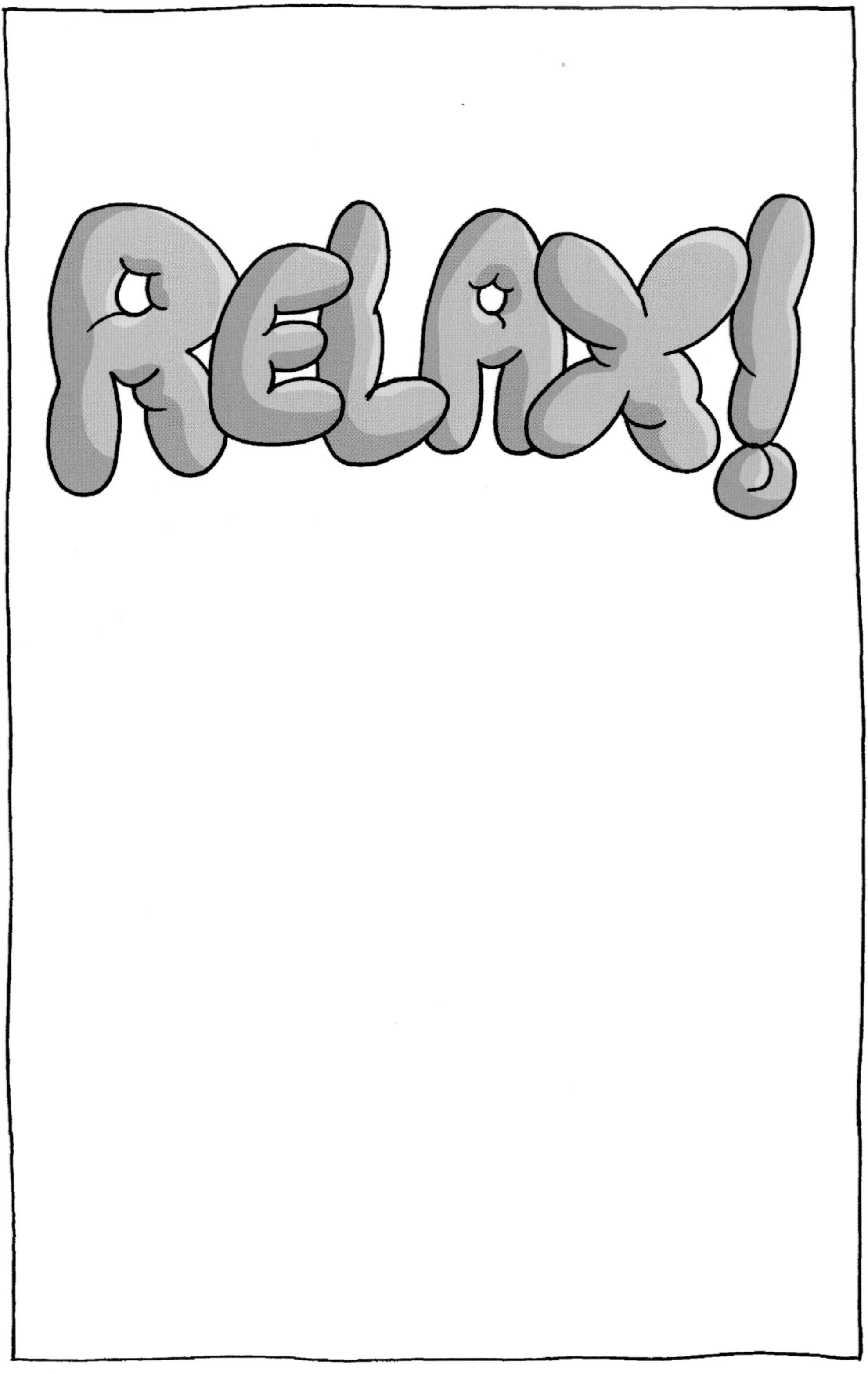
RELAX!

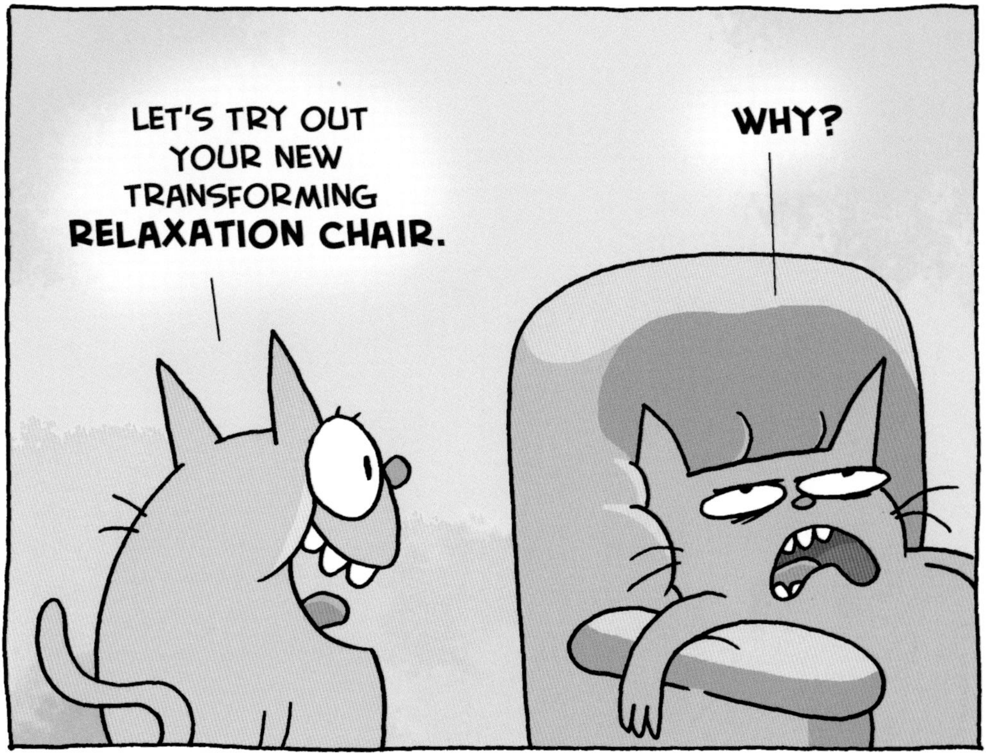
LET'S TRY OUT YOUR NEW TRANSFORMING **RELAXATION CHAIR.**
WHY?

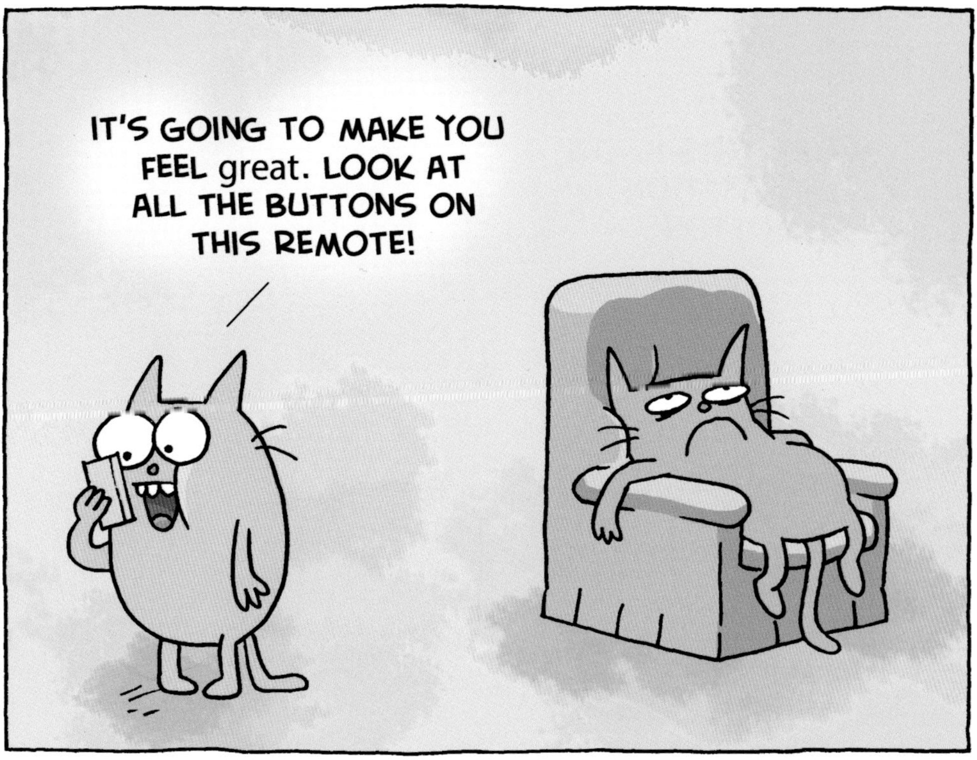
IT'S GOING TO MAKE YOU FEEL great. LOOK AT ALL THE BUTTONS ON THIS REMOTE!

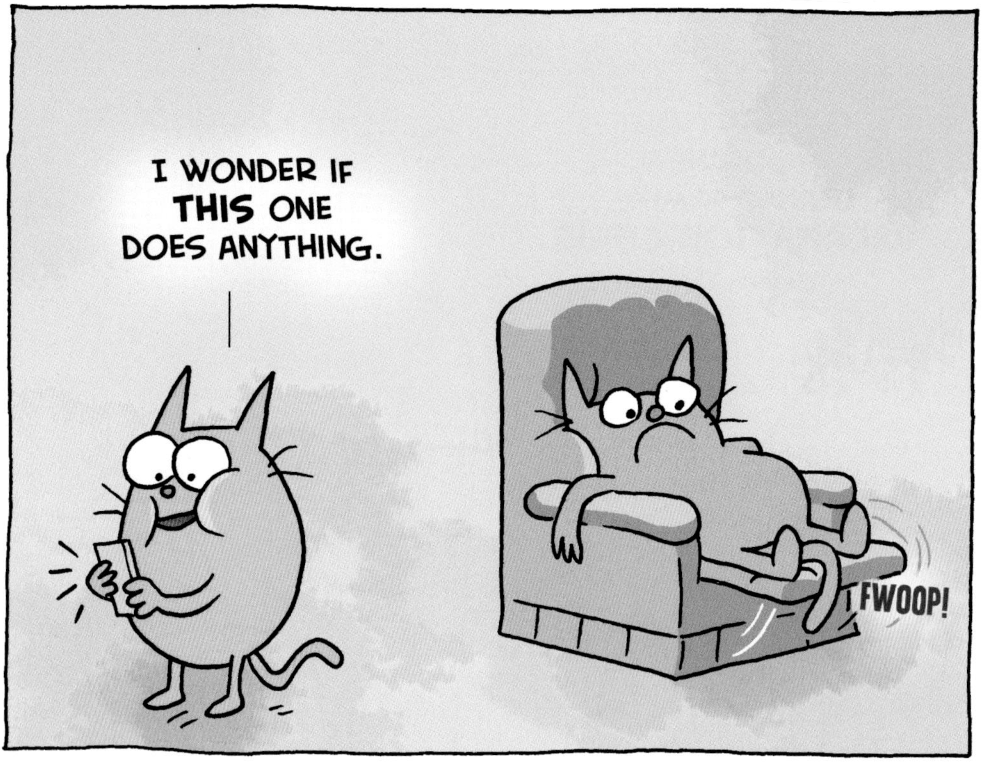
I WONDER IF THIS ONE DOES ANYTHING.
FWOOP!

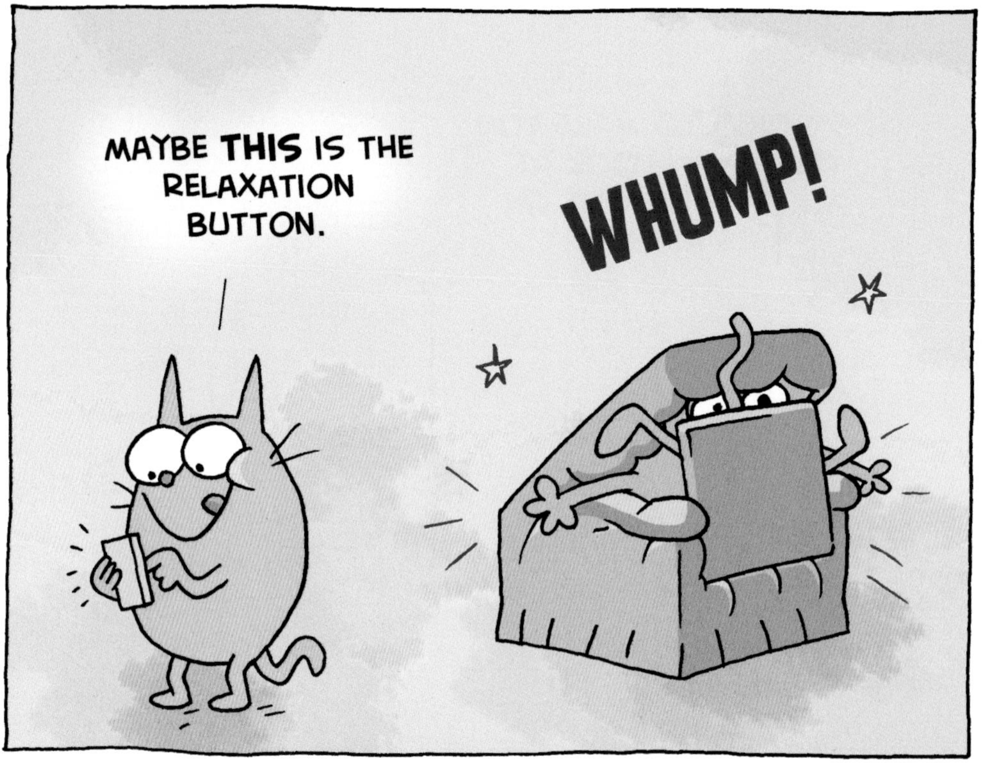
MAYBE THIS IS THE RELAXATION BUTTON.
WHUMP!

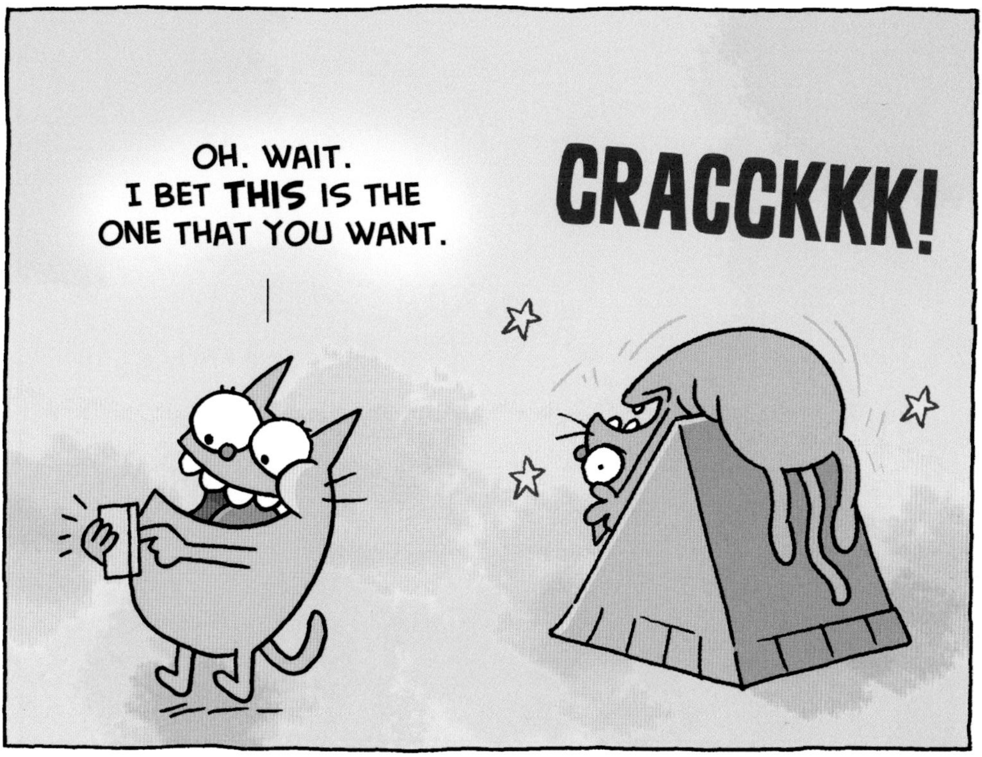
OH. WAIT.
I BET THIS IS THE
ONE THAT YOU WANT.
CRACCKKK!

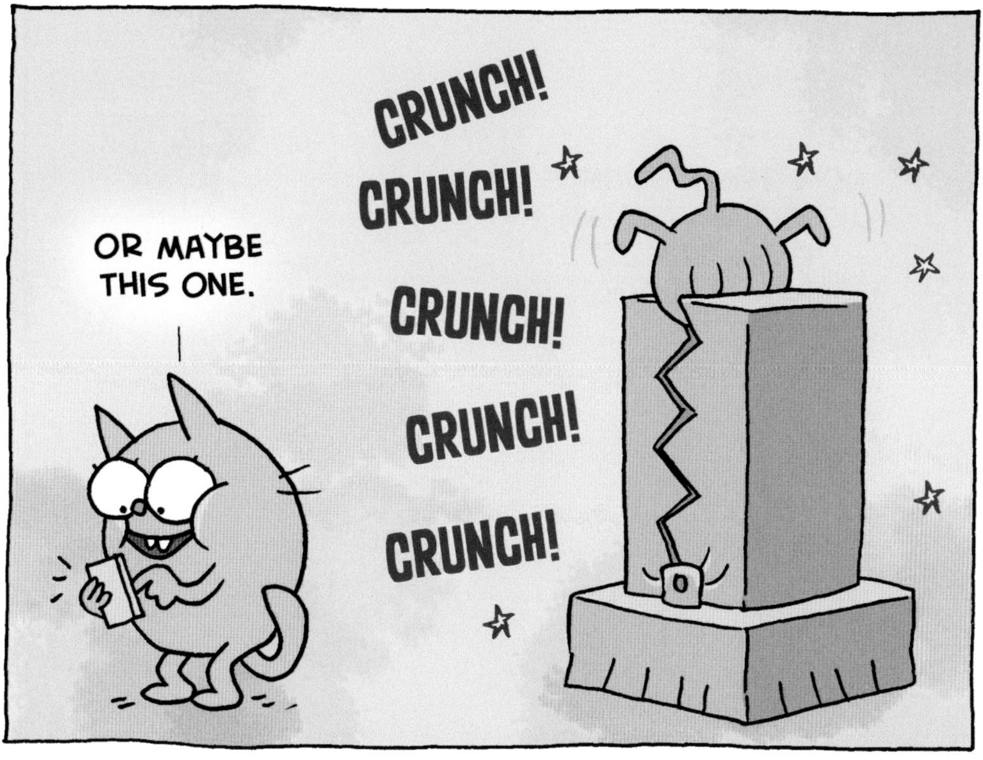
OR MAYBE
THIS ONE.
CRUNCH!
CRUNCH!
CRUNCH!
CRUNCH!
CRUNCH!

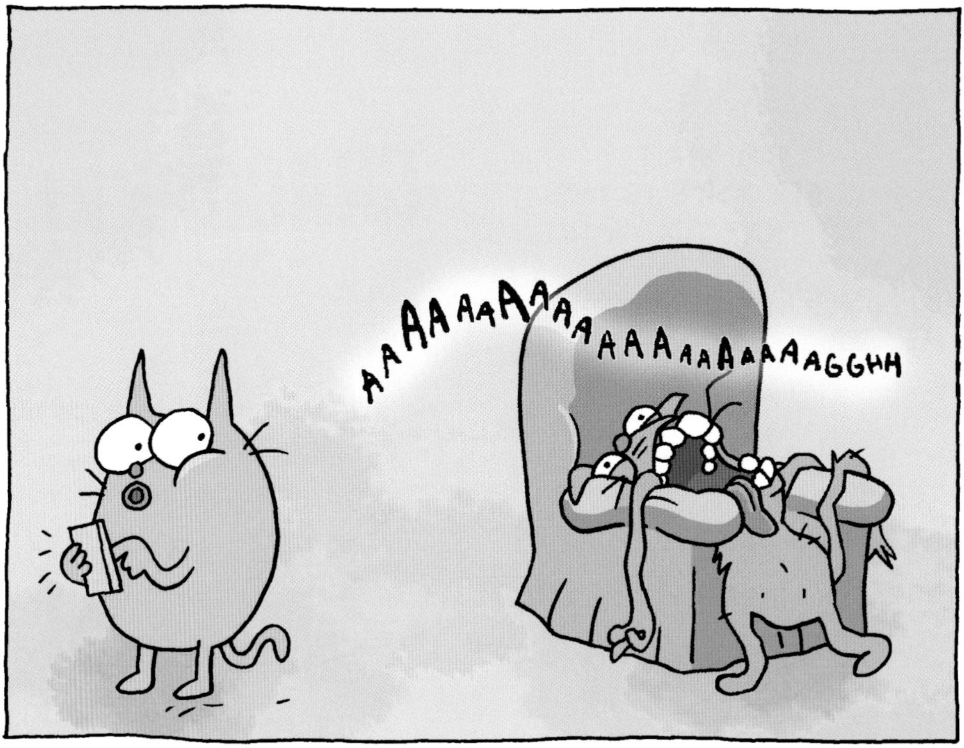
AAAAAAAAAAAAAAAAAAAAAAGGHH

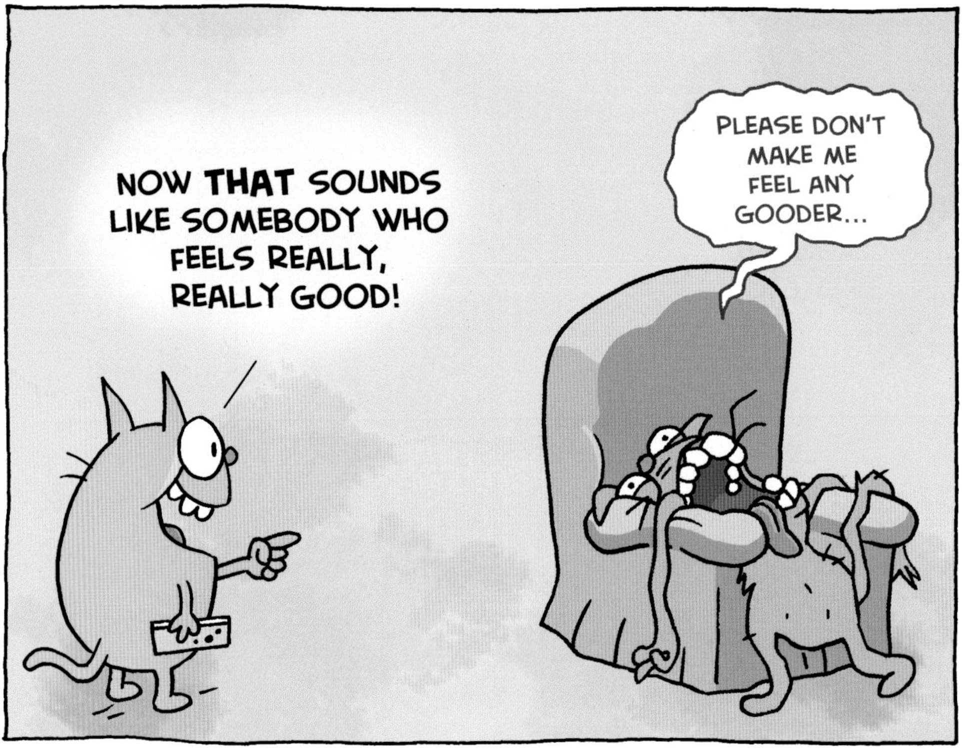
NOW **THAT** SOUNDS LIKE SOMEBODY WHO FEELS REALLY, REALLY GOOD!
PLEASE DON'T MAKE ME FEEL ANY GOODER...

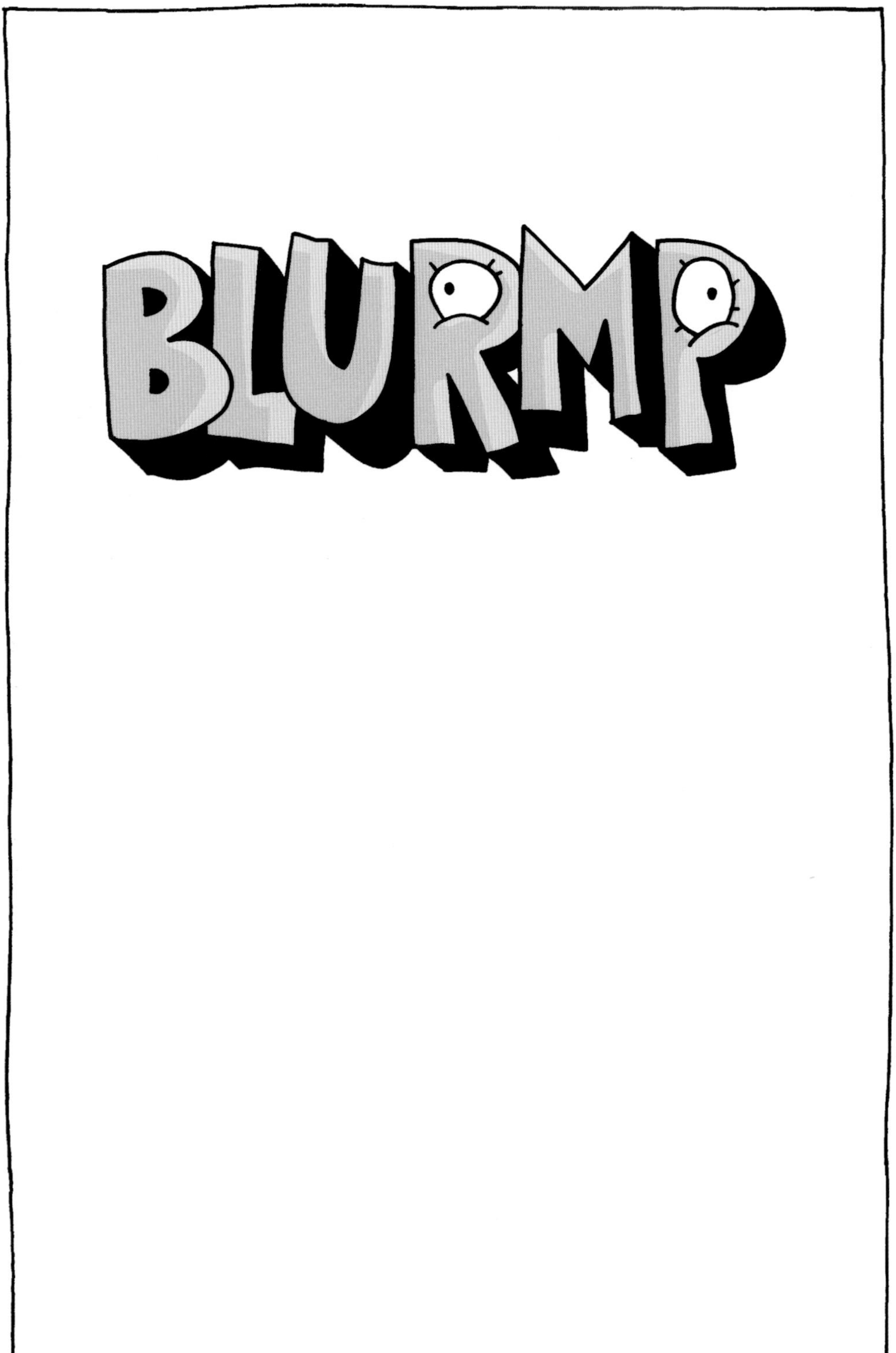
BLURMP

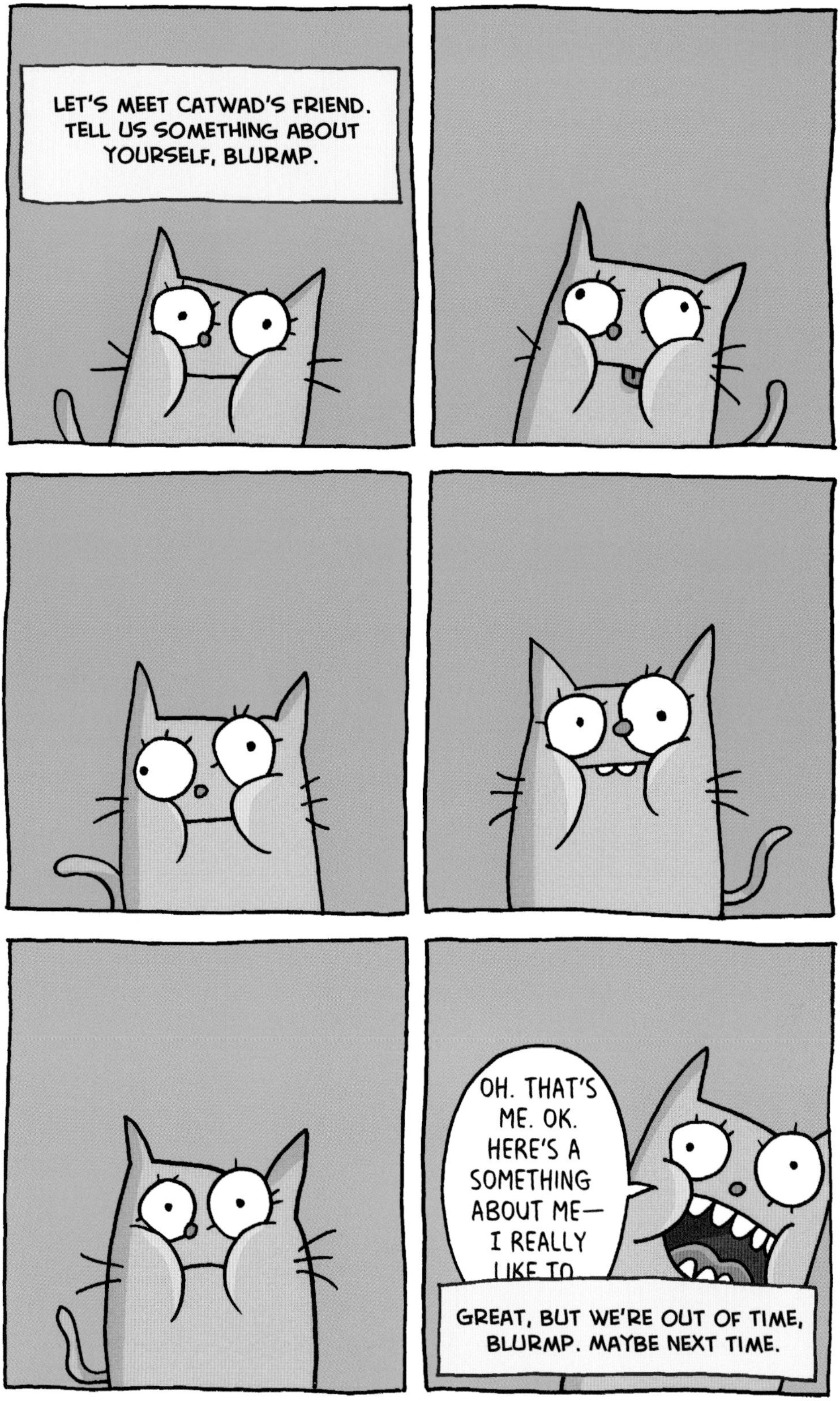
LET'S MEET CATWAD'S FRIEND. TELL US SOMETHING ABOUT YOURSELF, BLURMP.
OH. THAT'S ME. OK. HERE'S A SOMETHING ABOUT ME— I REALLY LIKE TO
GREAT, BUT WE'RE OUT OF TIME, BLURMP. MAYBE NEXT TIME.

BRUSH

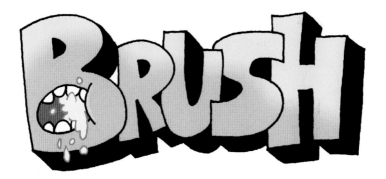

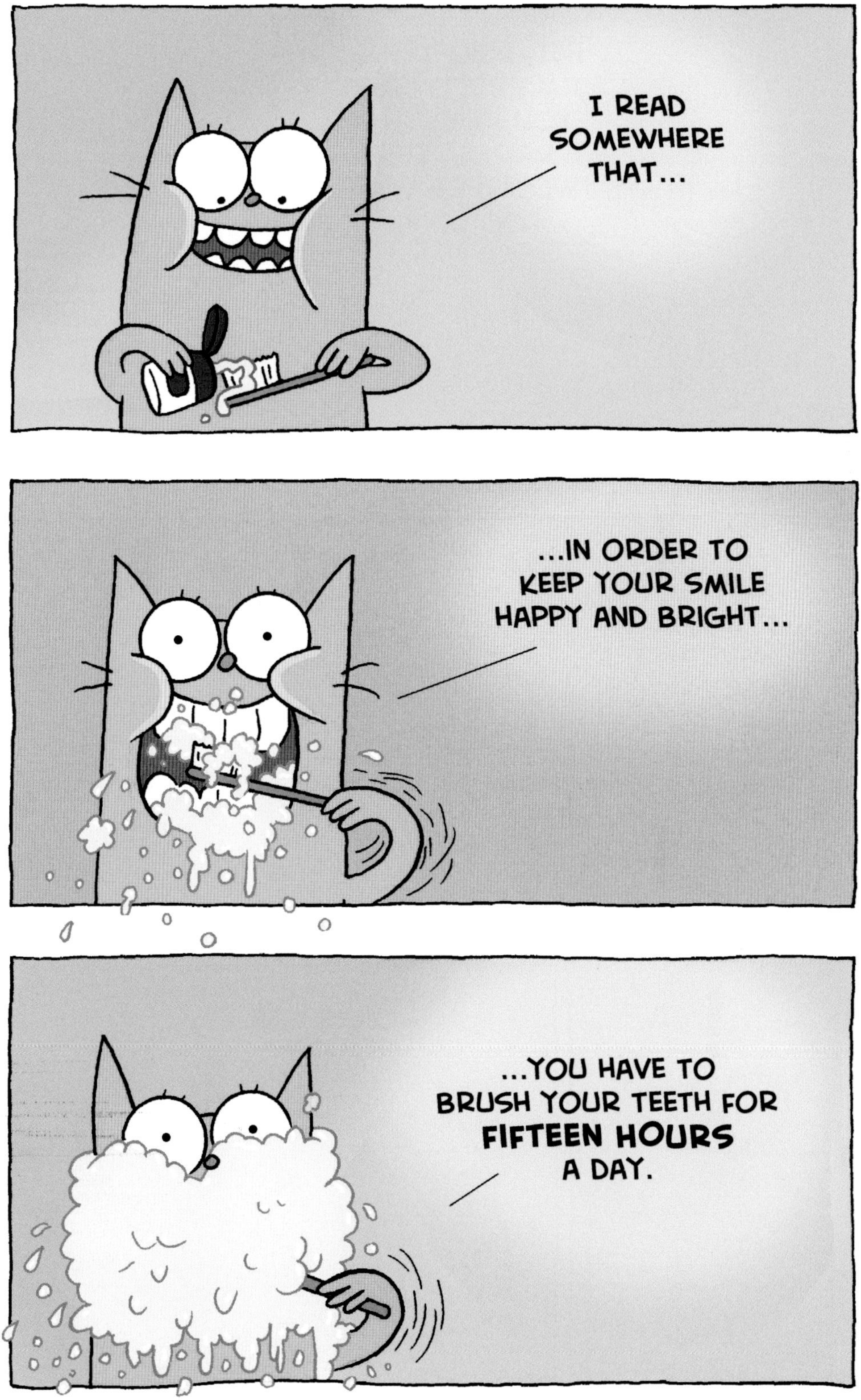
I READ SOMEWHERE THAT...
...IN ORDER TO KEEP YOUR SMILE HAPPY AND BRIGHT...
...YOU HAVE TO BRUSH YOUR TEETH FOR **FIFTEEN HOURS** A DAY.

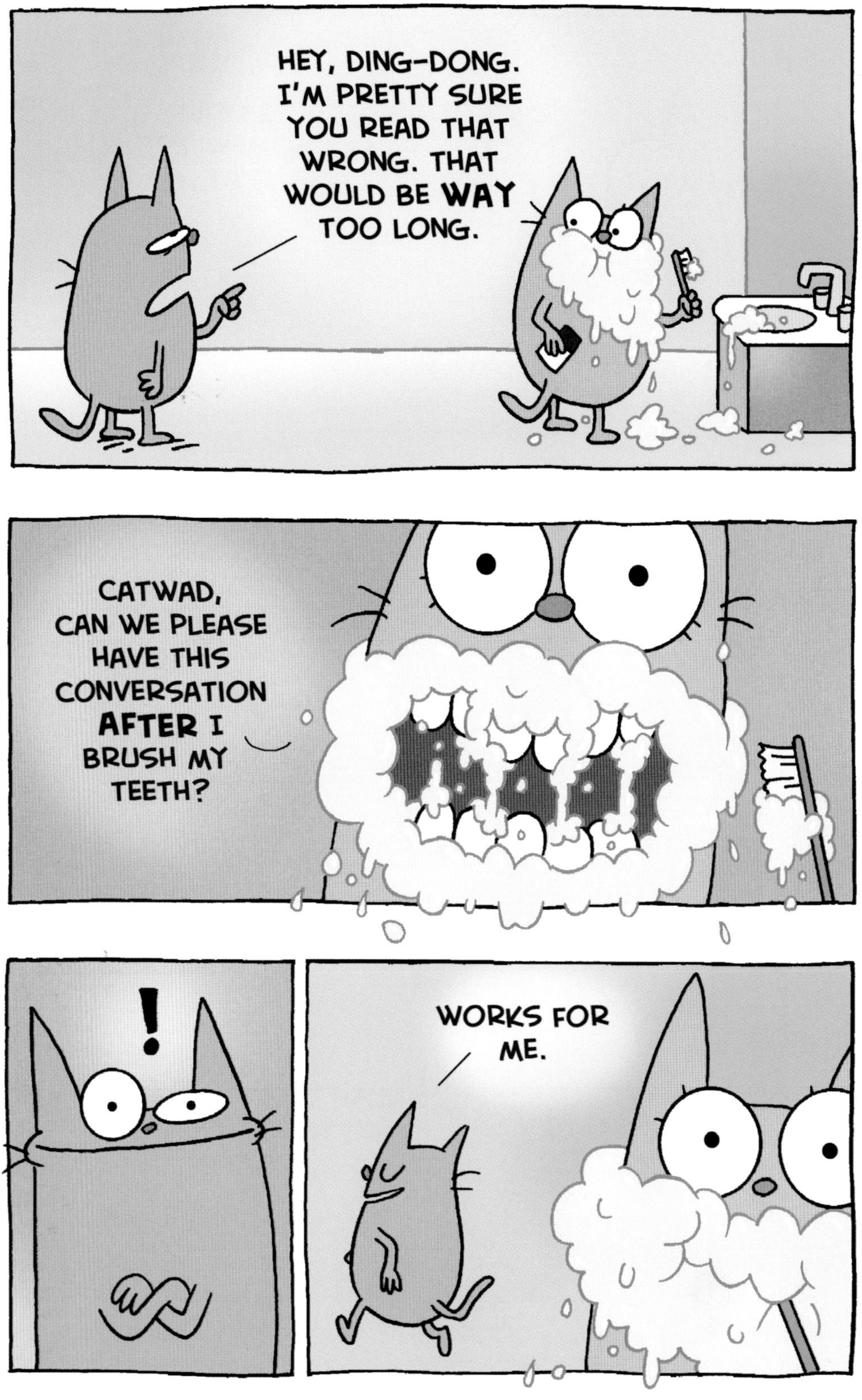
HEY, DING-DONG. I'M PRETTY SURE YOU READ THAT WRONG. THAT WOULD BE **WAY** TOO LONG.
CATWAD, CAN WE PLEASE HAVE THIS CONVERSATION **AFTER** I BRUSH MY TEETH?
!
WORKS FOR ME.

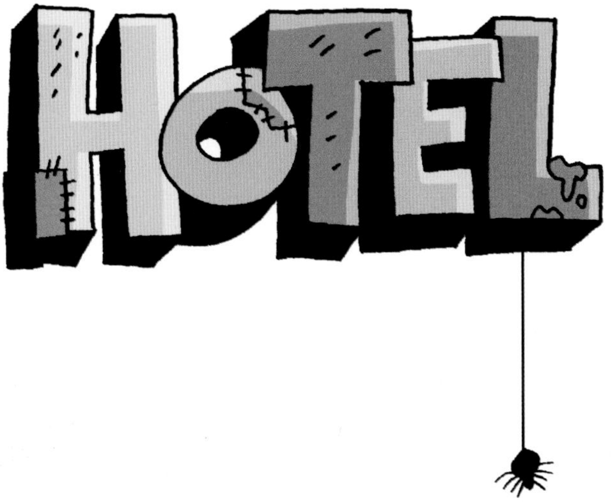
HOTEL

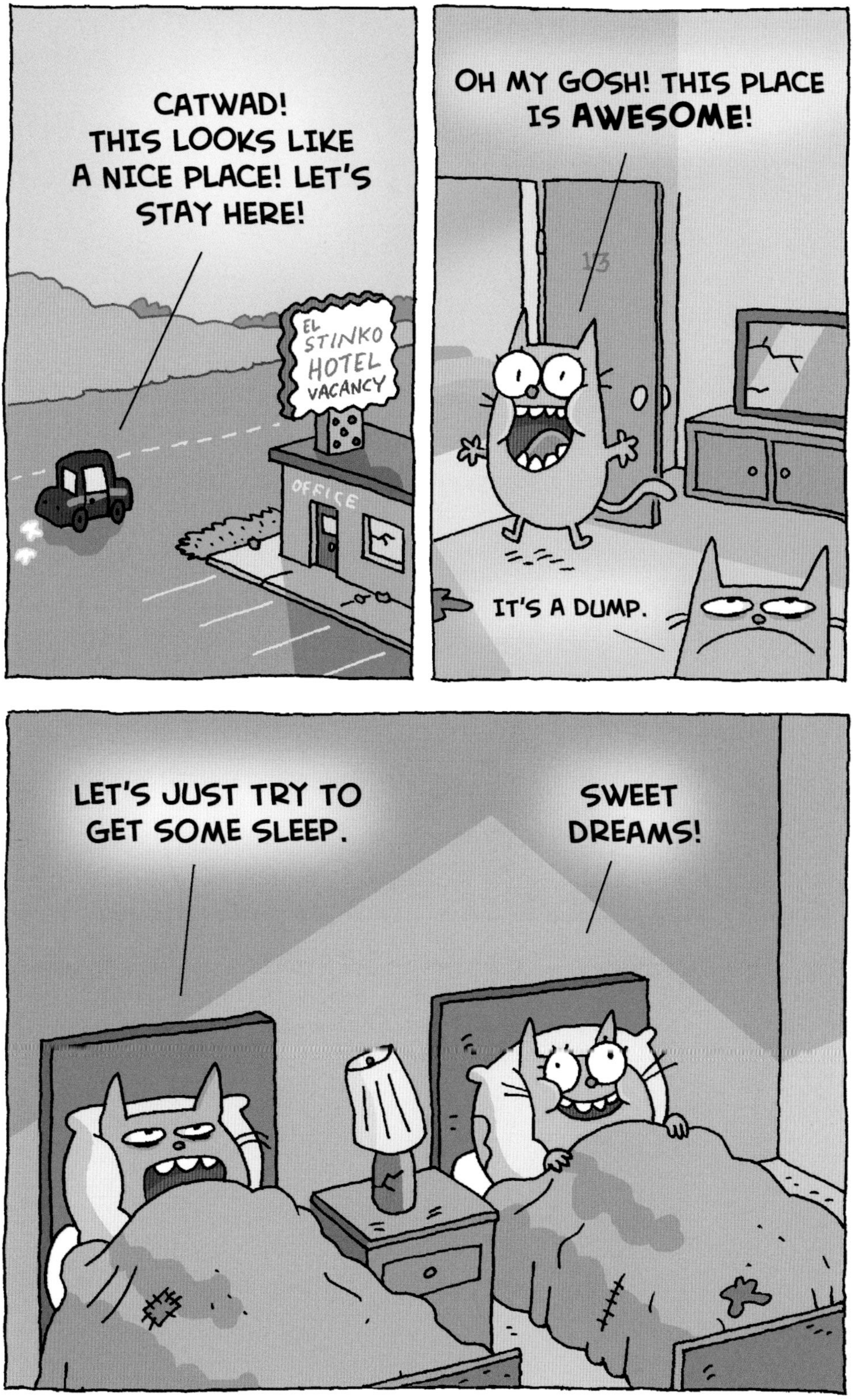
CATWAD! THIS LOOKS LIKE A NICE PLACE! LET'S STAY HERE!
EL STINKO HOTEL VACANCY
OFFICE
OH MY GOSH! THIS PLACE IS **AWESOME**!
13
IT'S A DUMP.
LET'S JUST TRY TO GET SOME SLEEP.
SWEET DREAMS!

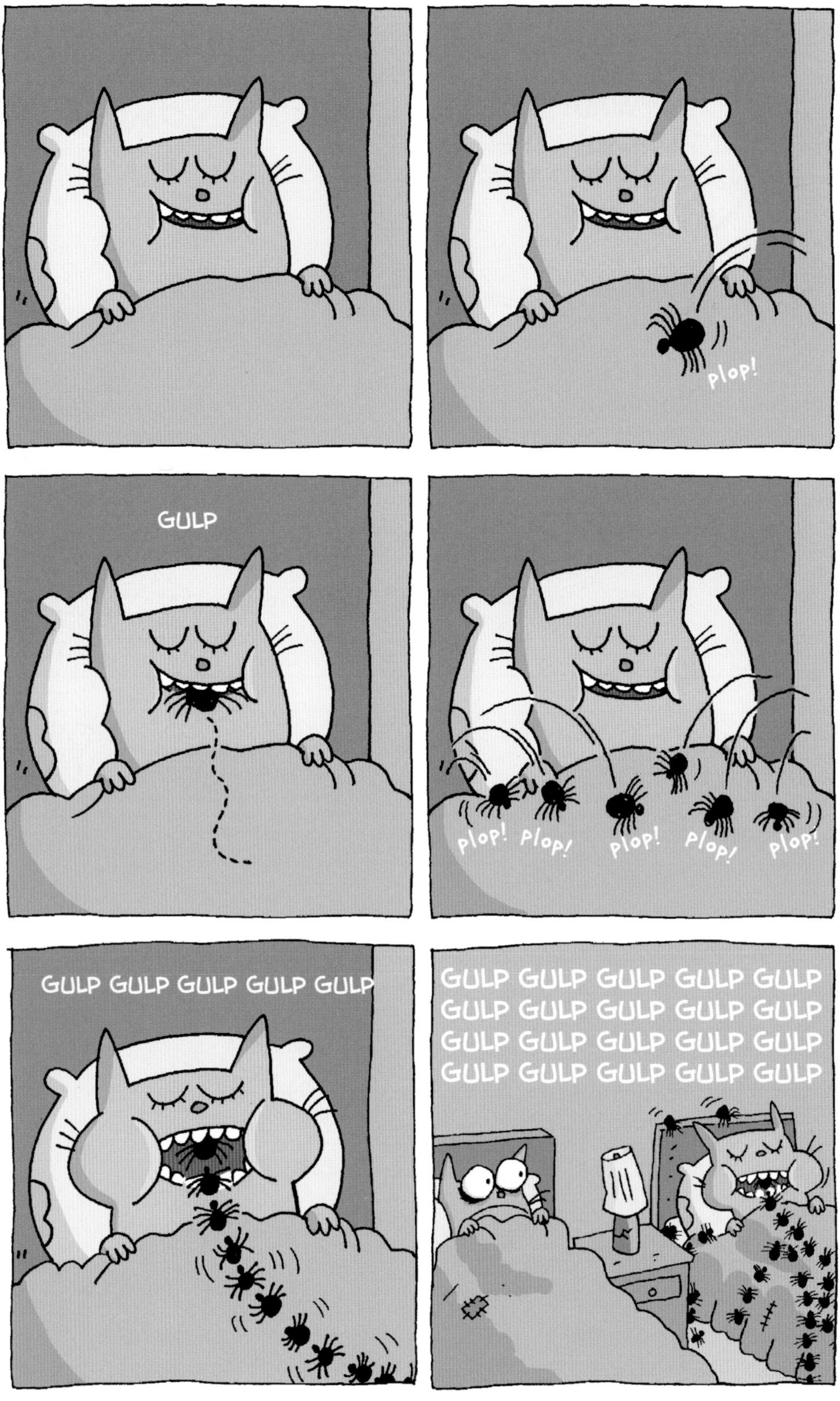
plop!
GULP
plop! plop! plop! plop! plop!
GULP GULP GULP GULP GULP
GULP GULP GULP GULP GULP
GULP GULP GULP GULP GULP
GULP GULP GULP GULP GULP
GULP GULP GULP GULP GULP

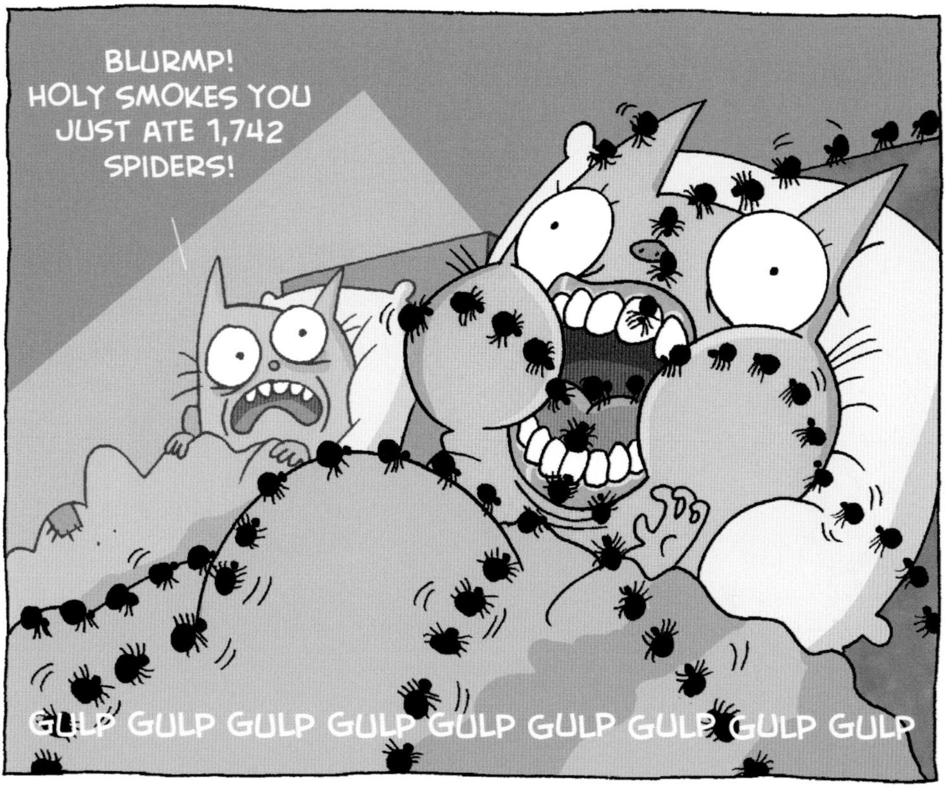
BLURMP!
HOLY SMOKES YOU JUST ATE 1,742 SPIDERS!
GULP GULP GULP GULP GULP GULP GULP GULP GULP

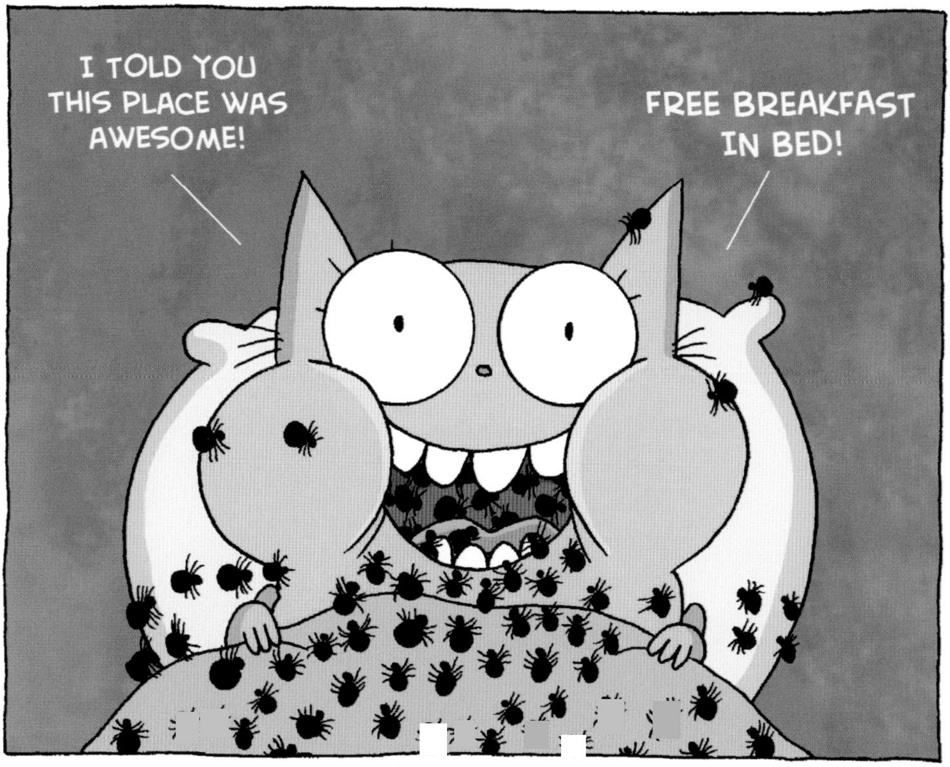
I TOLD YOU THIS PLACE WAS AWESOME!
FREE BREAKFAST IN BED!

GROW UP

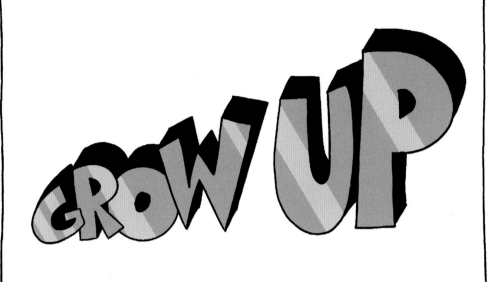

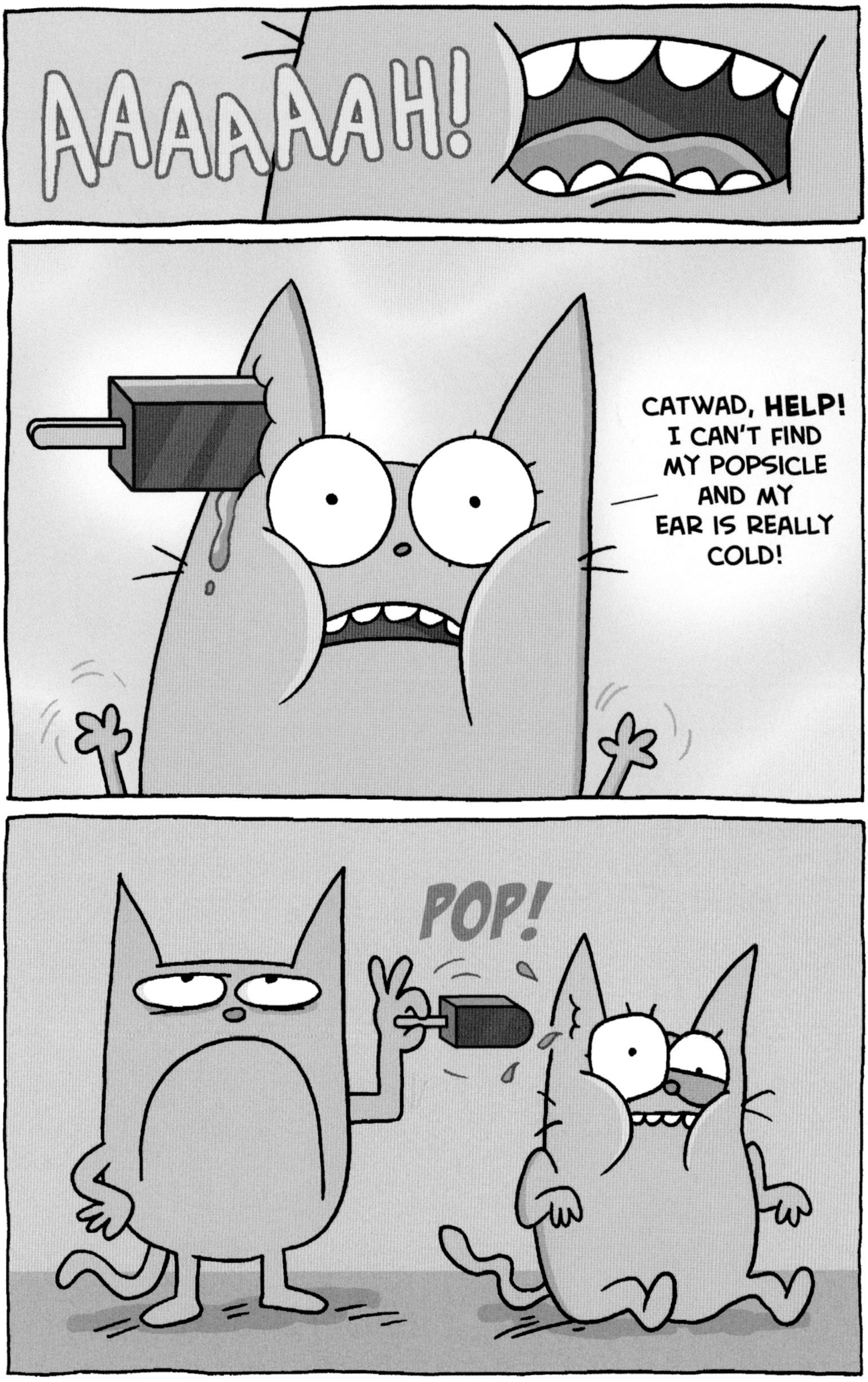
AAAAAAH!
CATWAD, **HELP!** I CAN'T FIND MY POPSICLE AND MY EAR IS REALLY COLD!
POP!

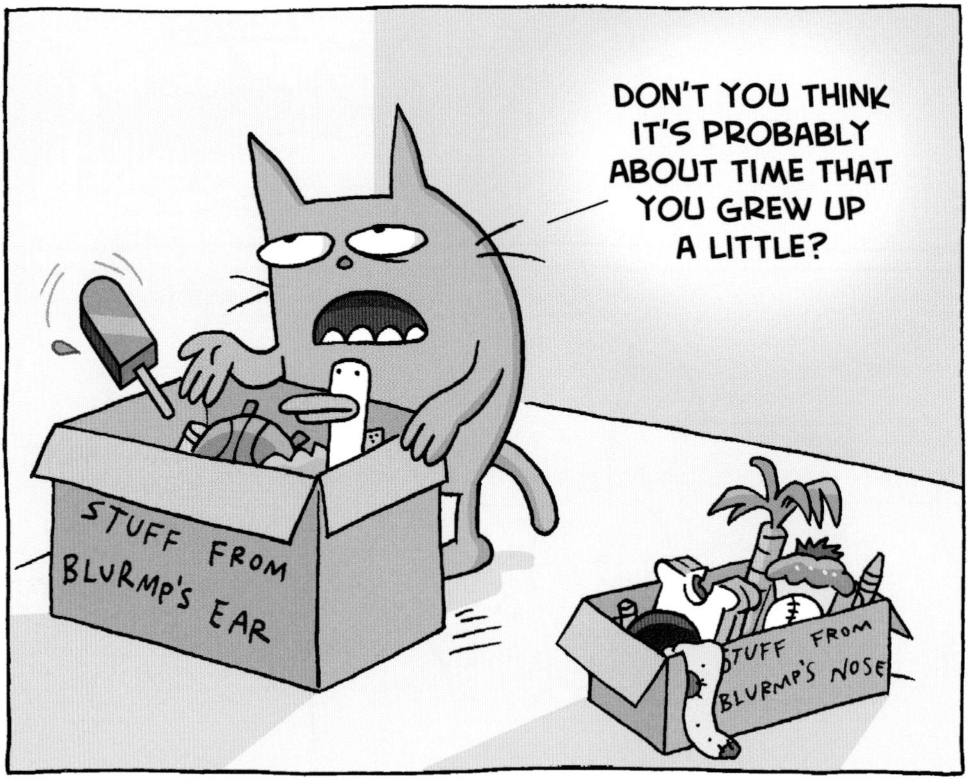
DON'T YOU THINK IT'S PROBABLY ABOUT TIME THAT YOU GREW UP A LITTLE?
STUFF FROM BLURMP'S EAR
STUFF FROM BLURMP'S NOSE

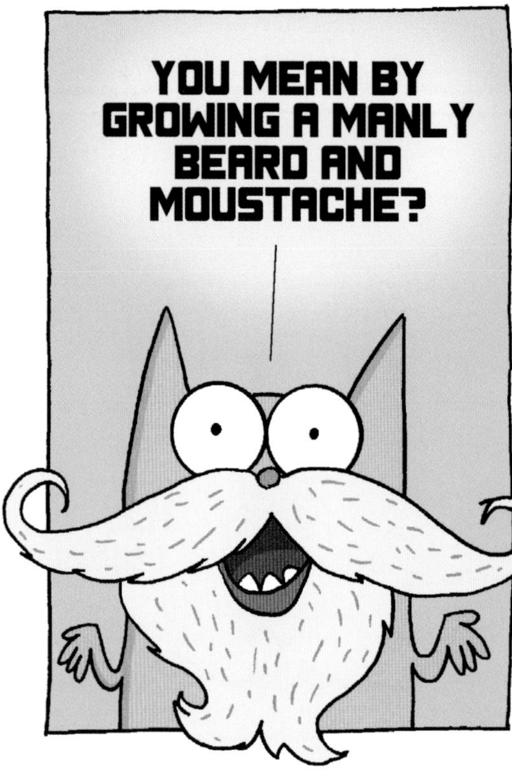
YOU MEAN BY GROWING A MANLY BEARD AND MOUSTACHE?

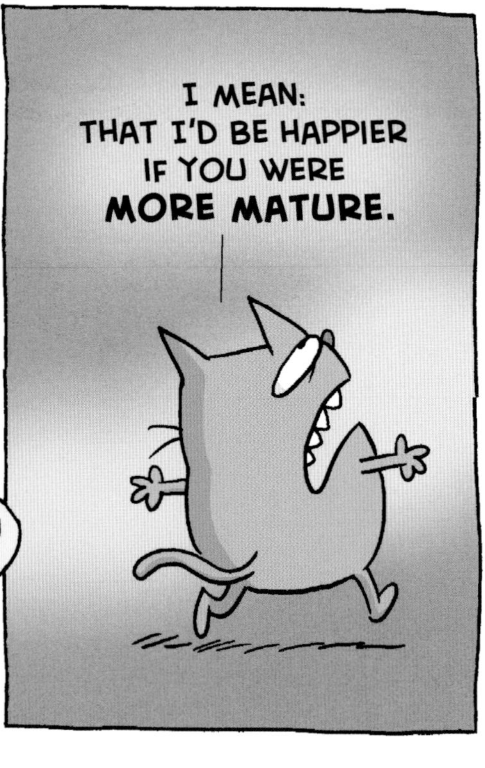
I MEAN: THAT I'D BE HAPPIER IF YOU WERE MORE MATURE.

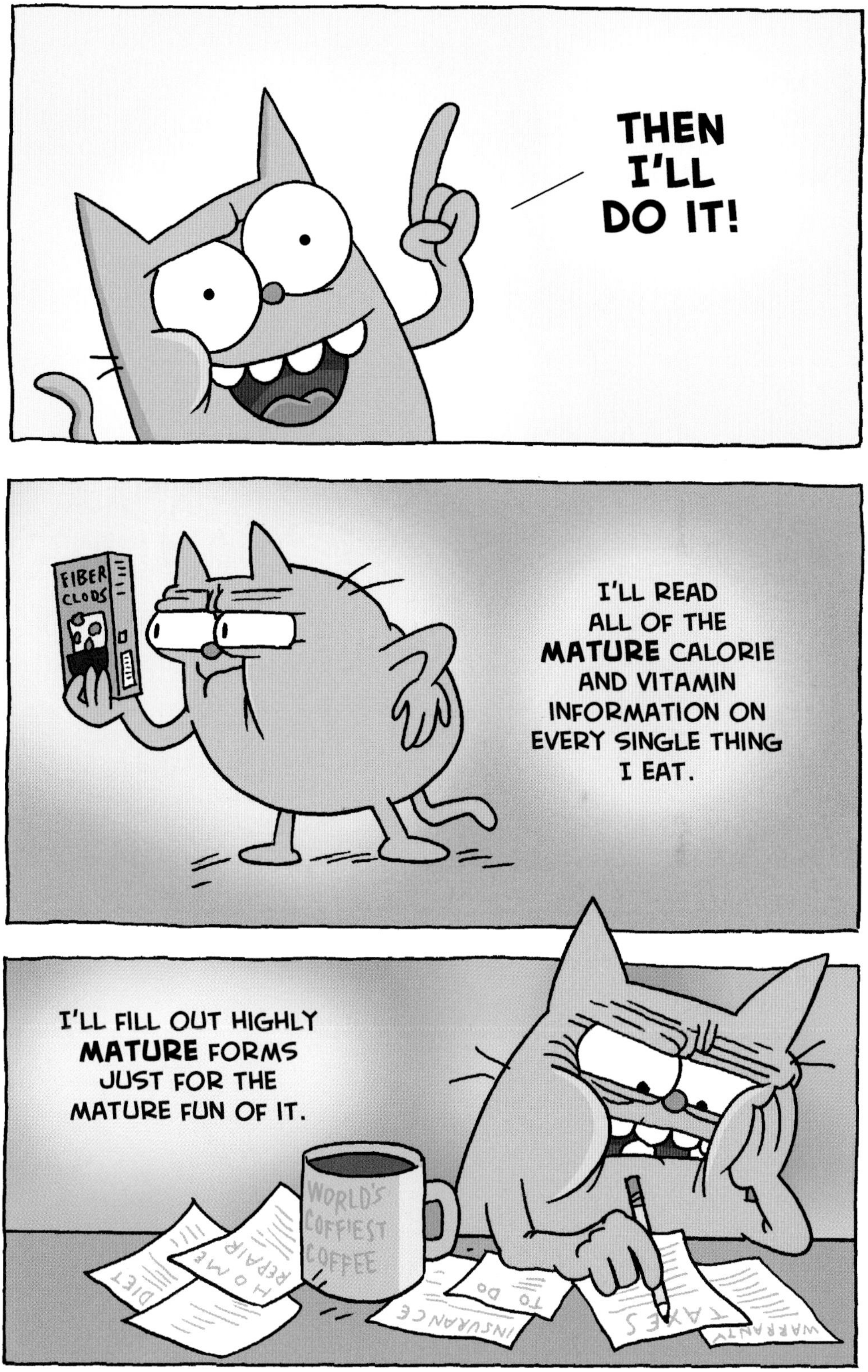
THEN I'LL DO IT!
FIBER CLODS
I'LL READ ALL OF THE **MATURE** CALORIE AND VITAMIN INFORMATION ON EVERY SINGLE THING I EAT.
I'LL FILL OUT HIGHLY **MATURE** FORMS JUST FOR THE MATURE FUN OF IT.
WORLD'S COFFIEST COFFEE
DIET
HOME REPAIR
INSURANCE
TO DO
TAXES
WARRANTY

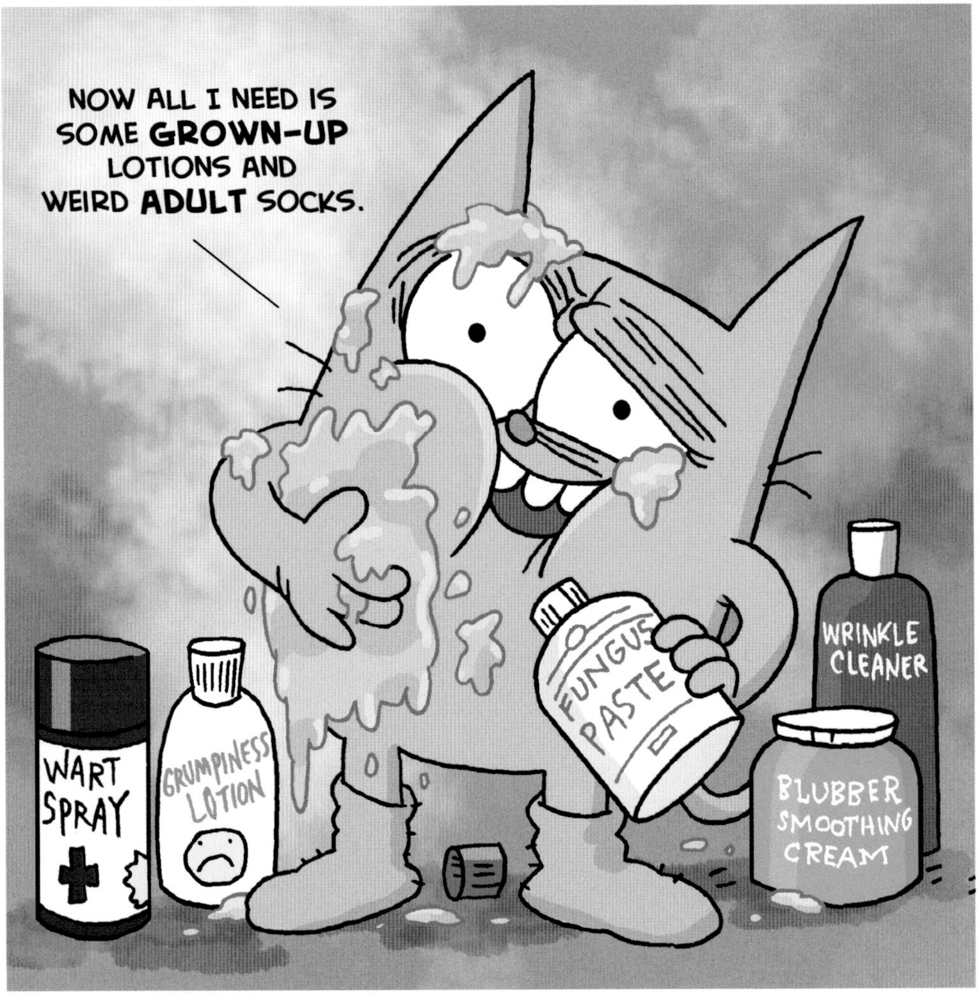
NOW ALL I NEED IS SOME **GROWN-UP** LOTIONS AND WEIRD **ADULT** SOCKS.
WART SPRAY
GRUMPINESS LOTION
FUNGUS PASTE
WRINKLE CLEANER
BLUBBER SMOOTHING CREAM

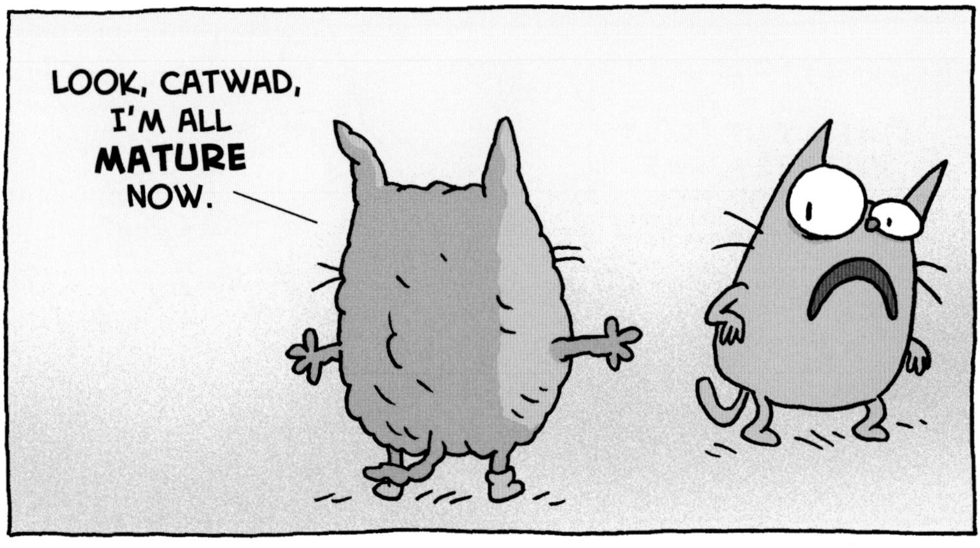
LOOK, CATWAD, I'M ALL **MATURE** NOW.

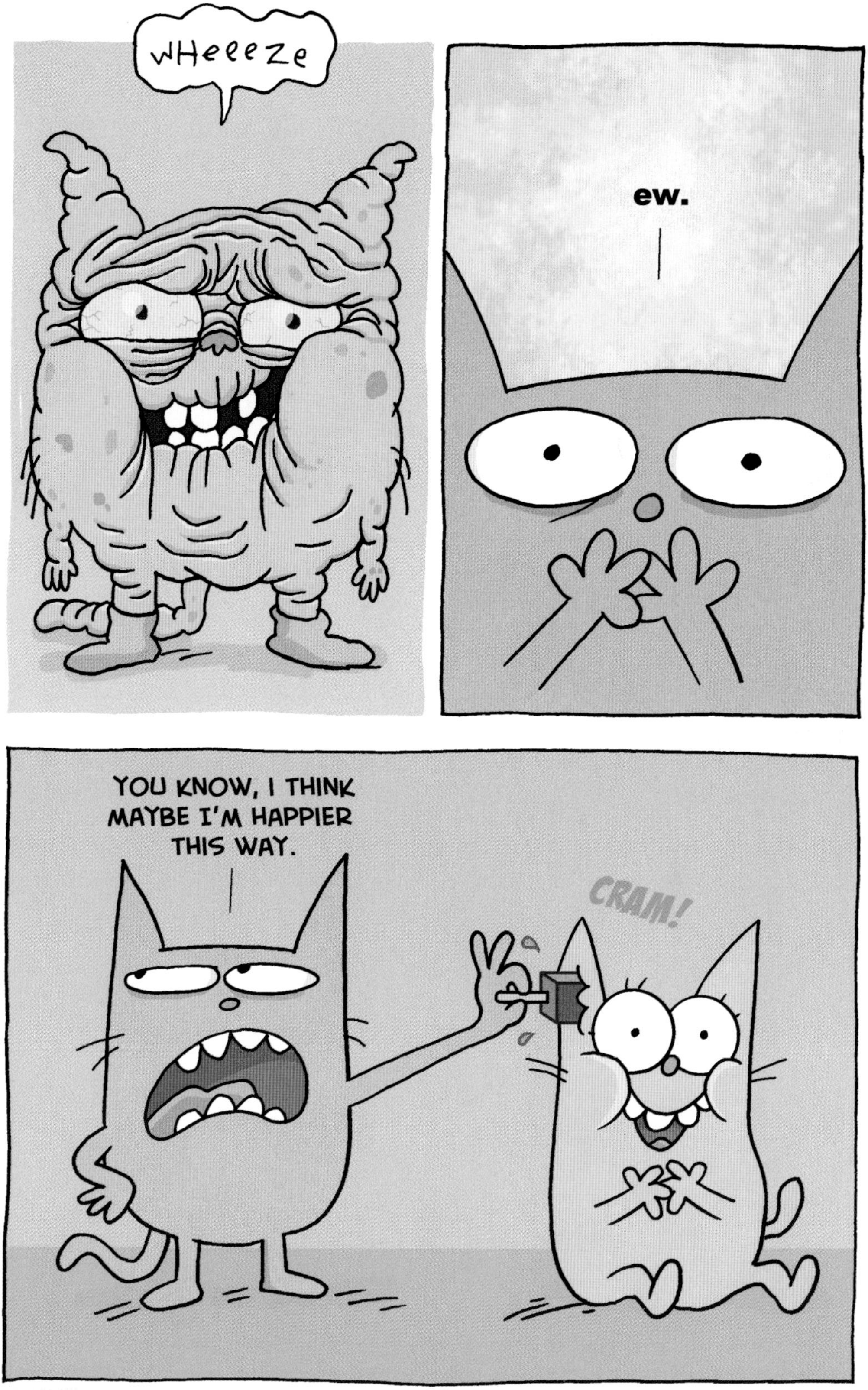
WHEEEZE
ew.
YOU KNOW, I THINK MAYBE I'M HAPPIER THIS WAY.
CRAM!

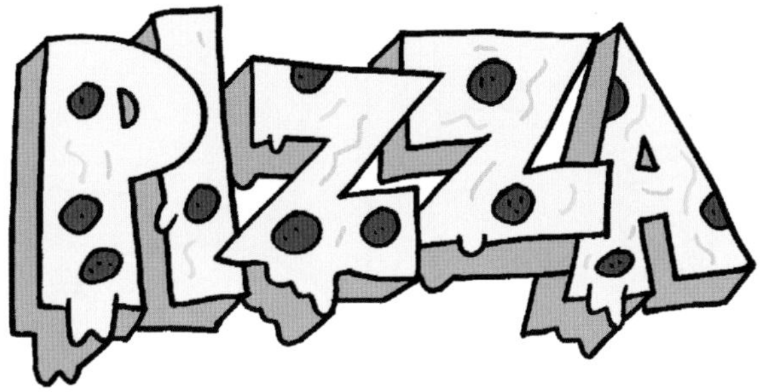
PIZZA

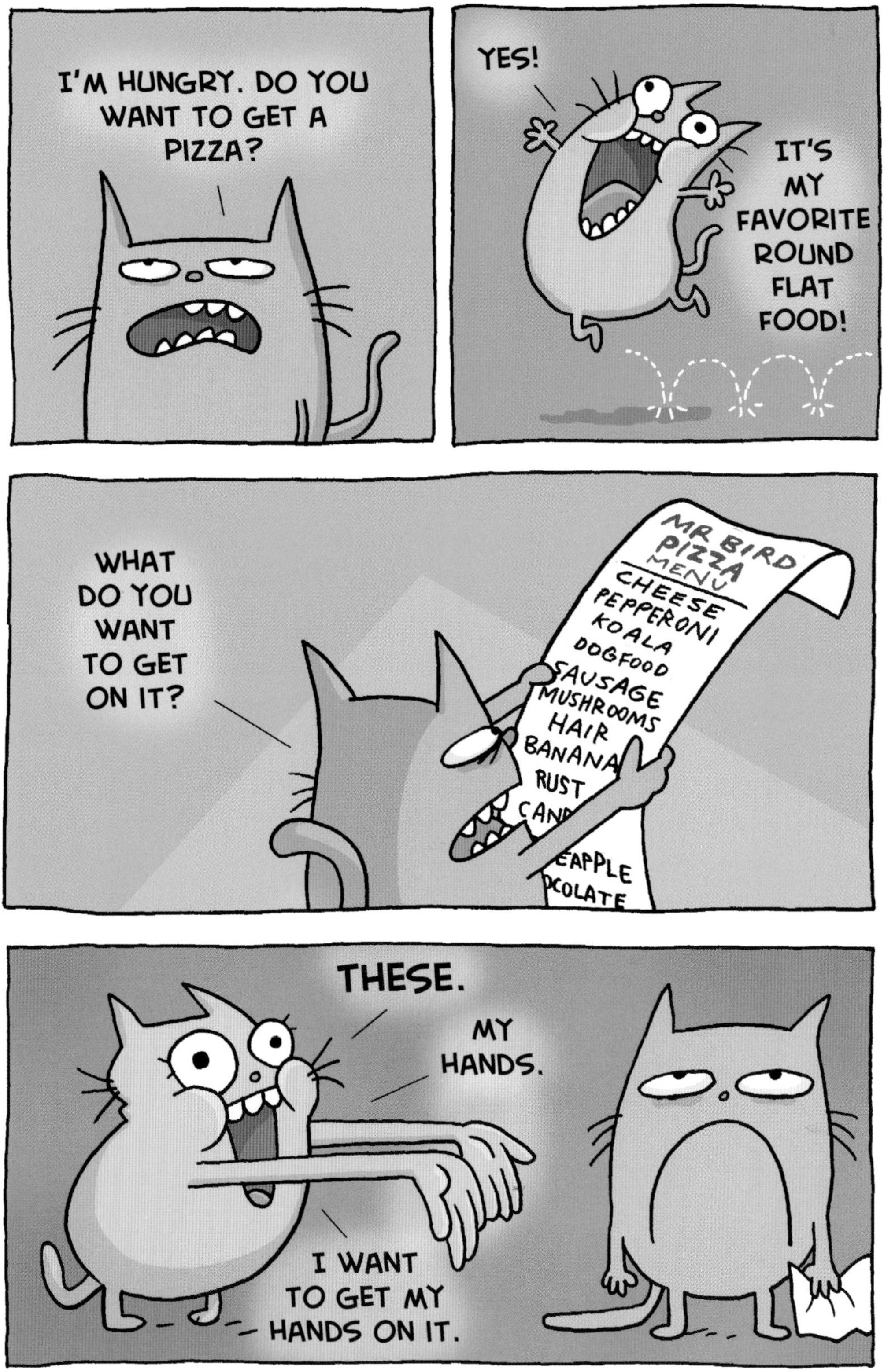
I'M HUNGRY. DO YOU WANT TO GET A PIZZA?
YES!
IT'S MY FAVORITE ROUND FLAT FOOD!
WHAT DO YOU WANT TO GET ON IT?
MR BIRD PIZZA MENU
CHEESE
PEPPERONI
KOALA
DOGFOOD
SAUSAGE
MUSHROOMS
HAIR
BANANA
RUST
THESE.
MY HANDS.
I WANT TO GET MY HANDS ON IT.

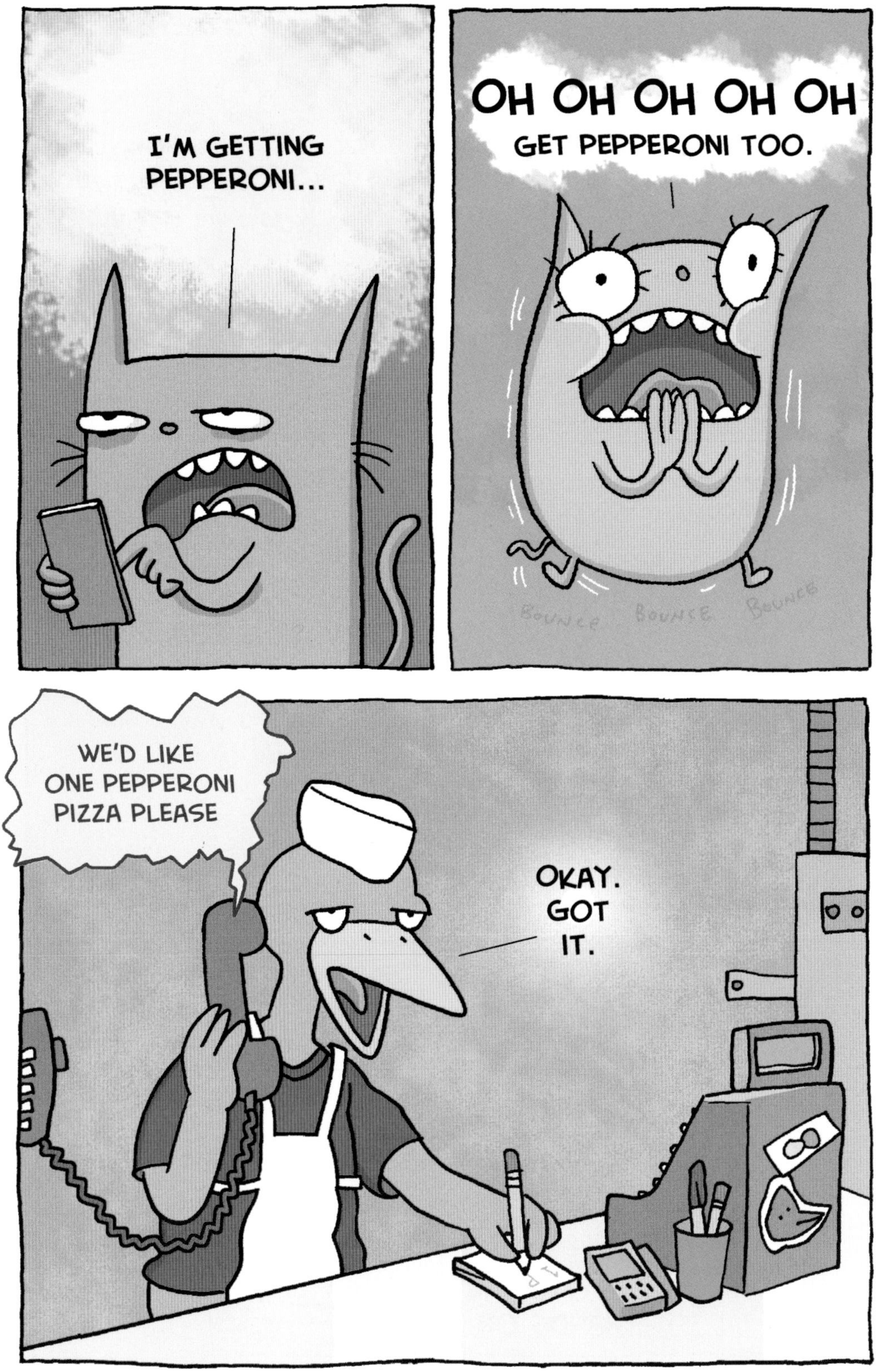
I'M GETTING
PEPPERONI...
OH OH OH OH OH
GET PEPPERONI TOO.
BOUNCE BOUNCE BOUNCE
WE'D LIKE
ONE PEPPERONI
PIZZA PLEASE
OKAY.
GOT
IT.

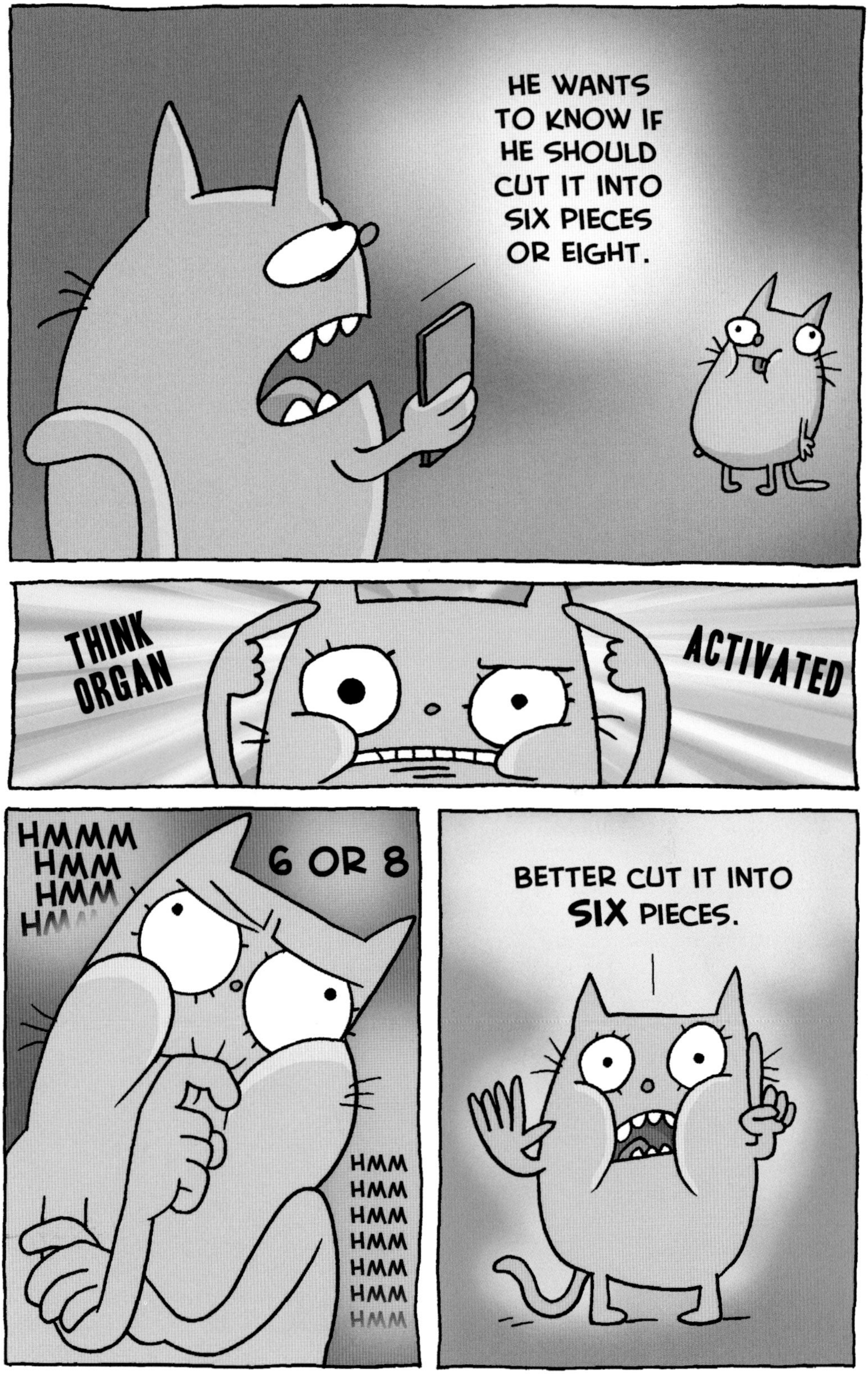
HE WANTS TO KNOW IF HE SHOULD CUT IT INTO SIX PIECES OR EIGHT.
THINK ORGAN
ACTIVATED
HMMM HMM HMM
6 OR 8
HMM HMM HMM HMM HMM HMM HMM
BETTER CUT IT INTO SIX PIECES.

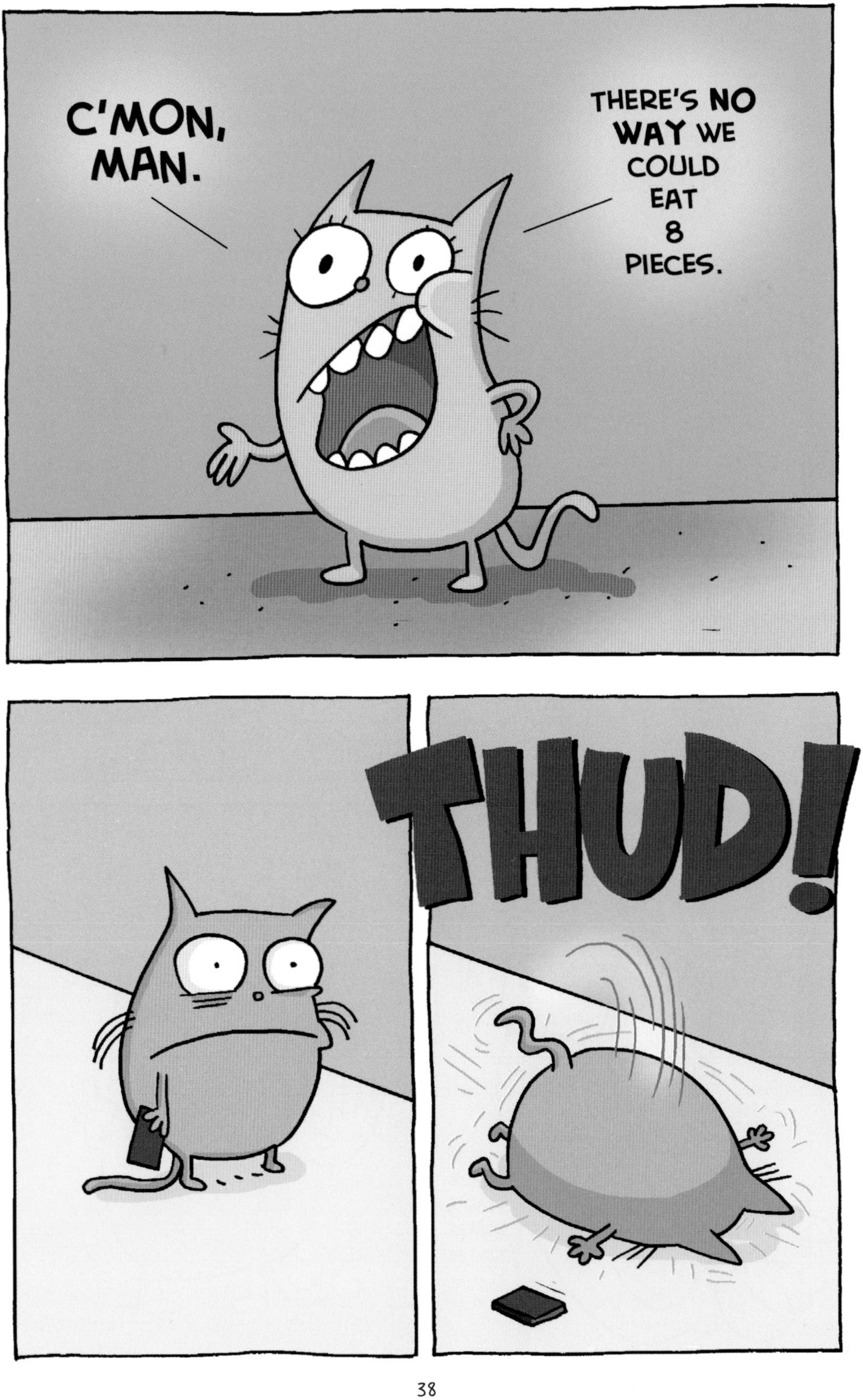
C'MON, MAN.
THERE'S NO WAY WE COULD EAT 8 PIECES.
THUD!

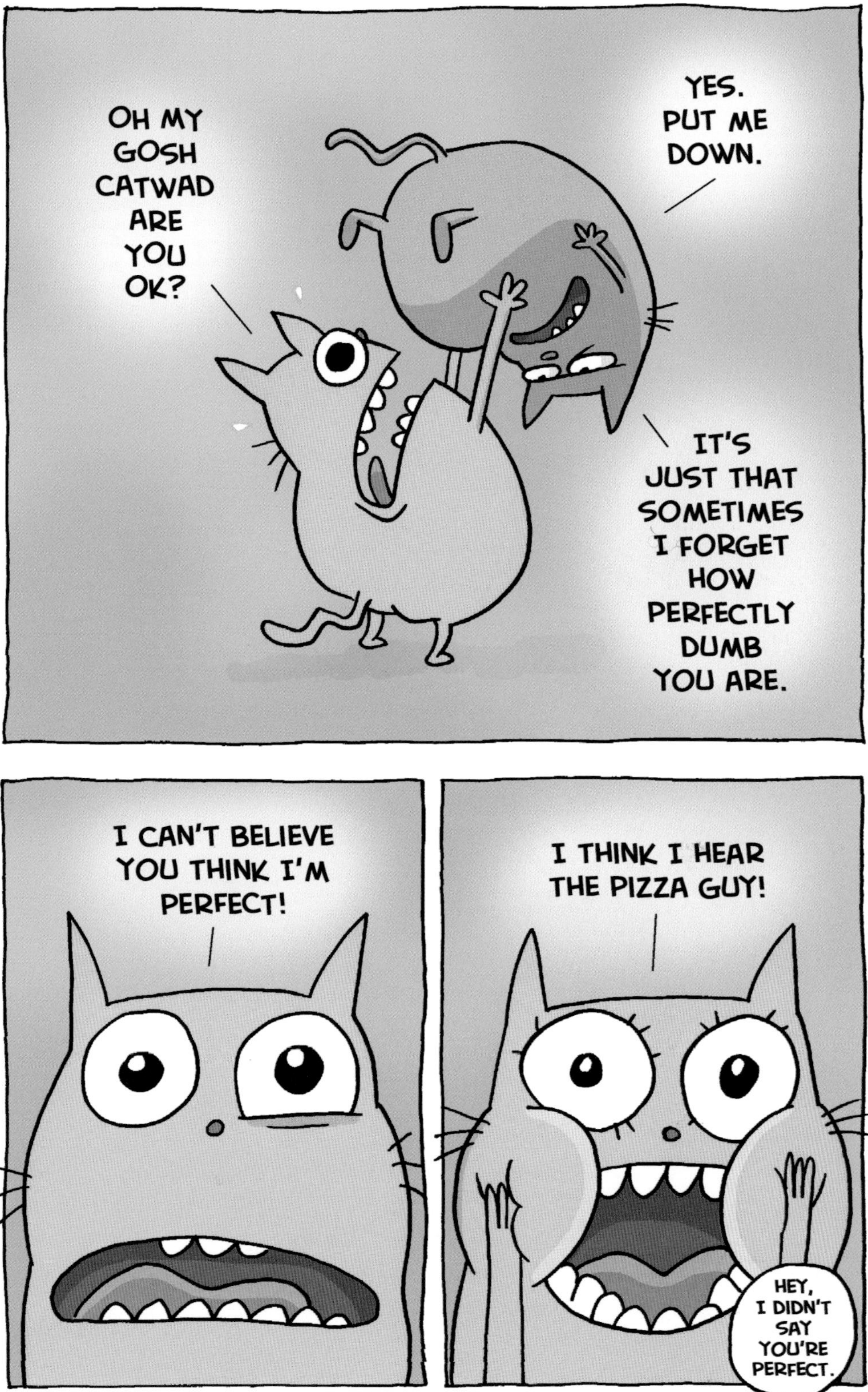
OH MY GOSH CATWAD ARE YOU OK?
YES. PUT ME DOWN.
IT'S JUST THAT SOMETIMES I FORGET HOW PERFECTLY DUMB YOU ARE.
I CAN'T BELIEVE YOU THINK I'M PERFECT!
I THINK I HEAR THE PIZZA GUY!
HEY, I DIDN'T SAY YOU'RE PERFECT.

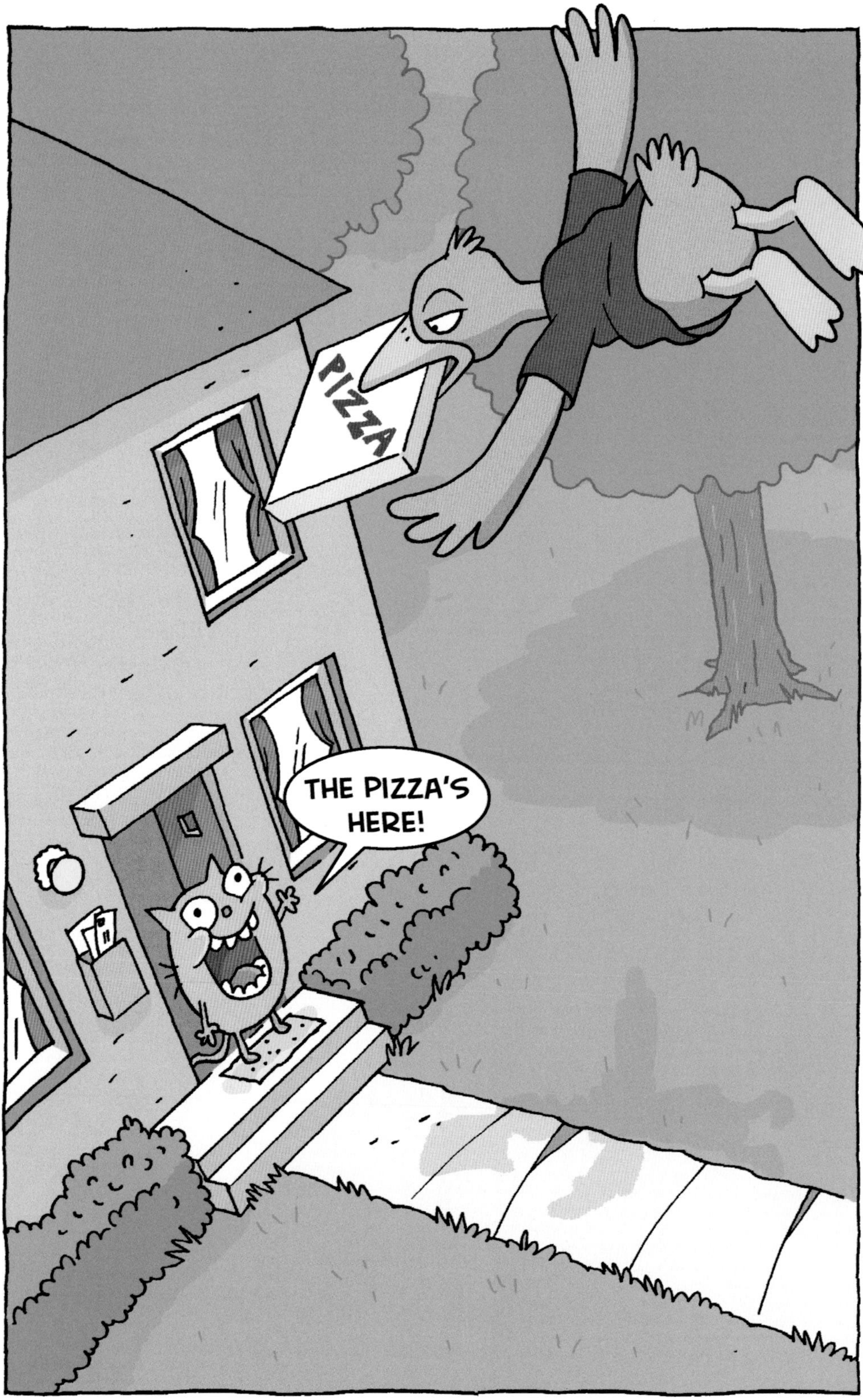
PIZZA
THE PIZZA'S HERE!

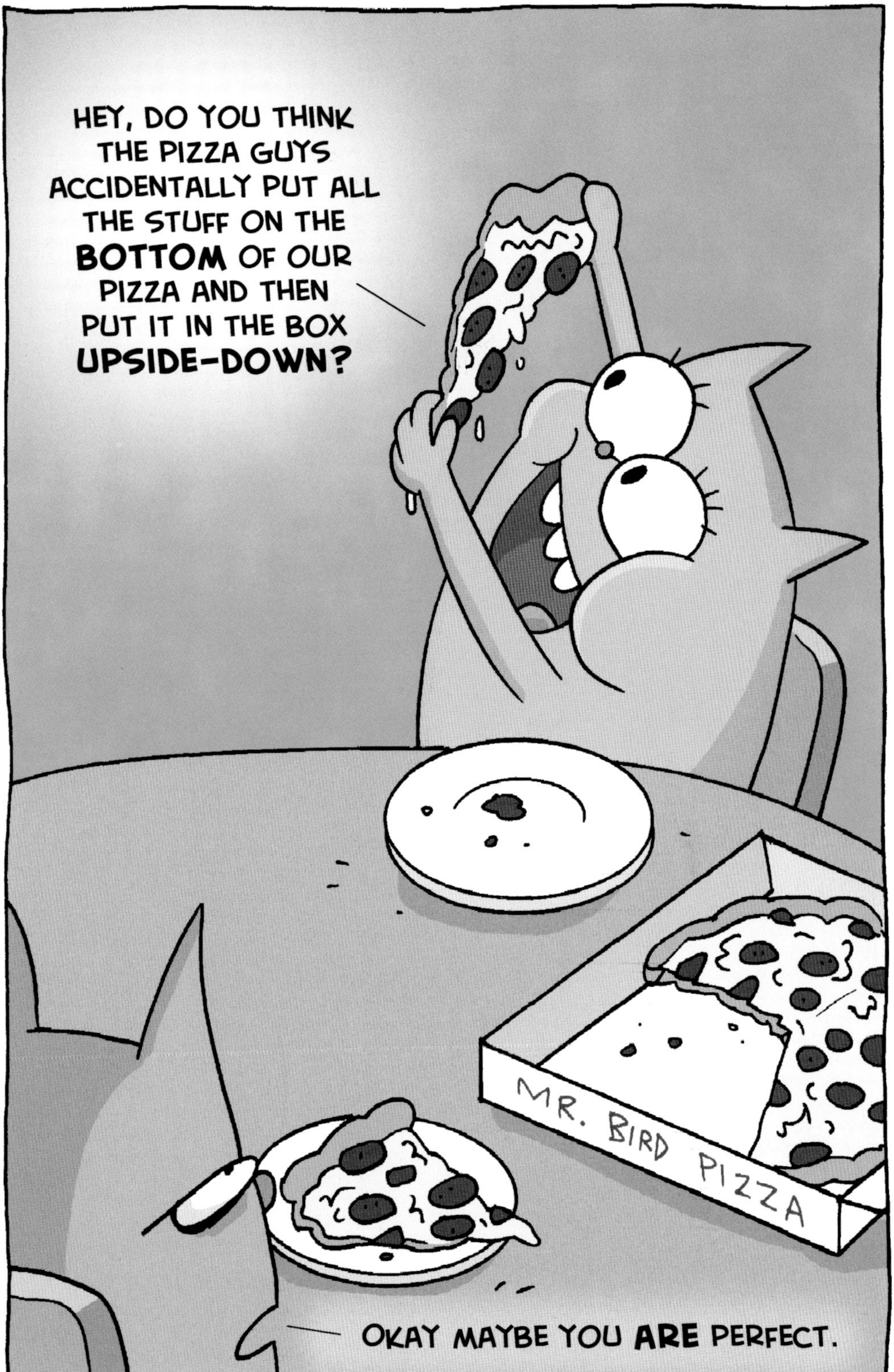
HEY, DO YOU THINK THE PIZZA GUYS ACCIDENTALLY PUT ALL THE STUFF ON THE **BOTTOM** OF OUR PIZZA AND THEN PUT IT IN THE BOX **UPSIDE-DOWN?**
MR. BIRD PIZZA
OKAY MAYBE YOU **ARE** PERFECT.

Do You?

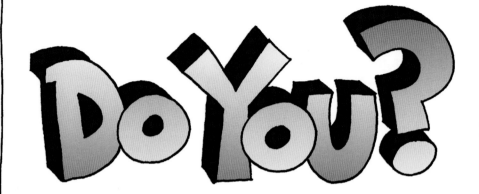

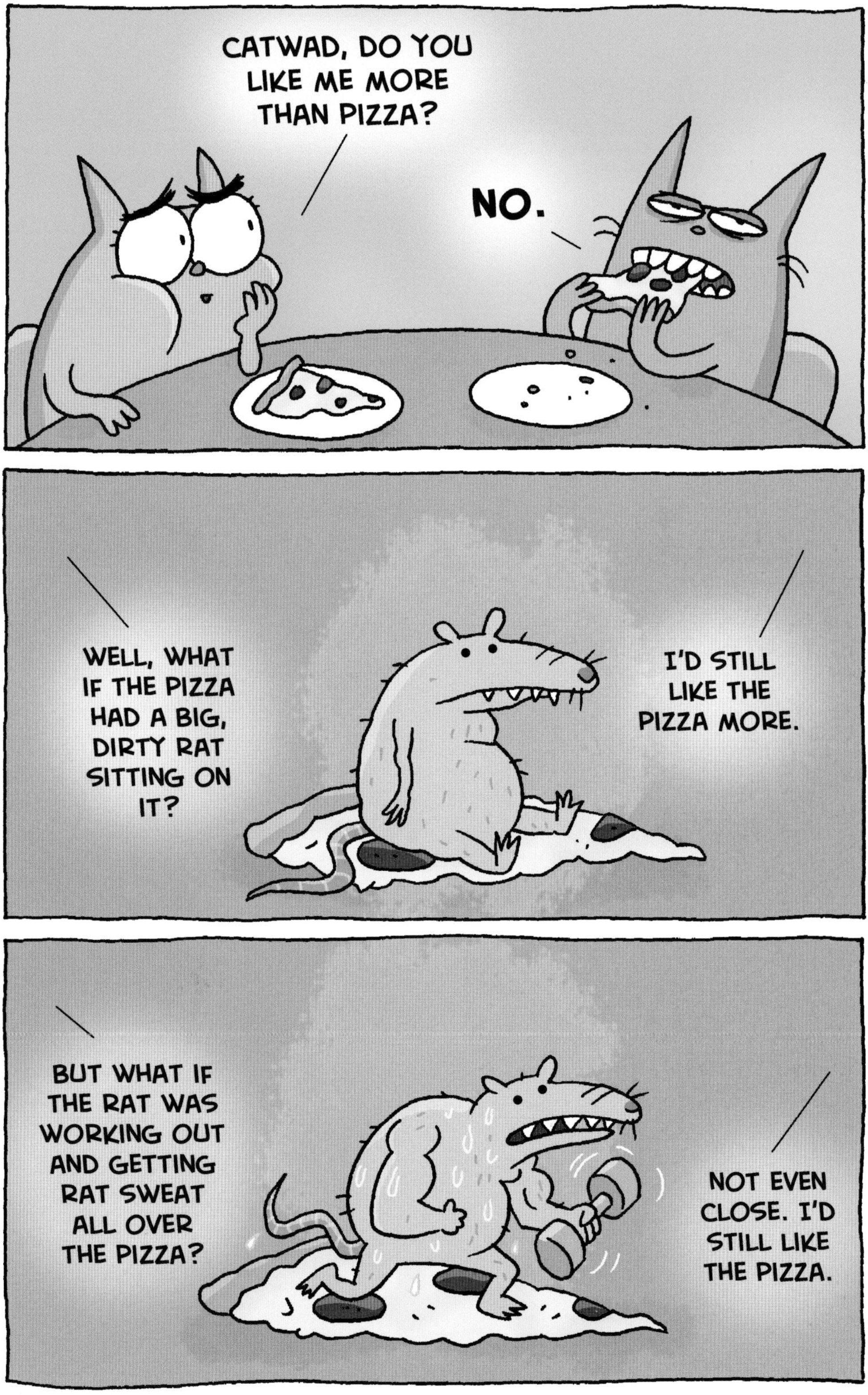
CATWAD, DO YOU LIKE ME MORE THAN PIZZA?
NO.
WELL, WHAT IF THE PIZZA HAD A BIG, DIRTY RAT SITTING ON IT?
I'D STILL LIKE THE PIZZA MORE.
BUT WHAT IF THE RAT WAS WORKING OUT AND GETTING RAT SWEAT ALL OVER THE PIZZA?
NOT EVEN CLOSE. I'D STILL LIKE THE PIZZA.

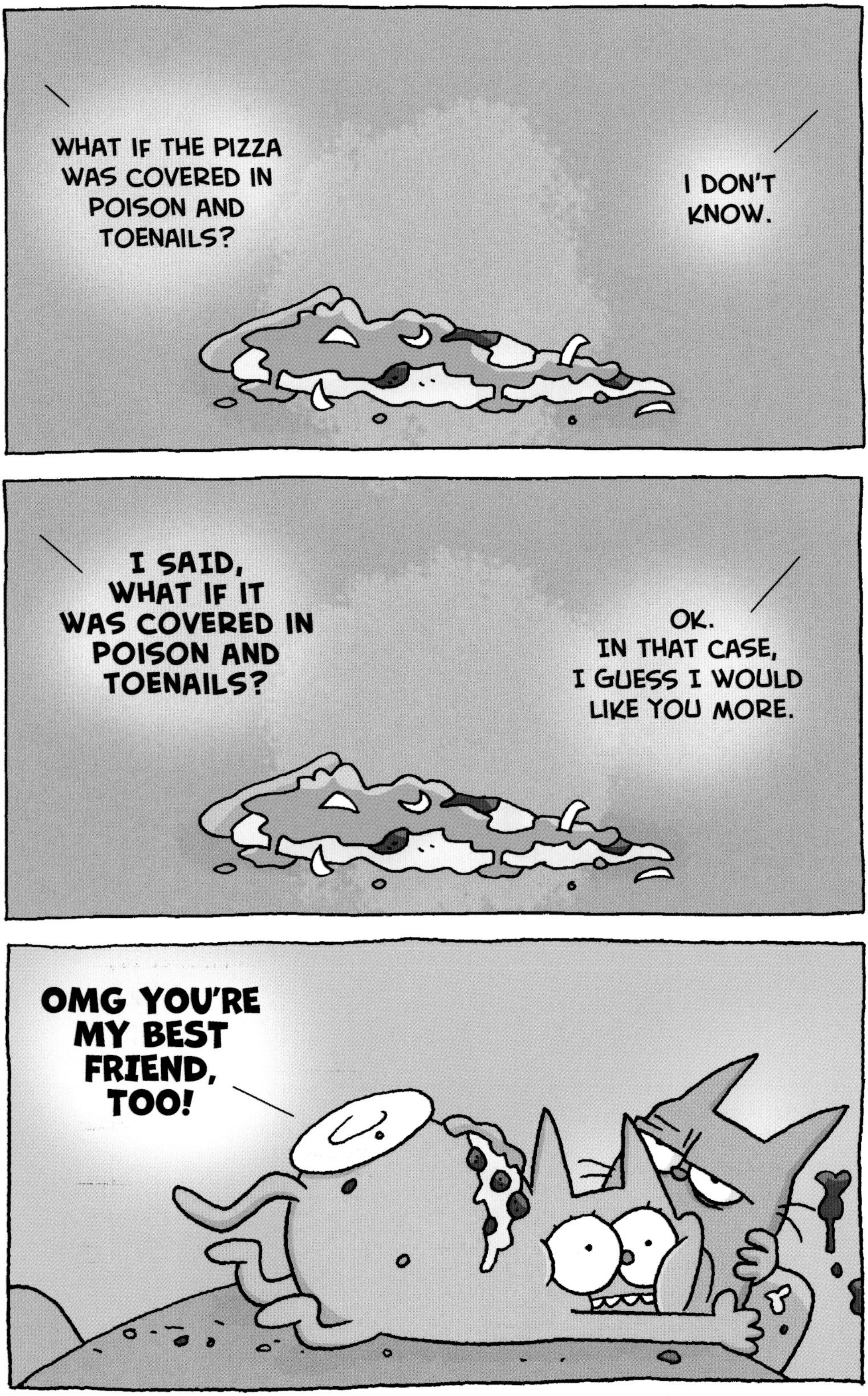
WHAT IF THE PIZZA WAS COVERED IN POISON AND TOENAILS?
I DON'T KNOW.
I SAID, WHAT IF IT WAS COVERED IN POISON AND TOENAILS?
OK. IN THAT CASE, I GUESS I WOULD LIKE YOU MORE.
OMG YOU'RE MY BEST FRIEND, TOO!

WHAT'S IN A NAME?

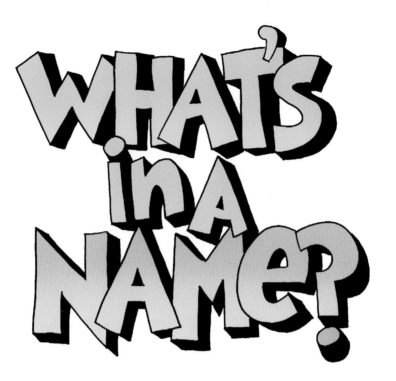

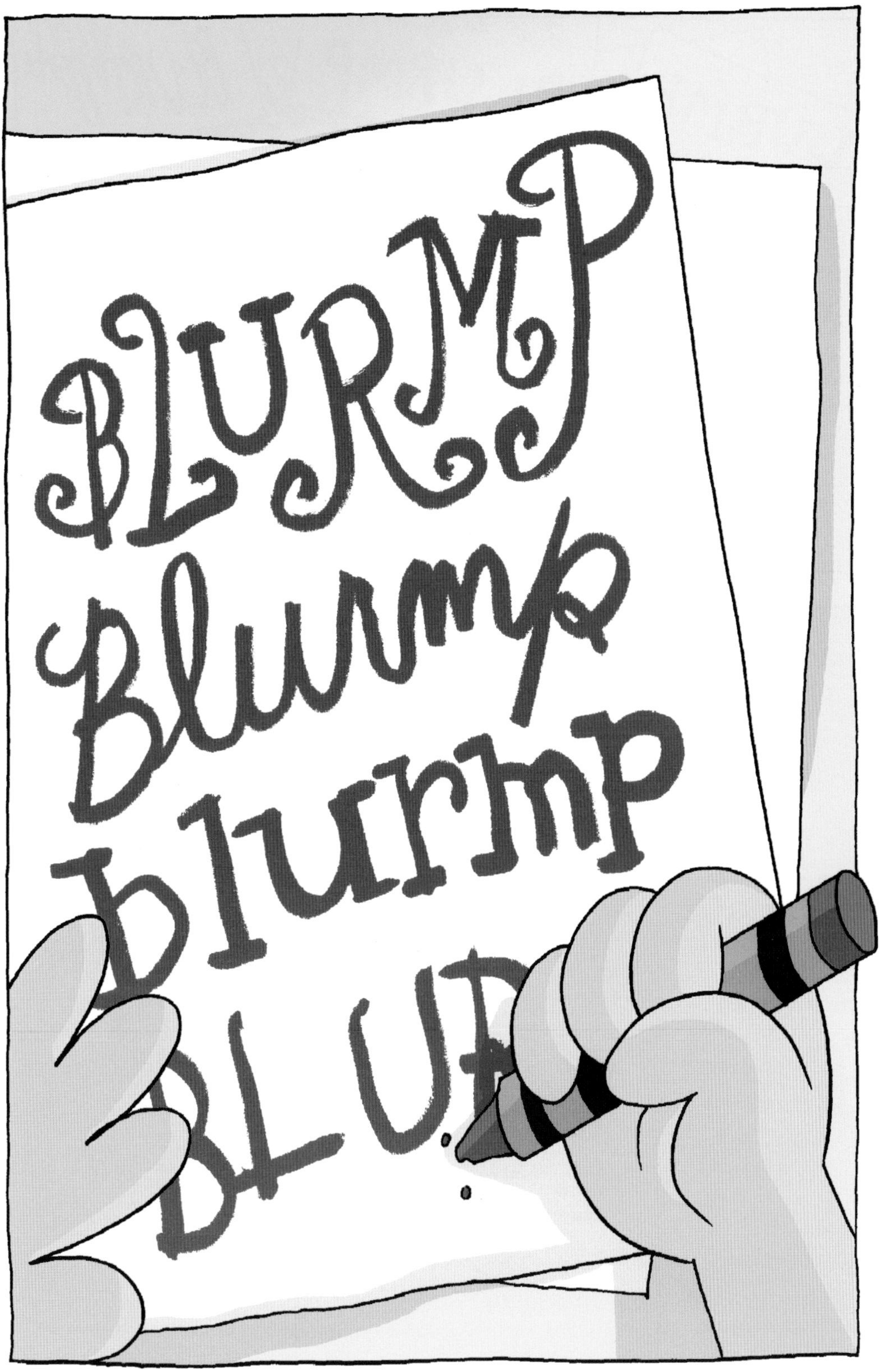
BLURMP
Blurmp
blurmp
BLUR

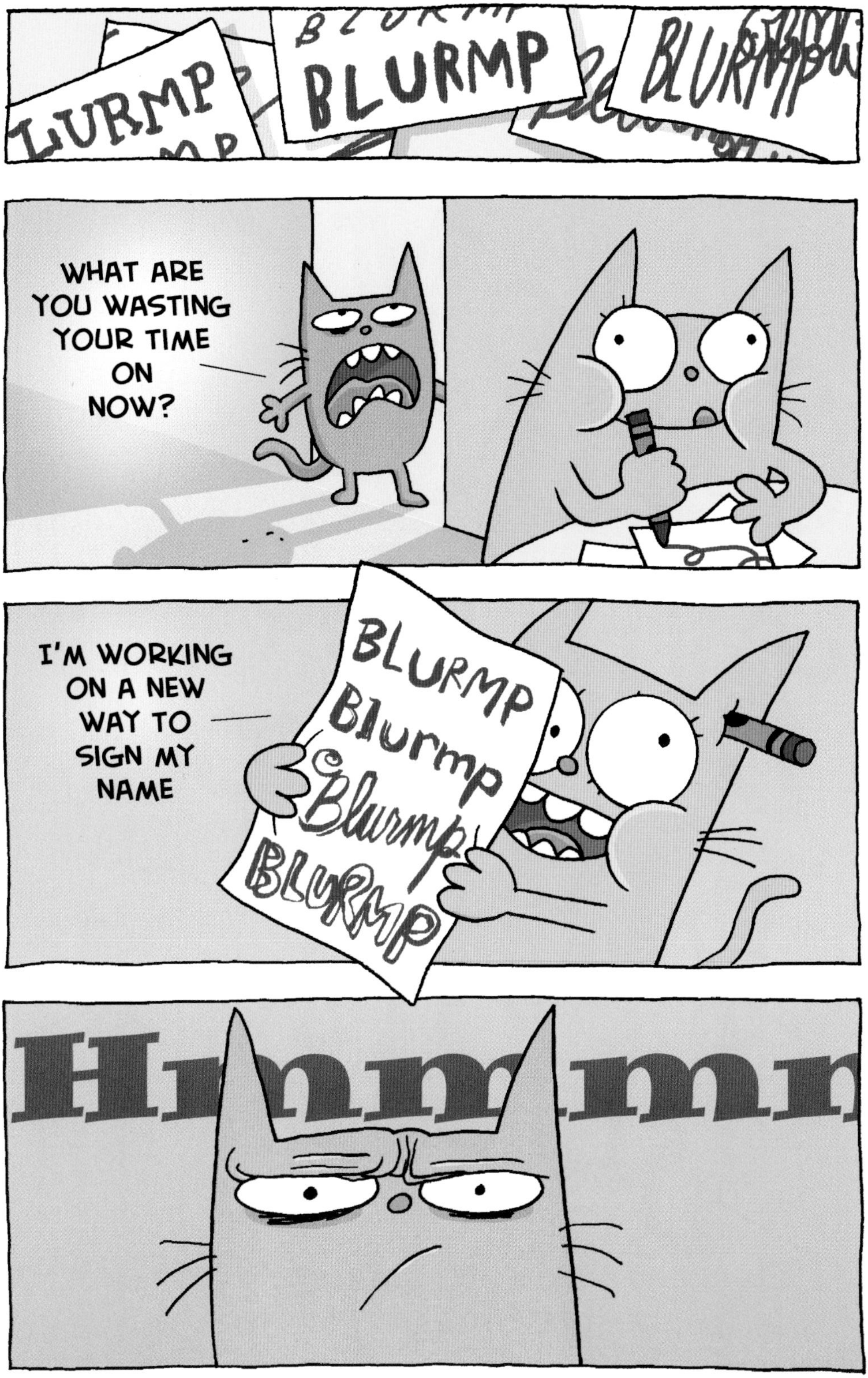
LURMP
BLURMP
BLURMP
WHAT ARE YOU WASTING YOUR TIME ON NOW?
I'M WORKING ON A NEW WAY TO SIGN MY NAME
BLURMP
Blurmp
Blurmp
BLURMP
Hmmmmm

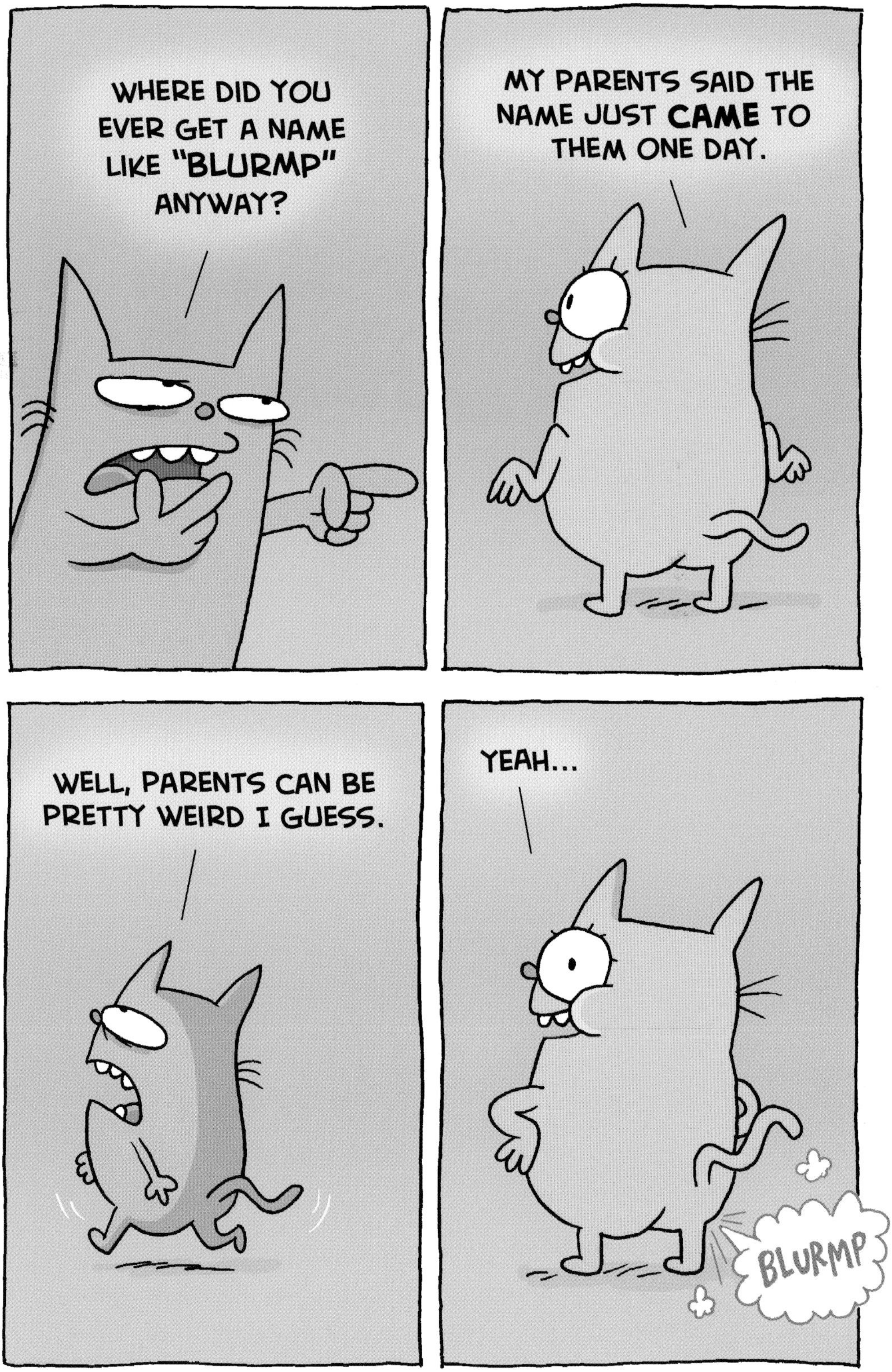
WHERE DID YOU EVER GET A NAME LIKE "BLURMP" ANYWAY?
MY PARENTS SAID THE NAME JUST CAME TO THEM ONE DAY.
WELL, PARENTS CAN BE PRETTY WEIRD I GUESS.
YEAH...
BLURMP

SURPRISE

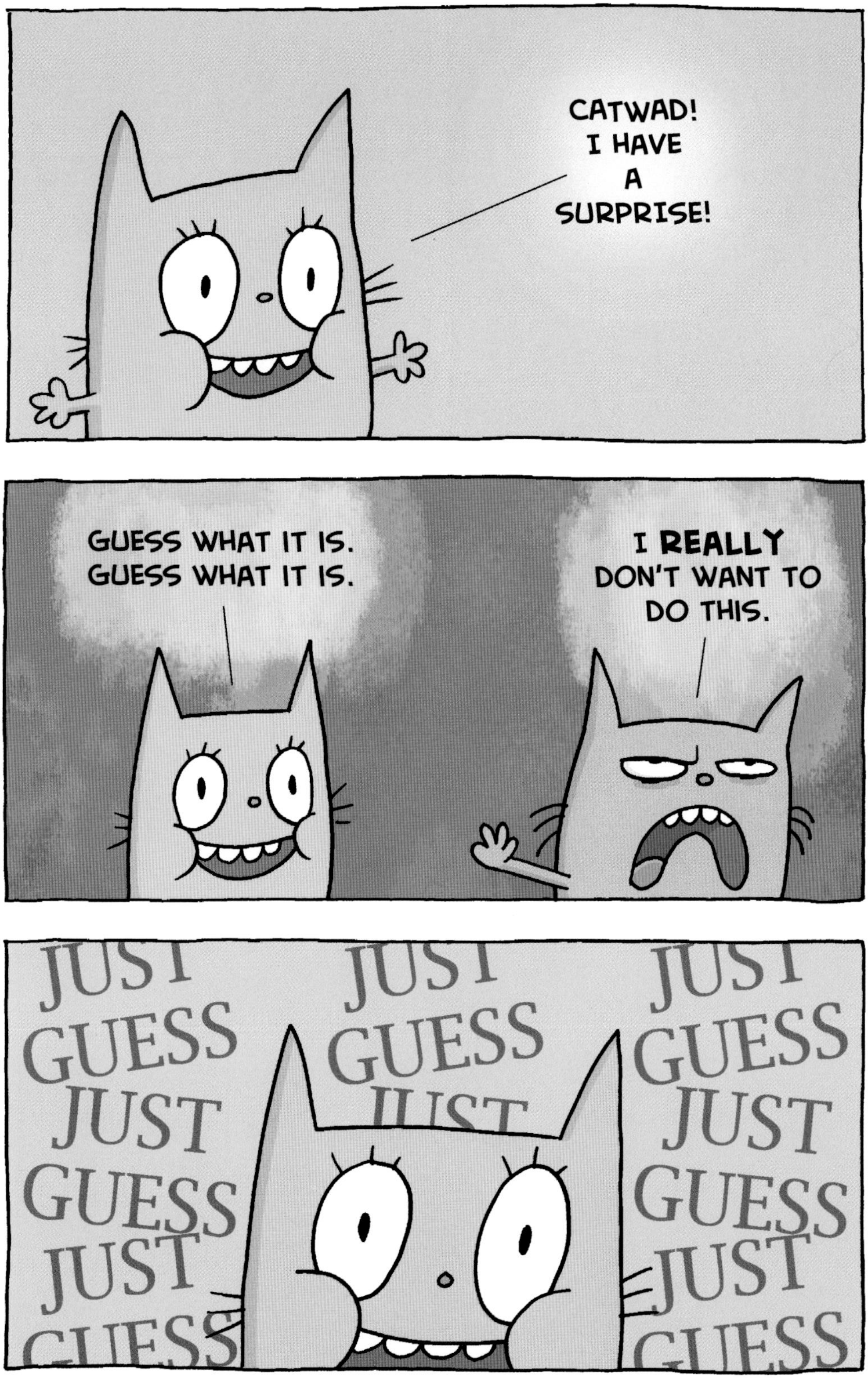
CATWAD! I HAVE A SURPRISE!
GUESS WHAT IT IS. GUESS WHAT IT IS.
I **REALLY** DON'T WANT TO DO THIS.
JUST GUESS JUST GUESS JUST GUESS

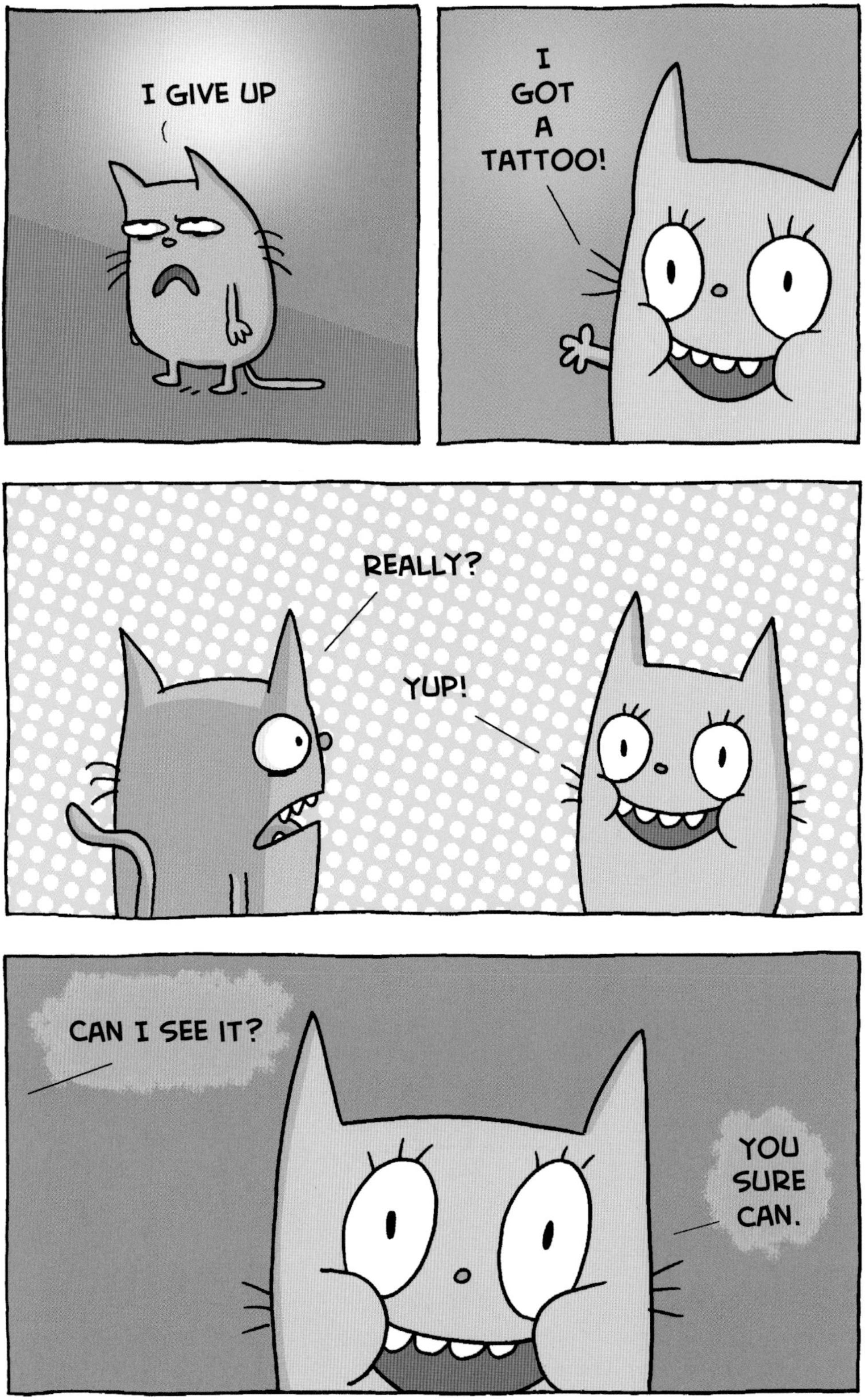
I GIVE UP
I GOT A TATTOO!
REALLY?
YUP!
CAN I SEE IT?
YOU SURE CAN.

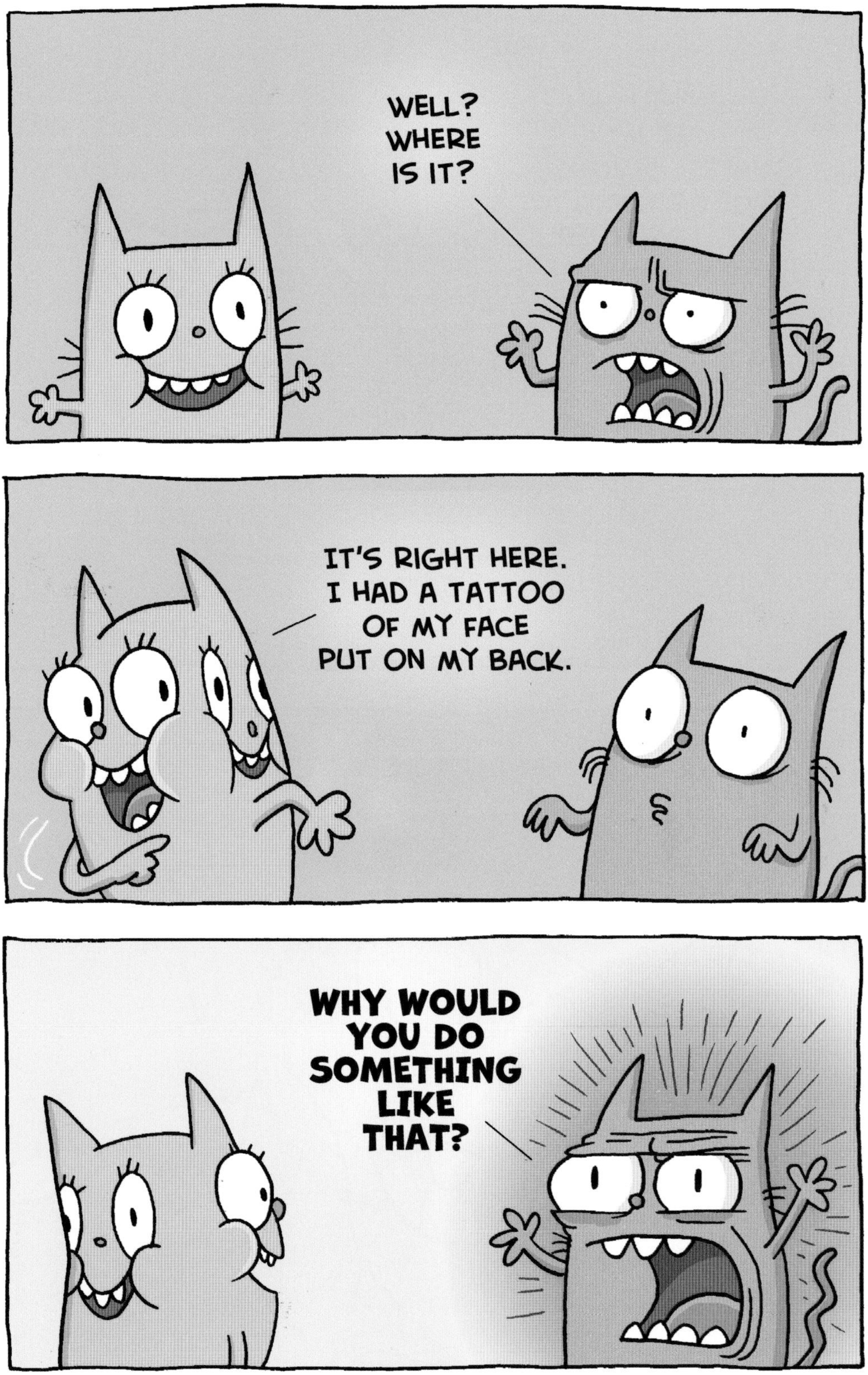
WELL? WHERE IS IT?
IT'S RIGHT HERE. I HAD A TATTOO OF MY FACE PUT ON MY BACK.
WHY WOULD YOU DO SOMETHING LIKE THAT?

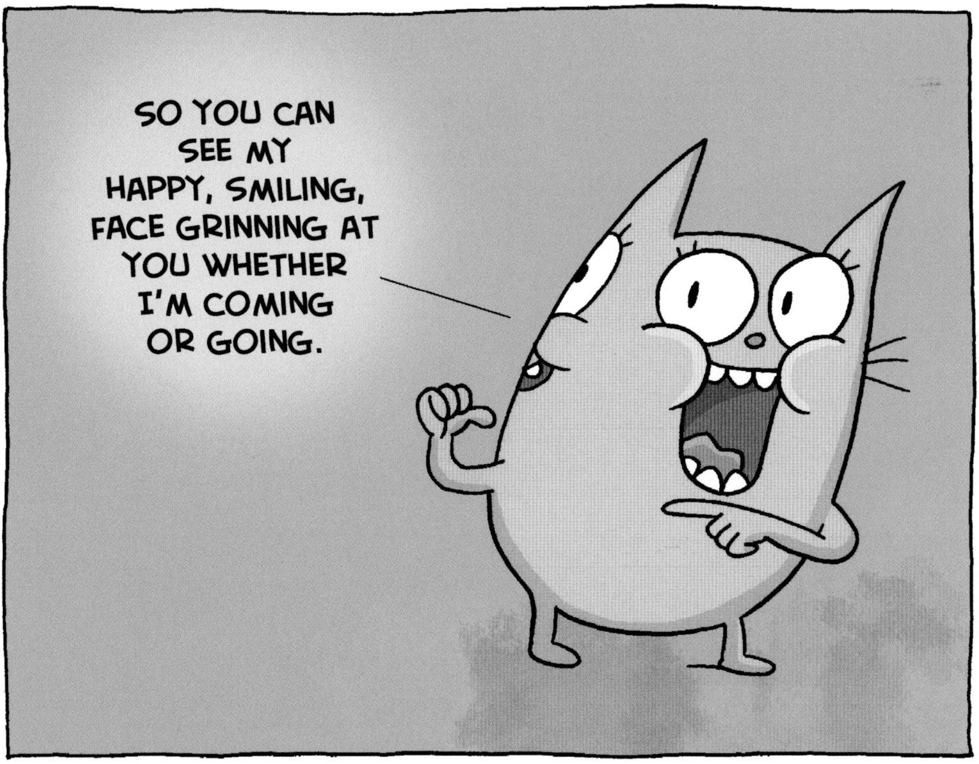
SO YOU CAN SEE MY HAPPY, SMILING, FACE GRINNING AT YOU WHETHER I'M COMING OR GOING.

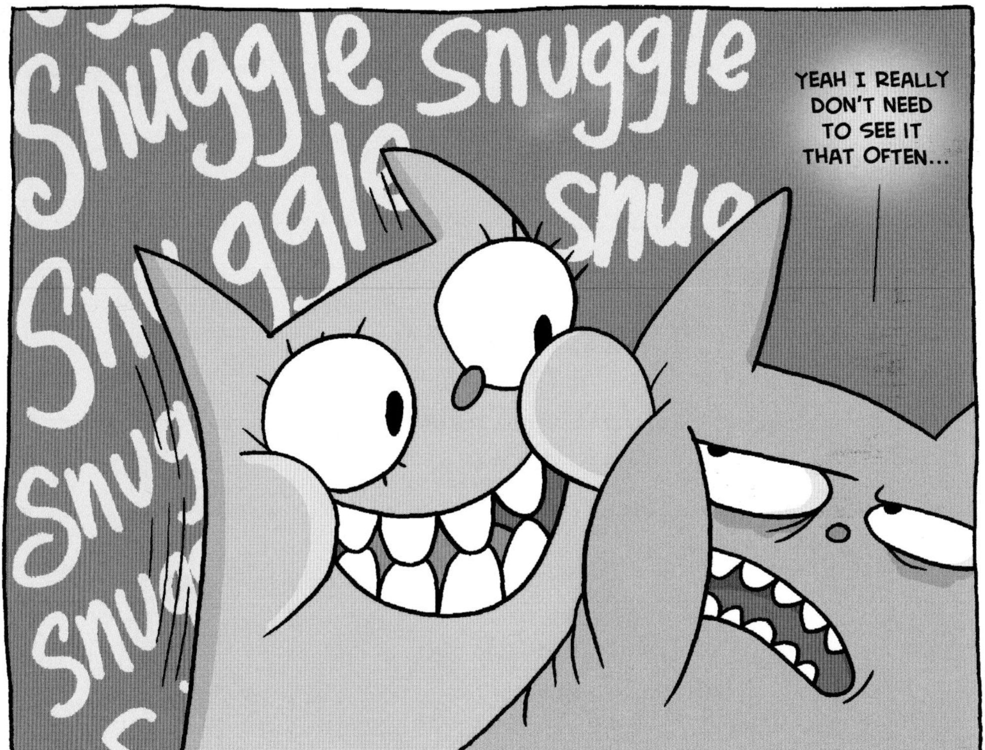
Snuggle Snuggle
YEAH I REALLY DON'T NEED TO SEE IT THAT OFTEN...

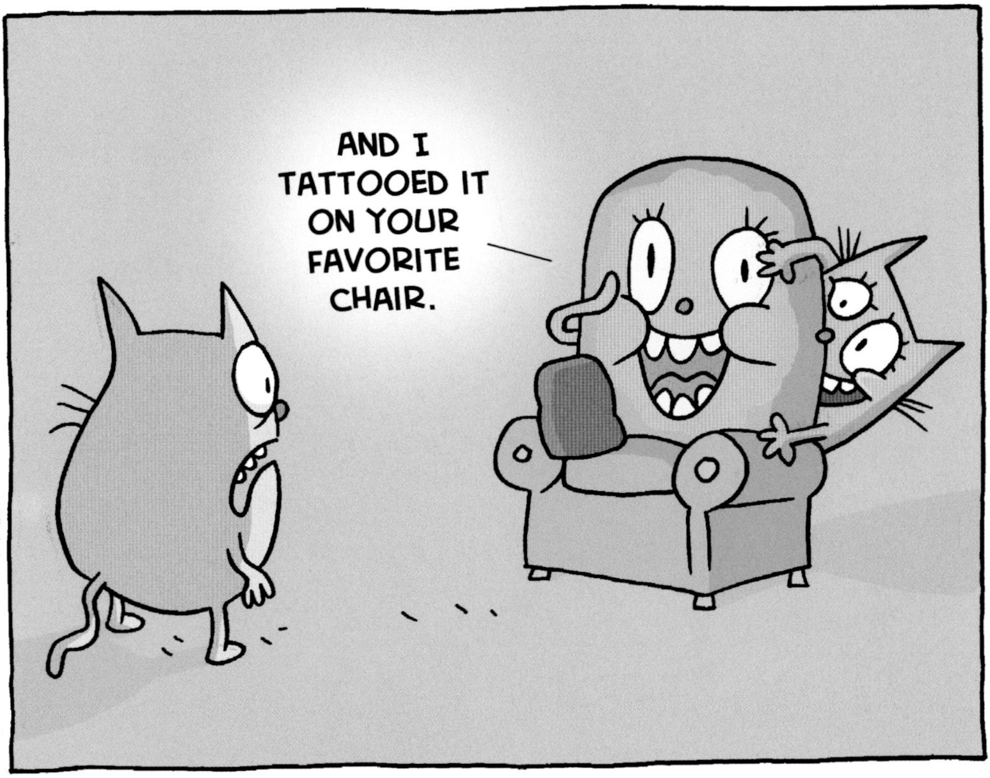
AND I TATTOOED IT ON YOUR FAVORITE CHAIR.

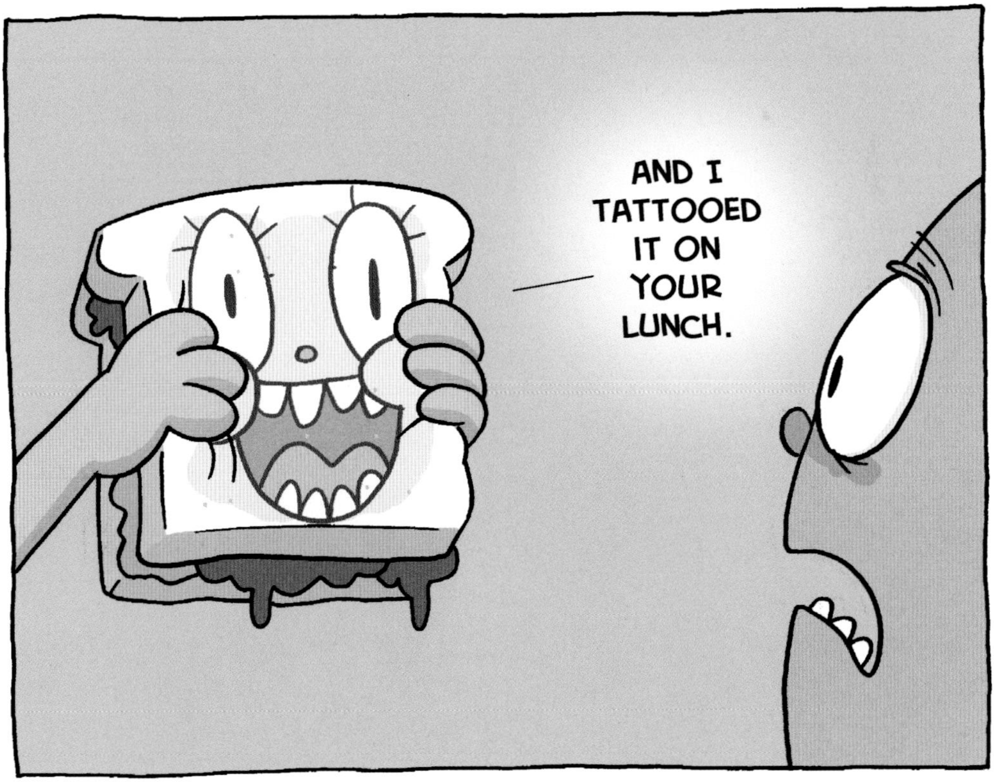
AND I TATTOOED IT ON YOUR LUNCH.

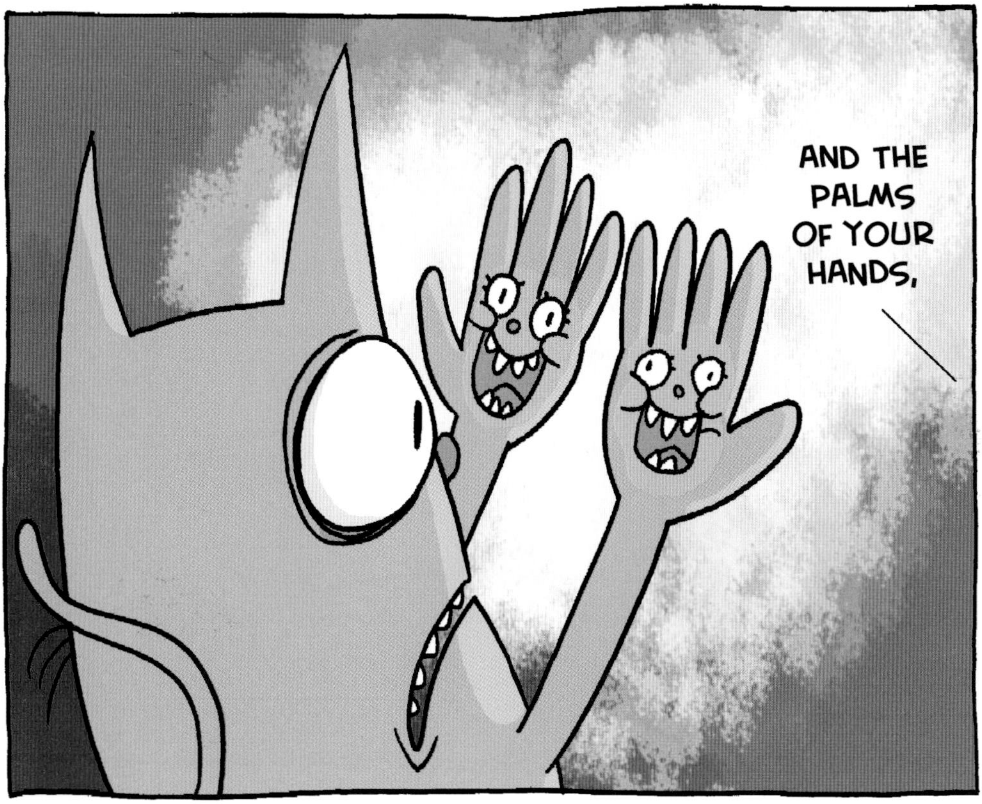
AND THE PALMS OF YOUR HANDS,

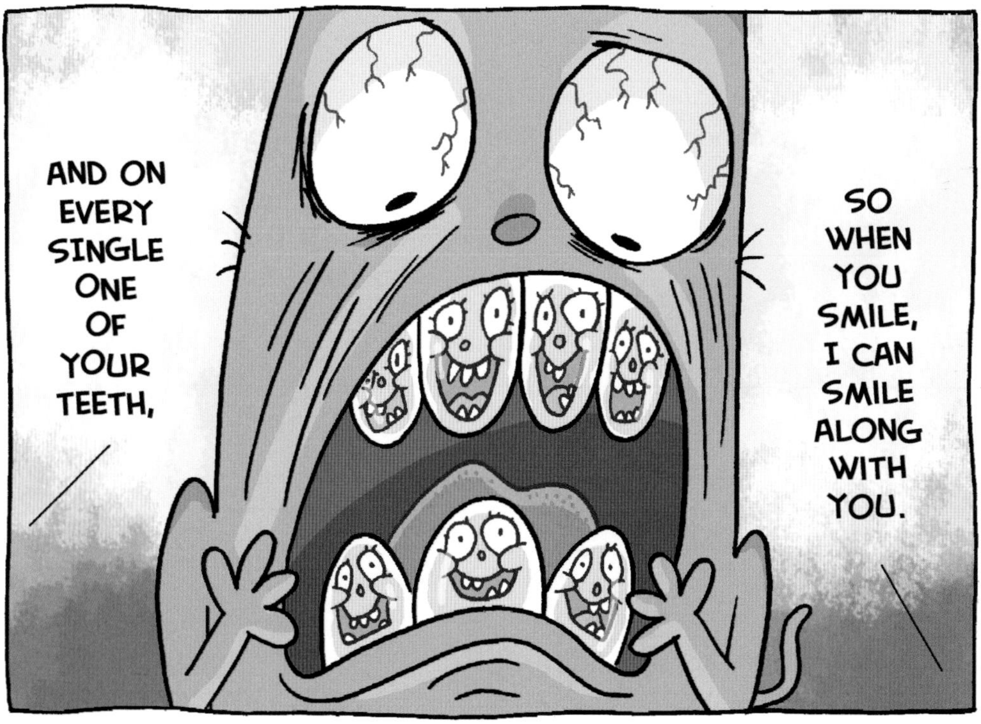
AND ON EVERY SINGLE ONE OF YOUR TEETH,
SO WHEN YOU SMILE, I CAN SMILE ALONG WITH YOU.

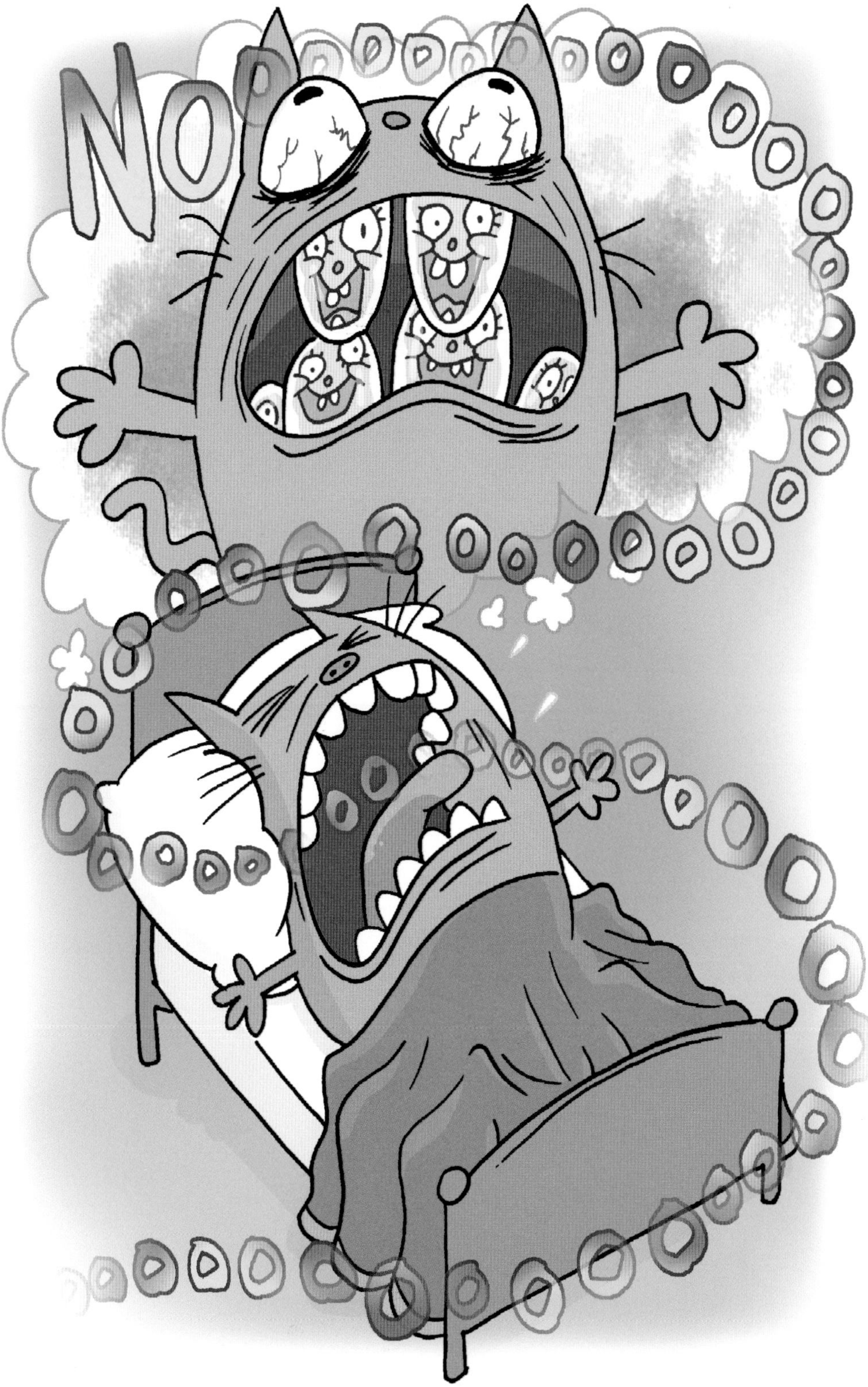
NOOOOOOOOOOOOOOOOOOOOOOOOOOOOOOOOOOOOOOOOOOOOOOOO

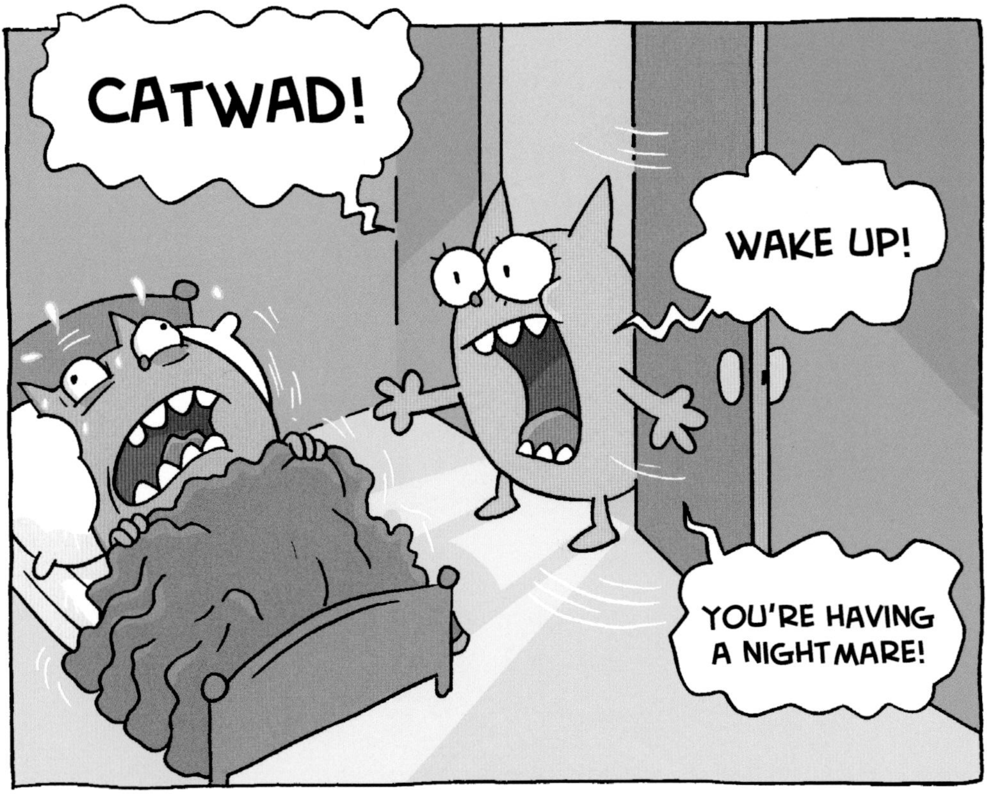
CATWAD!
WAKE UP!
YOU'RE HAVING A NIGHTMARE!

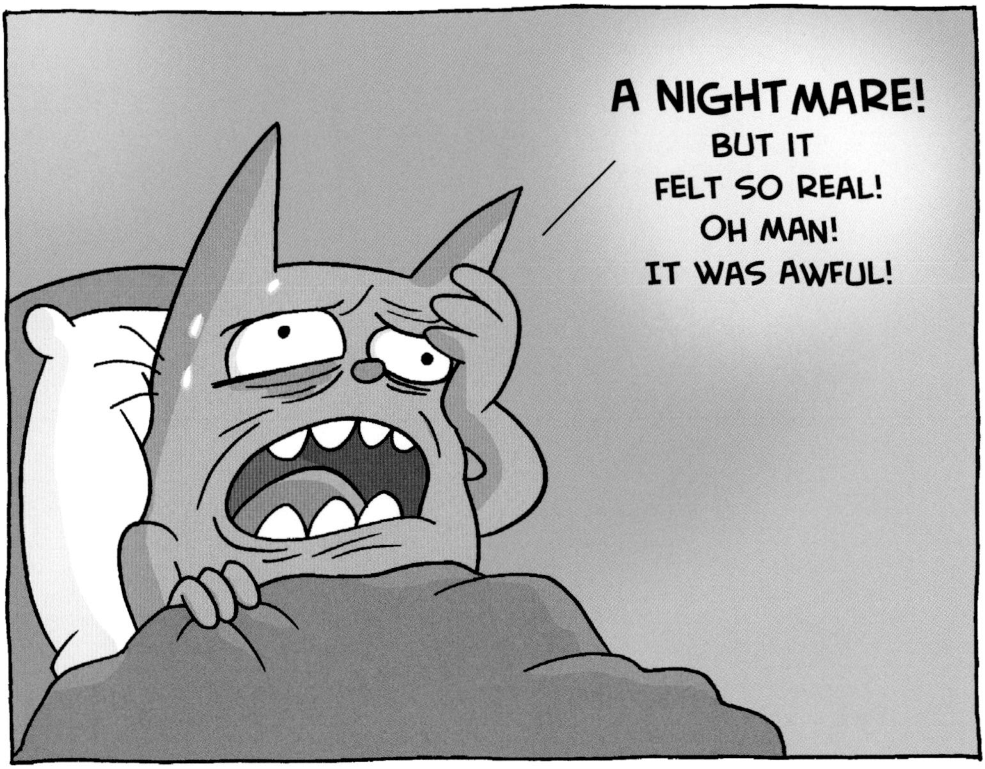
A NIGHTMARE!
BUT IT FELT SO REAL! OH MAN! IT WAS AWFUL!

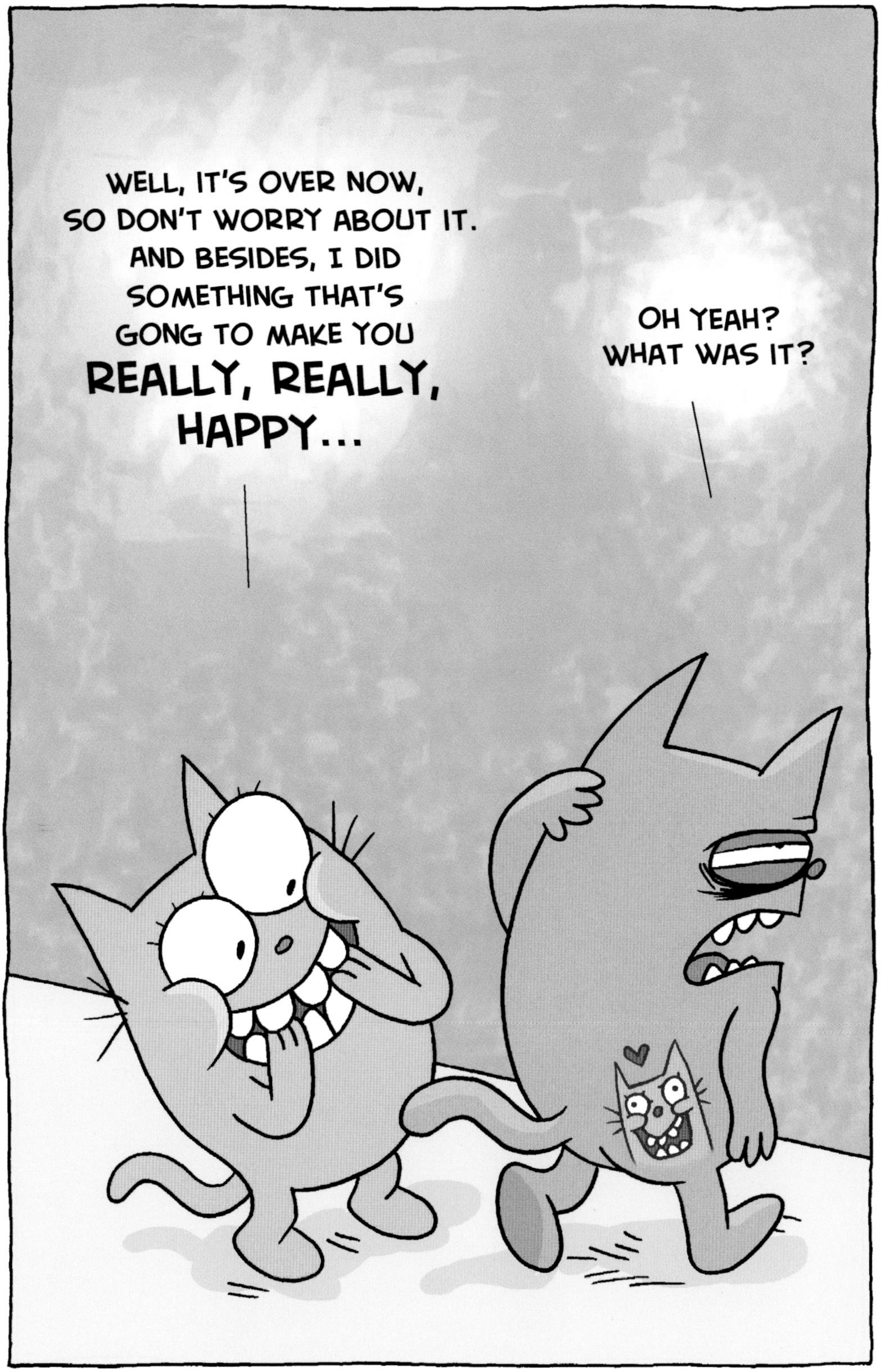
WELL, IT'S OVER NOW, SO DON'T WORRY ABOUT IT. AND BESIDES, I DID SOMETHING THAT'S GONG TO MAKE YOU REALLY, REALLY, HAPPY...
OH YEAH? WHAT WAS IT?

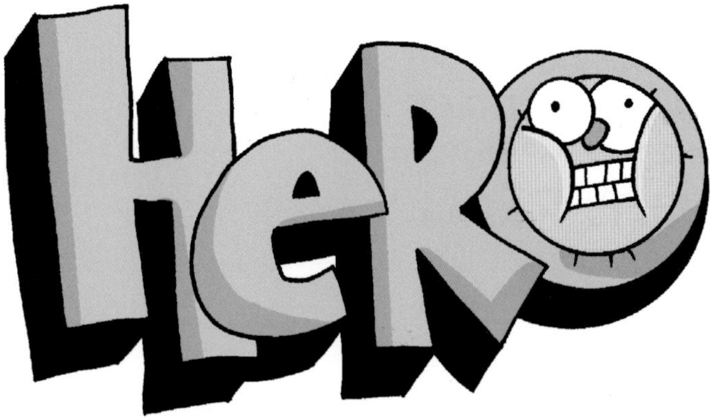
HERO

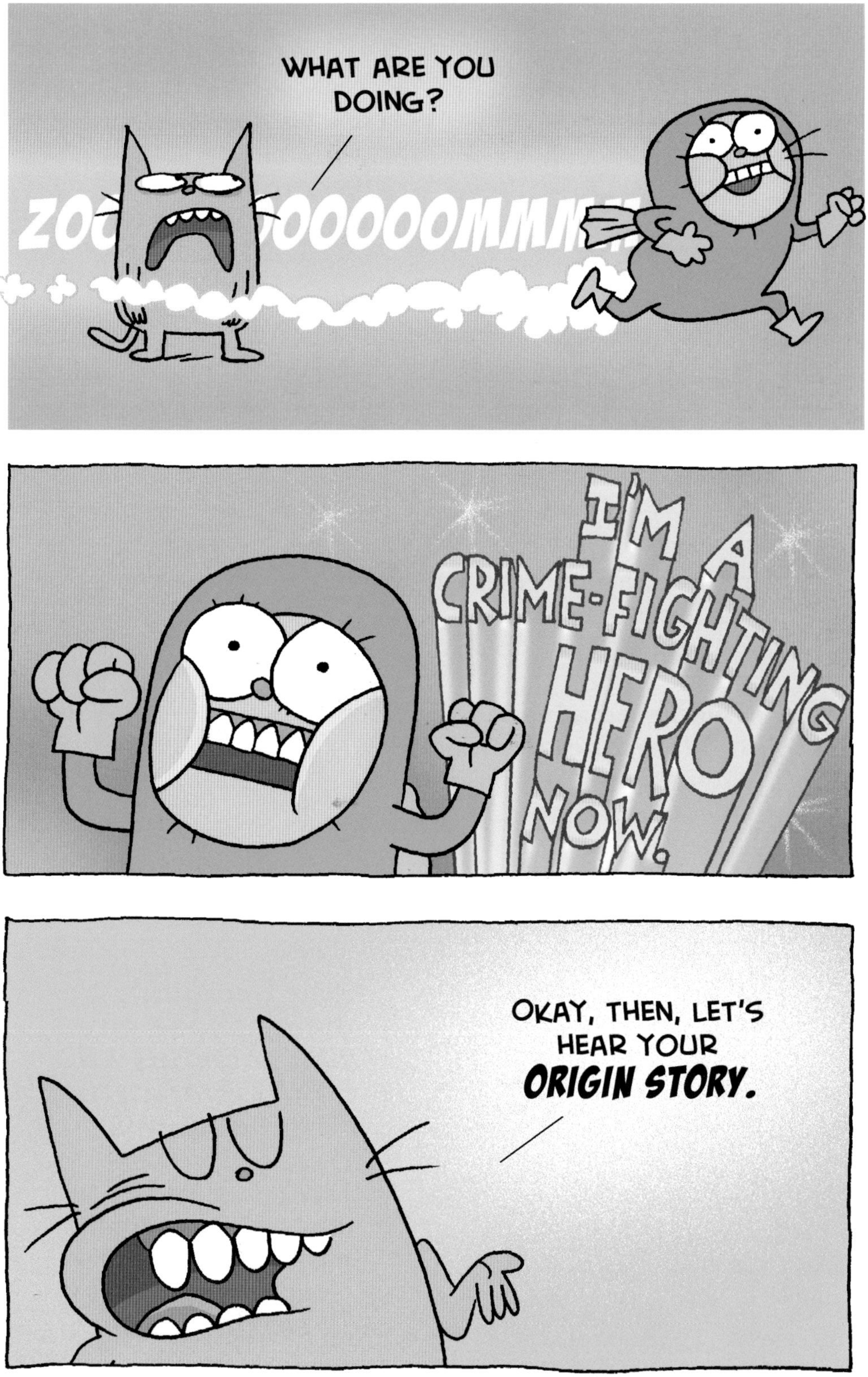
WHAT ARE YOU DOING?
I'M A CRIME-FIGHTING HERO NOW.
OKAY, THEN, LET'S HEAR YOUR ORIGIN STORY.

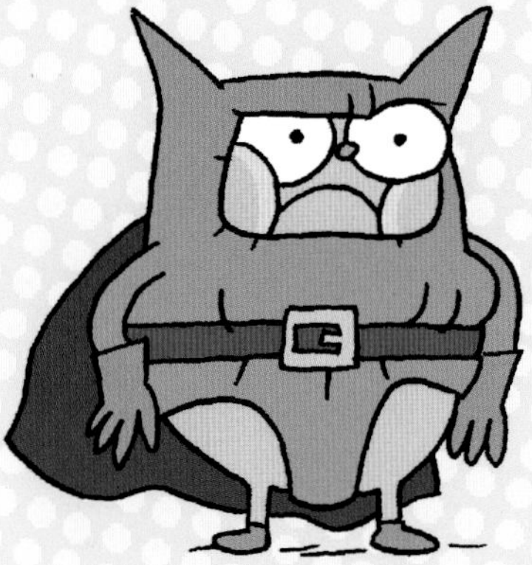

Well, I *thought* about being one of those mysterious and ANGRY HEROES OF THE NIGHT.

But my bedtime is too early for that.

I considered getting bitten by some RADIOACTIVE BUG.

But I was afraid it might be one of those dumb bugs that just crawls around on *dog poo.*

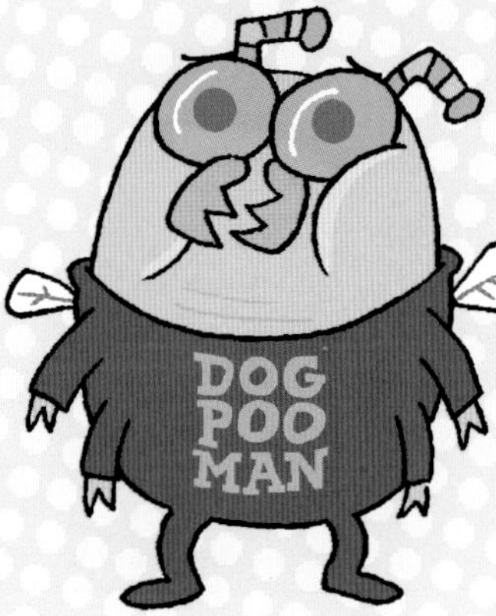
DOG
POO
MAN

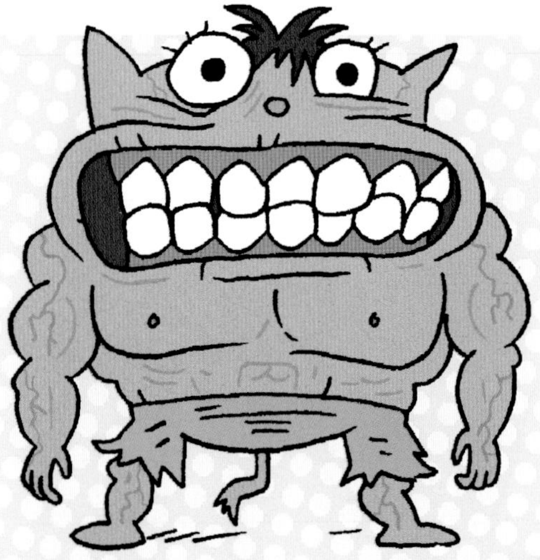

And I couldn't be one of those guys that gets BIG AND STRONG when he gets angry.

Because getting big and strong would make me so happy that I would just *shrink* again.

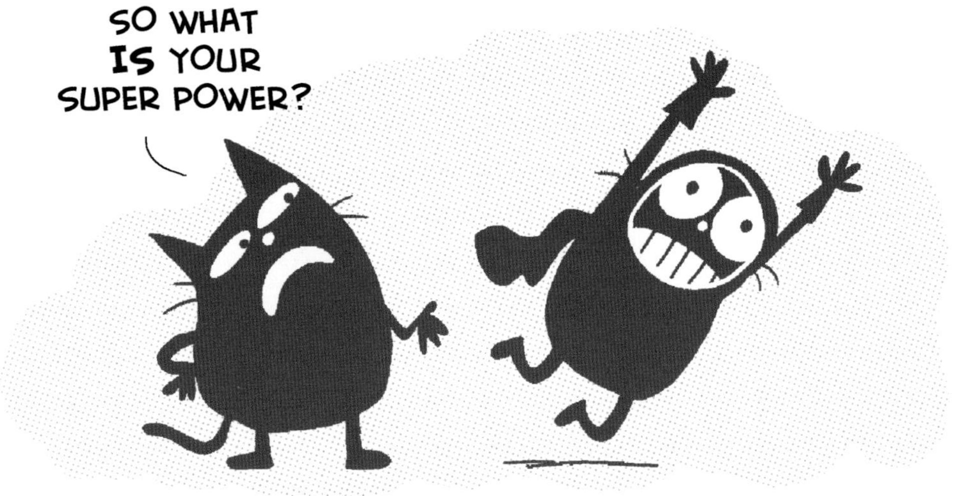
SO WHAT **IS** YOUR SUPER POWER?

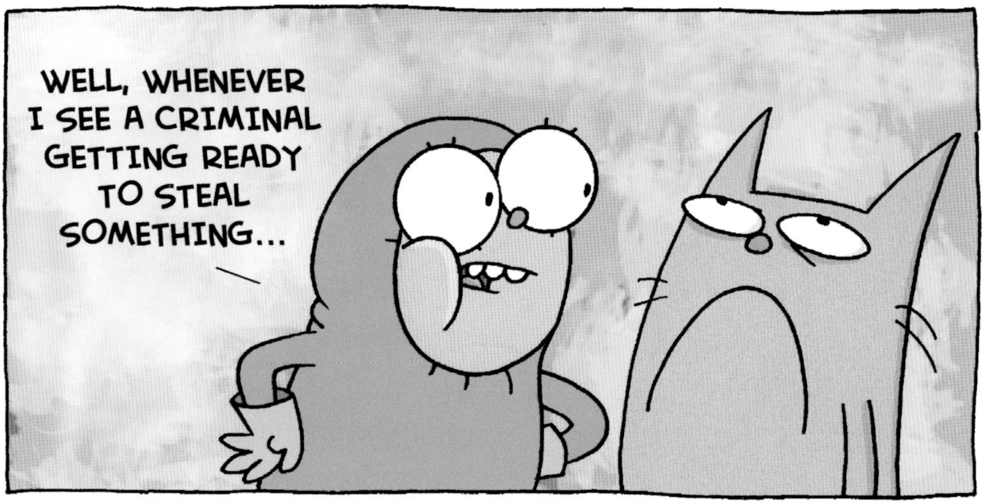
WELL, WHENEVER I SEE A CRIMINAL GETTING READY TO STEAL SOMETHING...

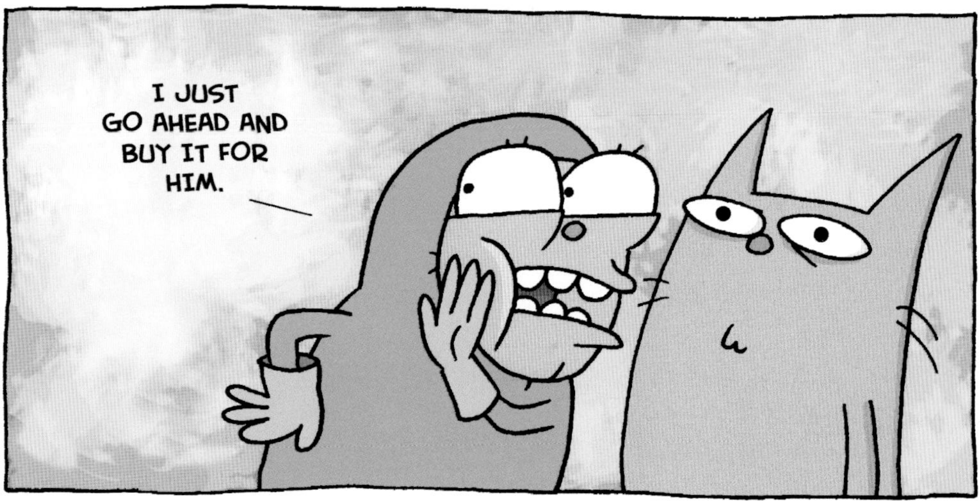
I JUST GO AHEAD AND BUY IT FOR HIM.

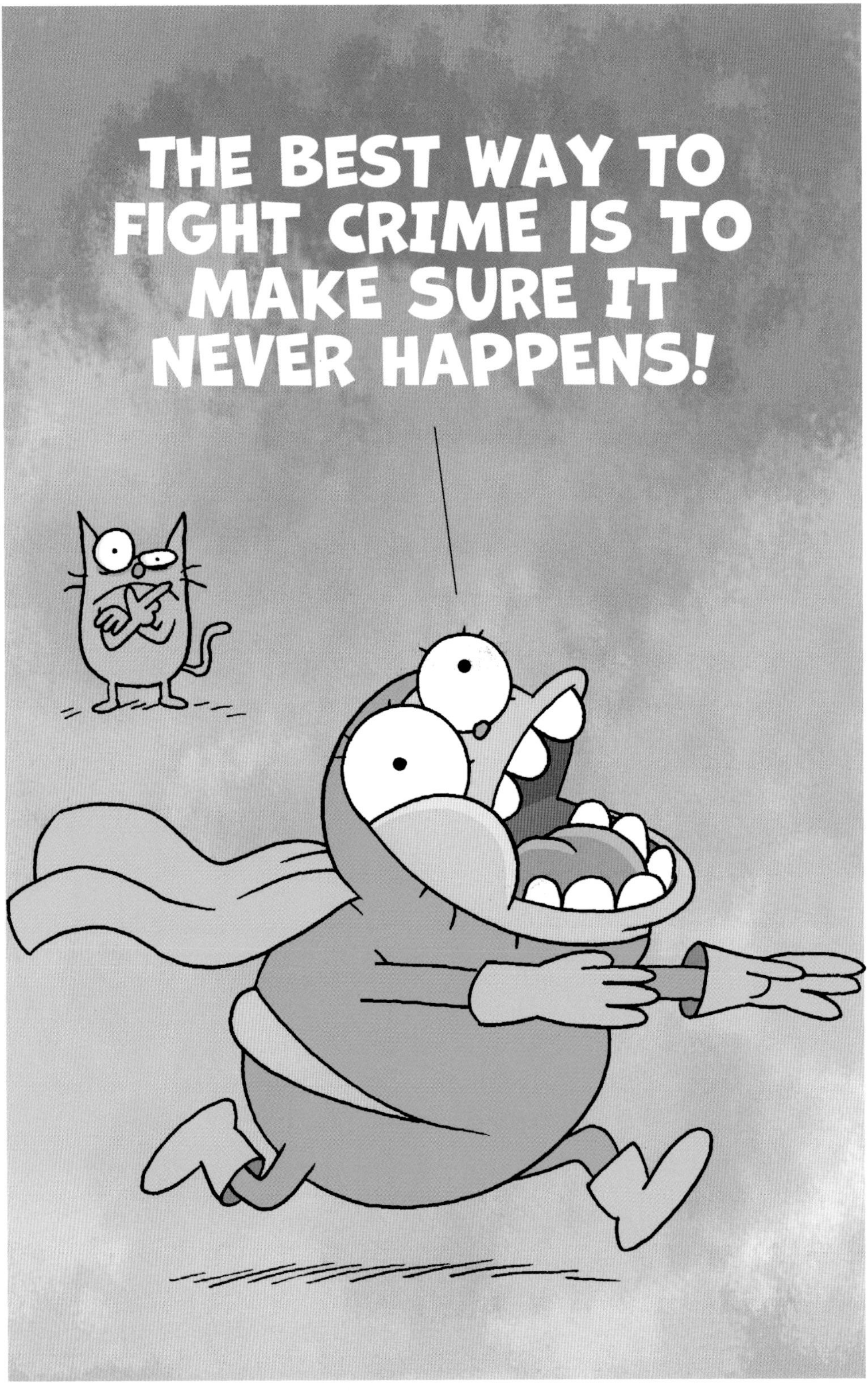
THE BEST WAY TO FIGHT CRIME IS TO MAKE SURE IT NEVER HAPPENS!

Legend

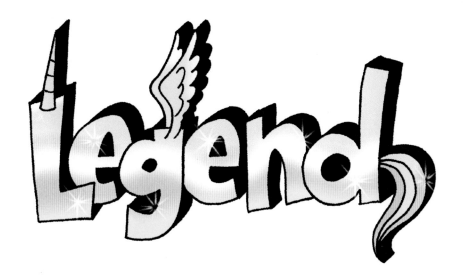

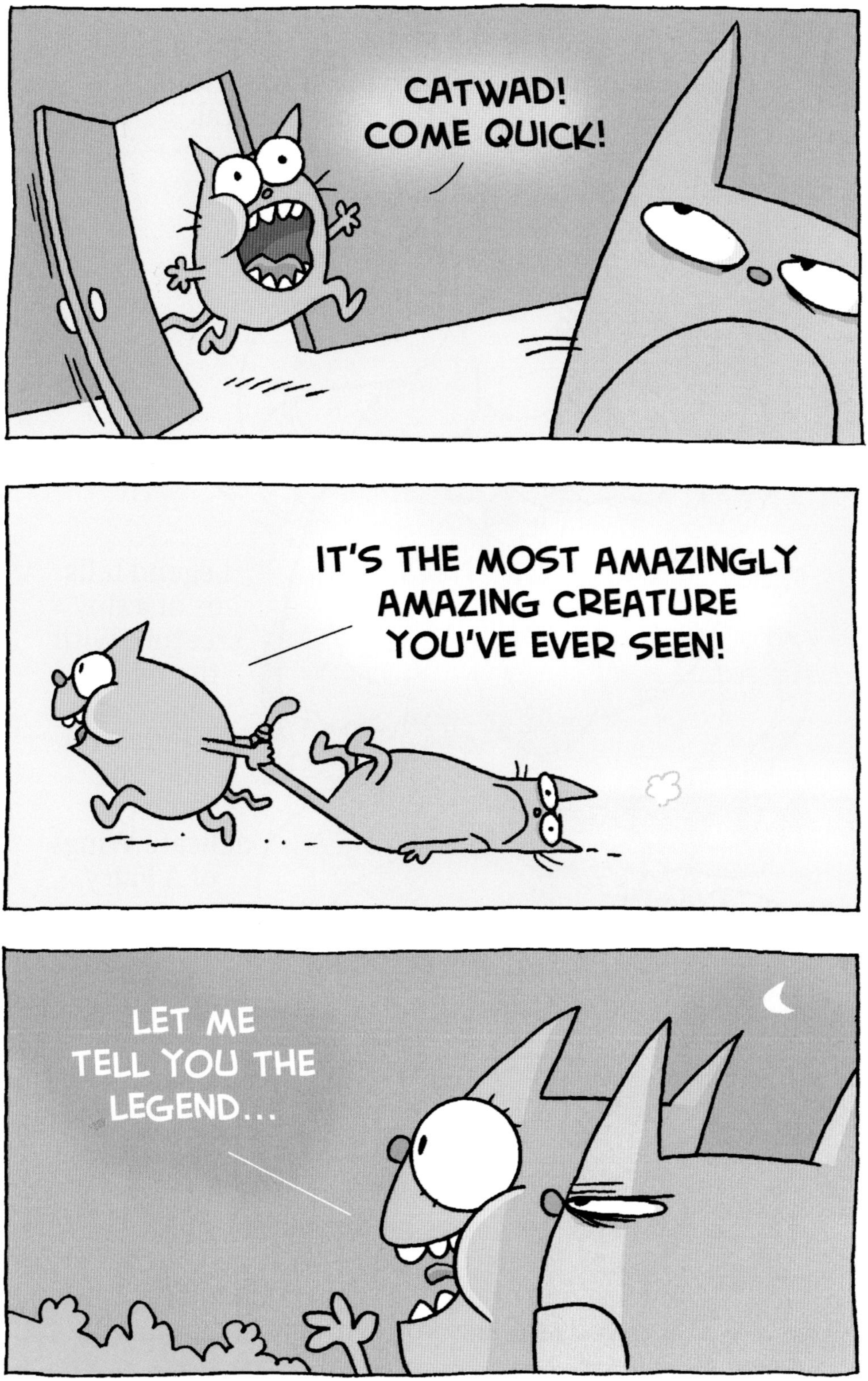
CATWAD! COME QUICK!
IT'S THE MOST AMAZINGLY AMAZING CREATURE YOU'VE EVER SEEN!
LET ME TELL YOU THE LEGEND...

Unicorns, as you know, are the most beautiful living things in the world, and Fairies are the most magical.

Such

A Beautiful

Legend

Legend tells us of a tiny creature with the pointy horn of A Unicorn, and the lovely, delicate Wings of A Fairy.

The story says on enchanted nights like this, if you're very, very, lucky, one of them might even land on you and kiss you with his horn.

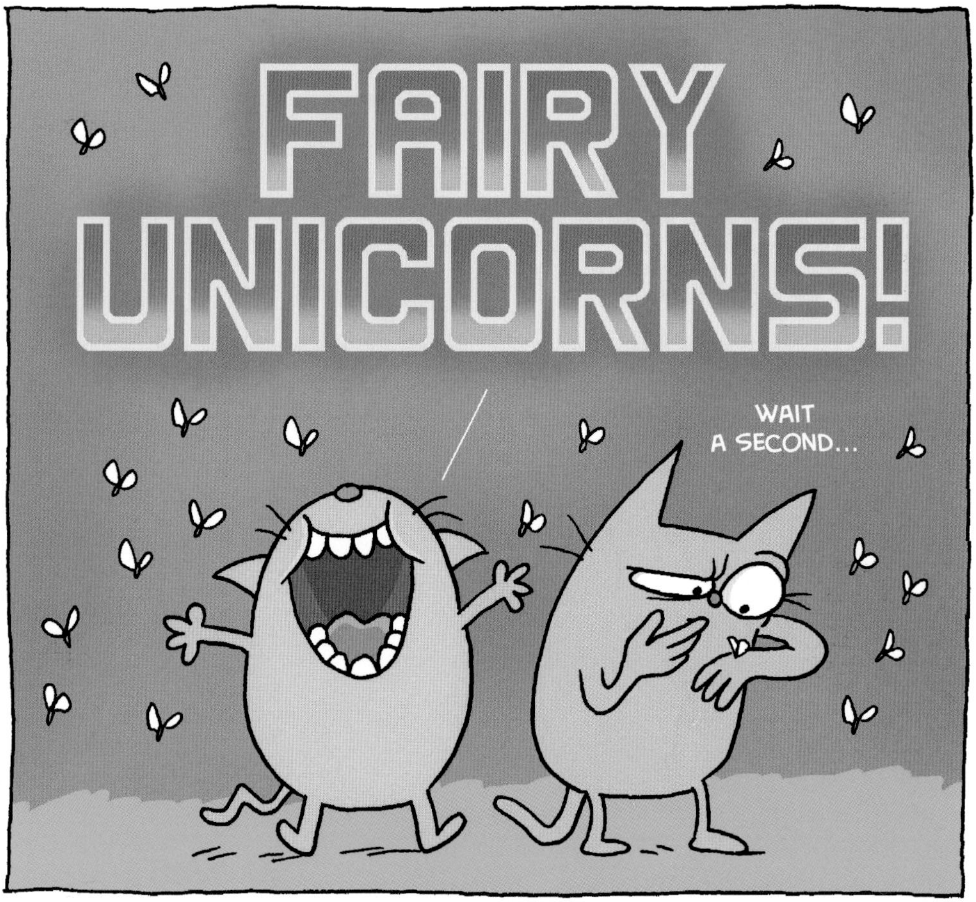
FAIRY UNICORNS!
WAIT A SECOND...

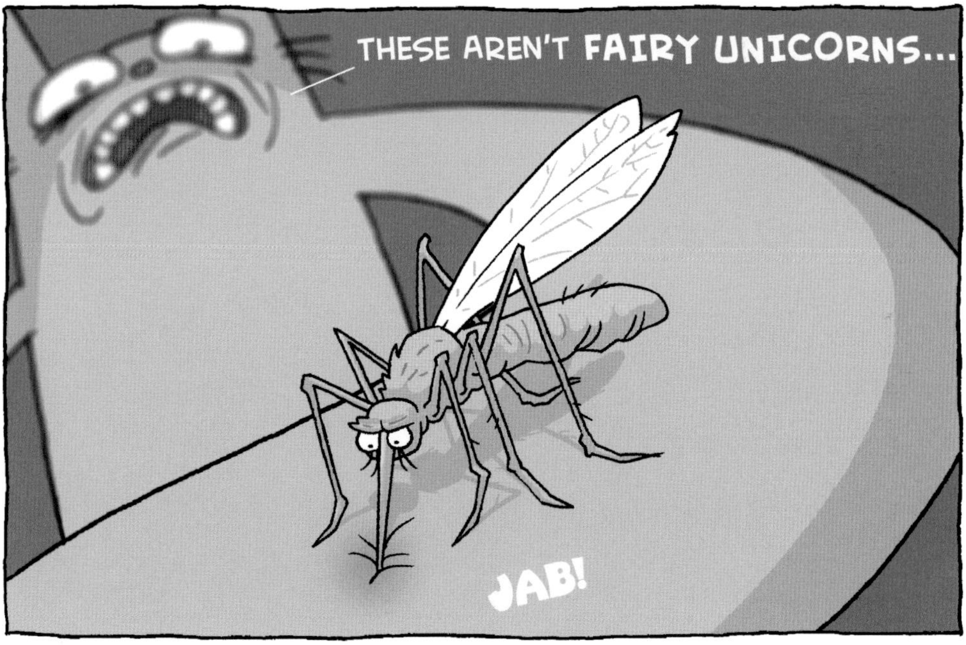
THESE AREN'T FAIRY UNICORNS...
JAB!

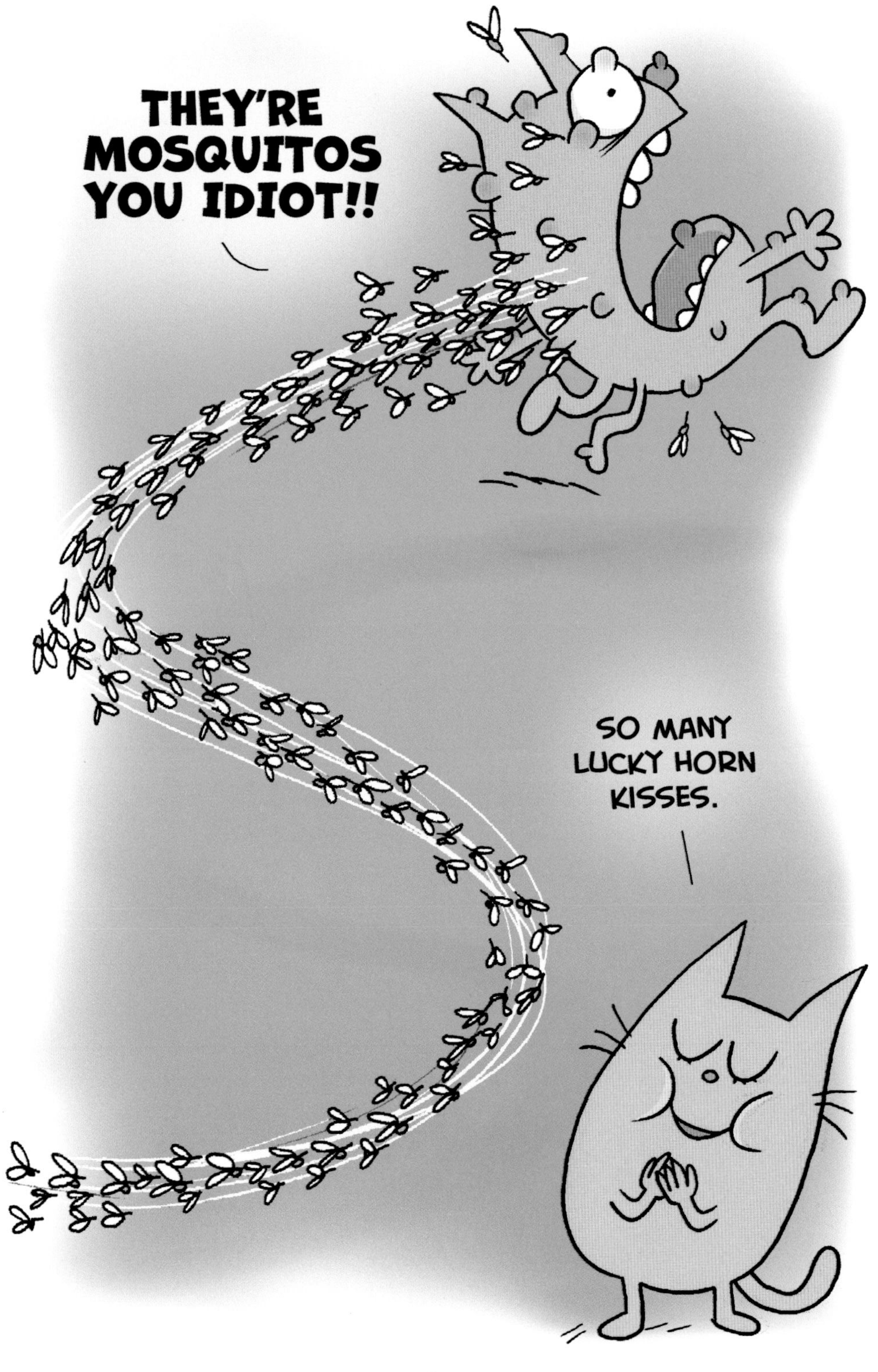
THEY'RE MOSQUITOS YOU IDIOT!!
SO MANY LUCKY HORN KISSES.

BURP

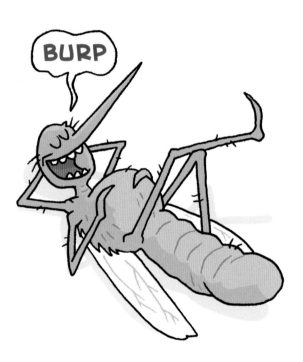

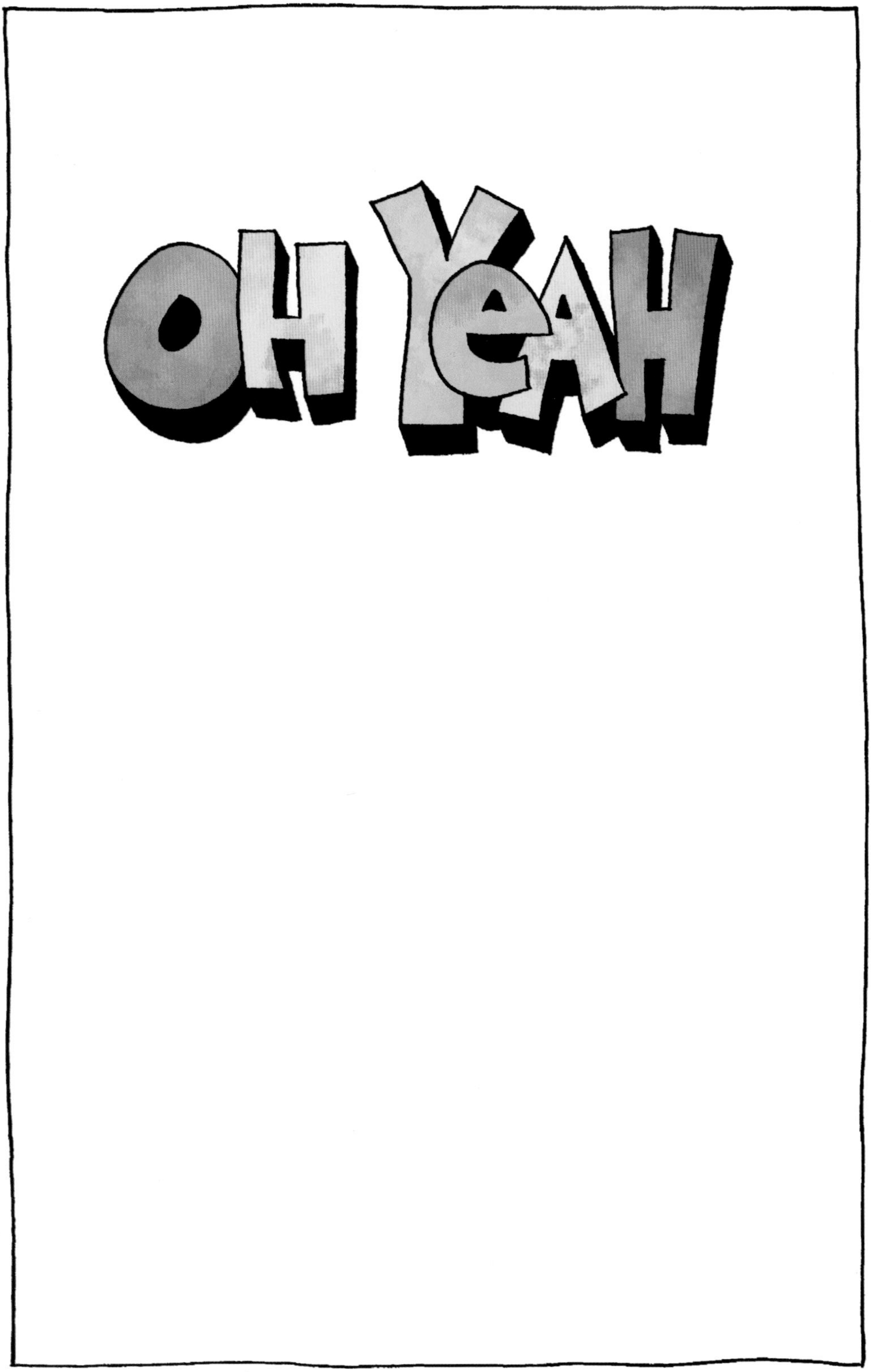
OH YEAH

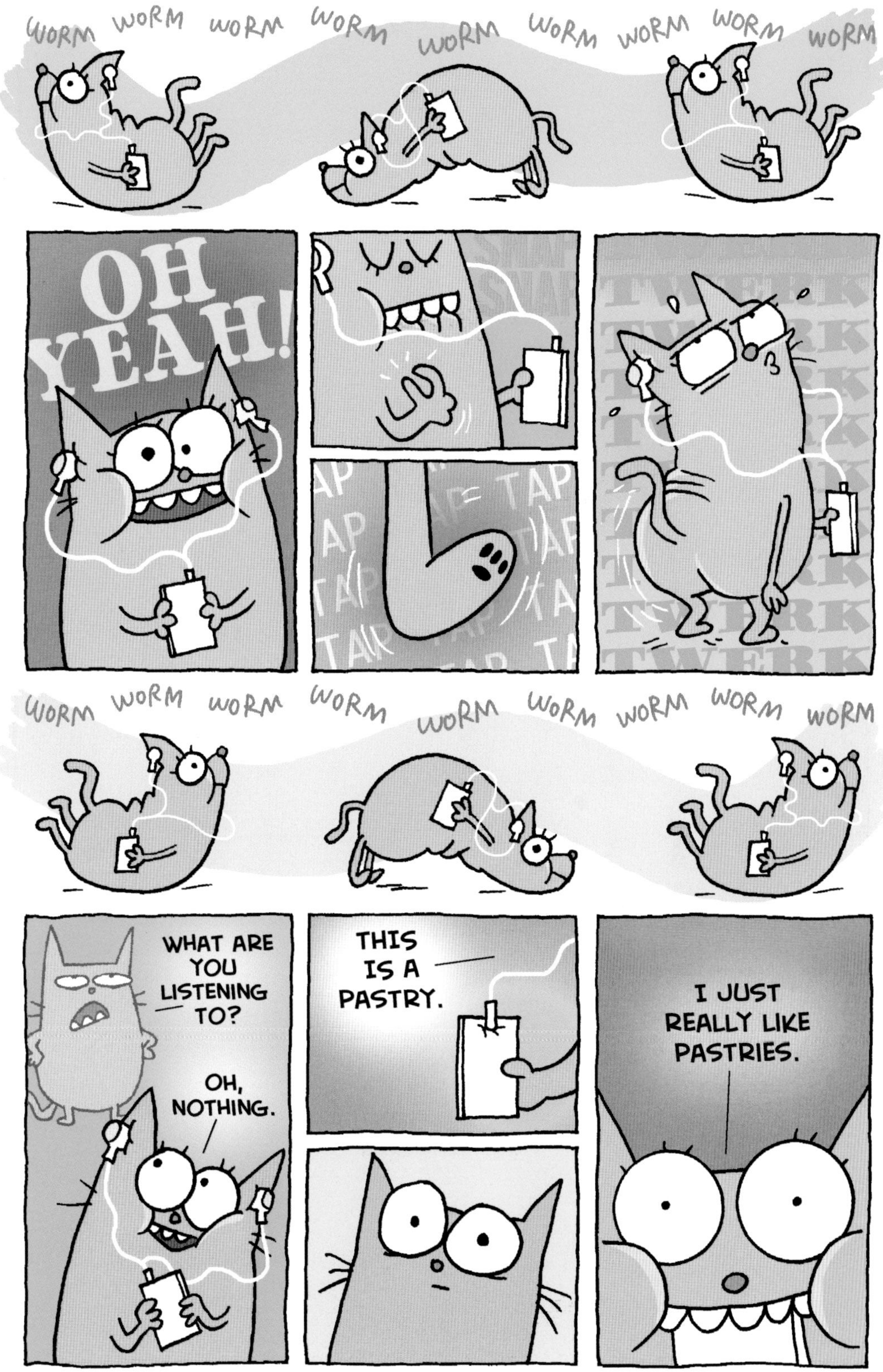
WORM WORM WORM WORM WORM WORM WORM WORM WORM
OH YEAH!
TAP TAP TAP TAP
TWERK
WORM WORM WORM WORM WORM WORM WORM WORM WORM
WHAT ARE YOU LISTENING TO?
OH, NOTHING.
THIS IS A PASTRY.
I JUST REALLY LIKE PASTRIES.

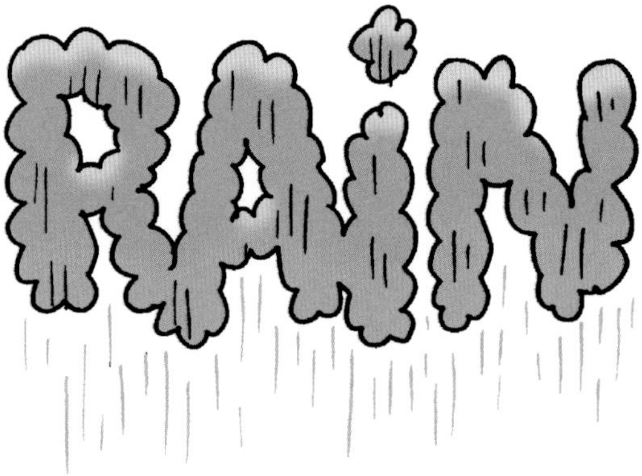
RAIN

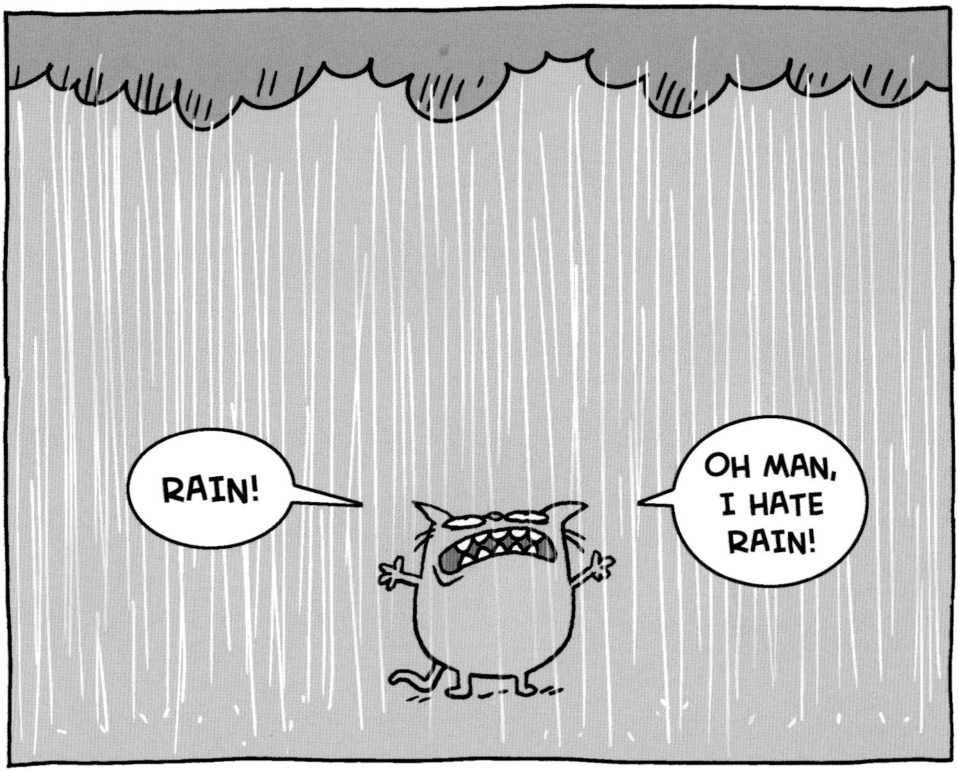
RAIN!
OH MAN, I HATE RAIN!

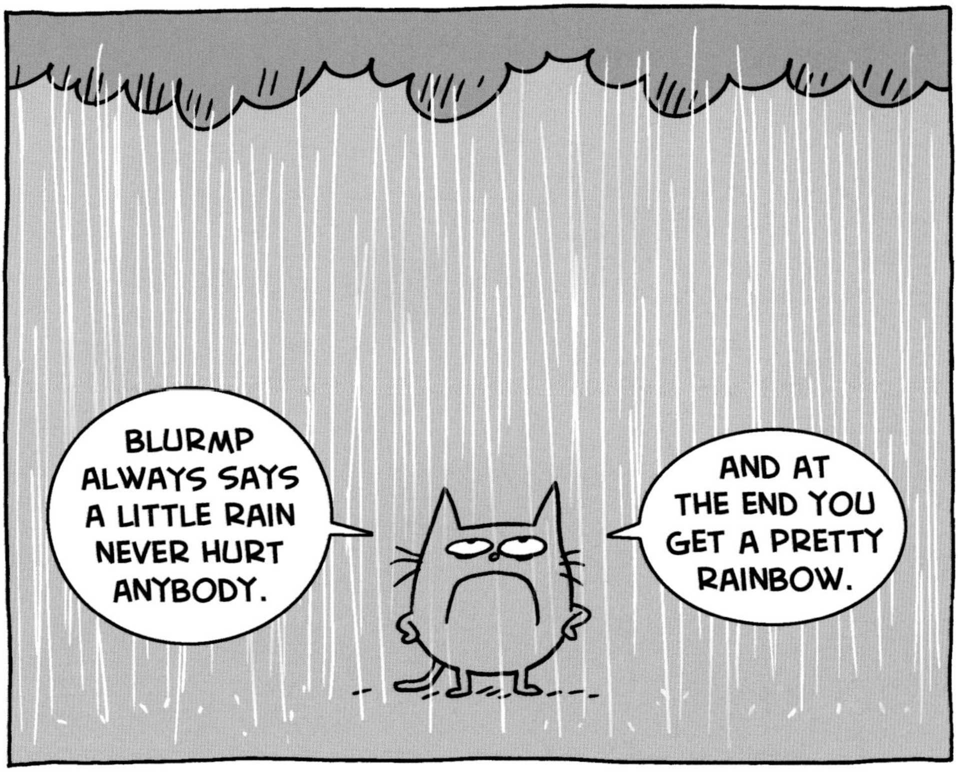
BLURMP ALWAYS SAYS A LITTLE RAIN NEVER HURT ANYBODY.
AND AT THE END YOU GET A PRETTY RAINBOW.

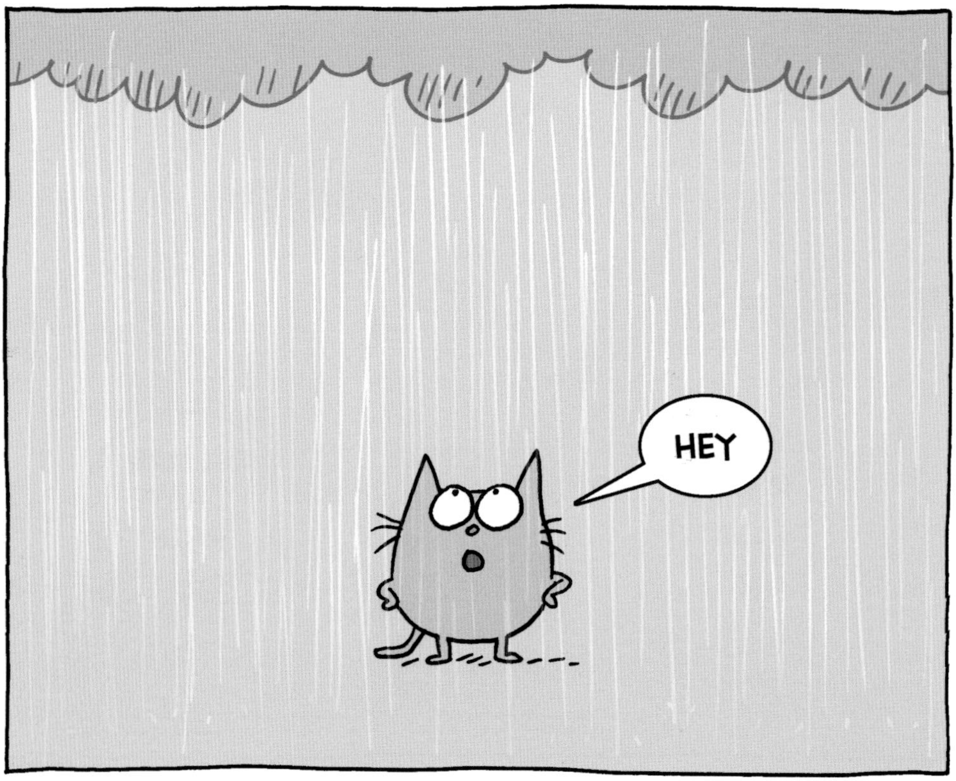
HEY

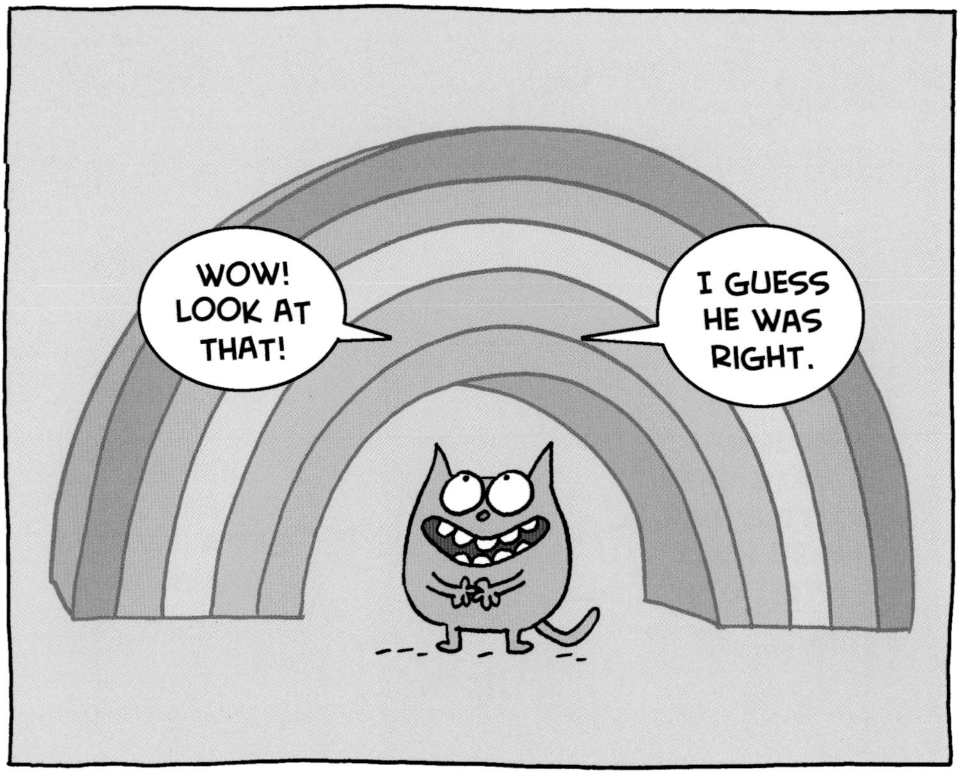
WOW! LOOK AT THAT!
I GUESS HE WAS RIGHT.

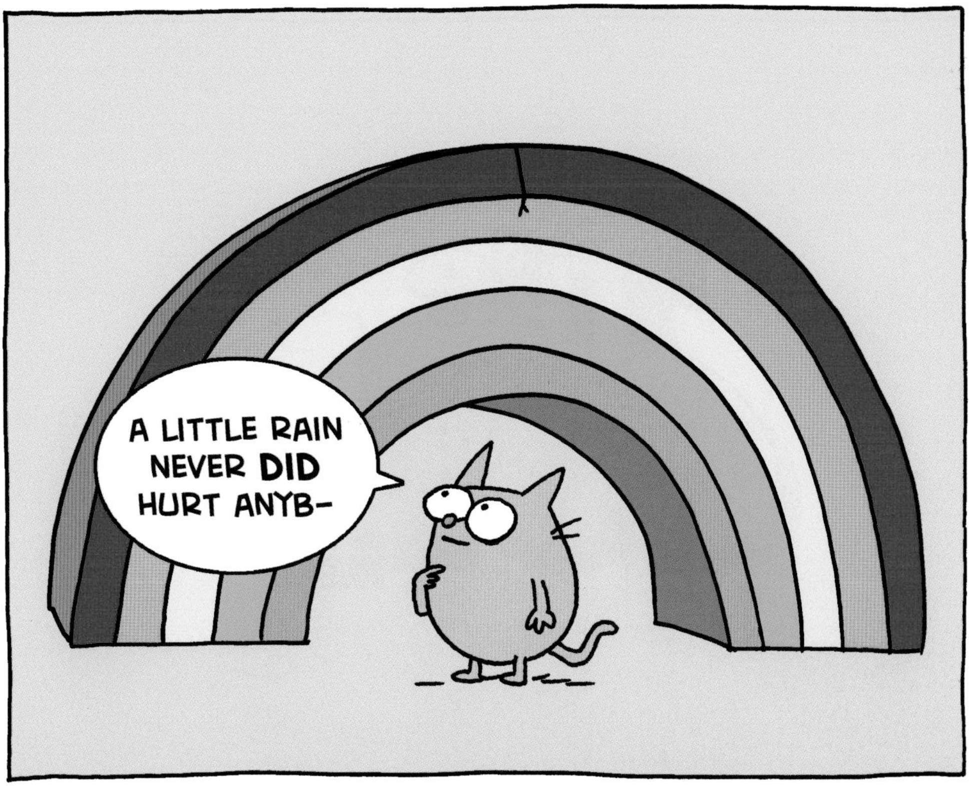
A LITTLE RAIN NEVER **DID** HURT ANYB-

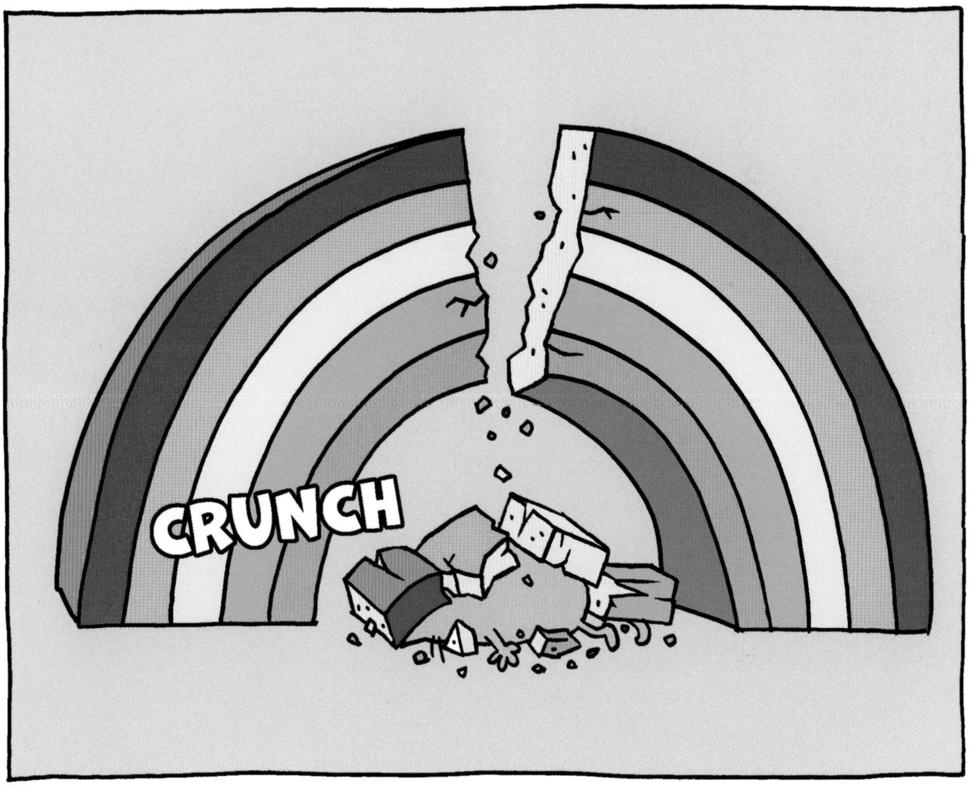
CRUNCH

THE COLD

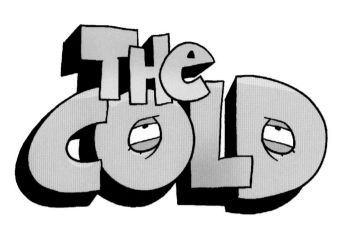

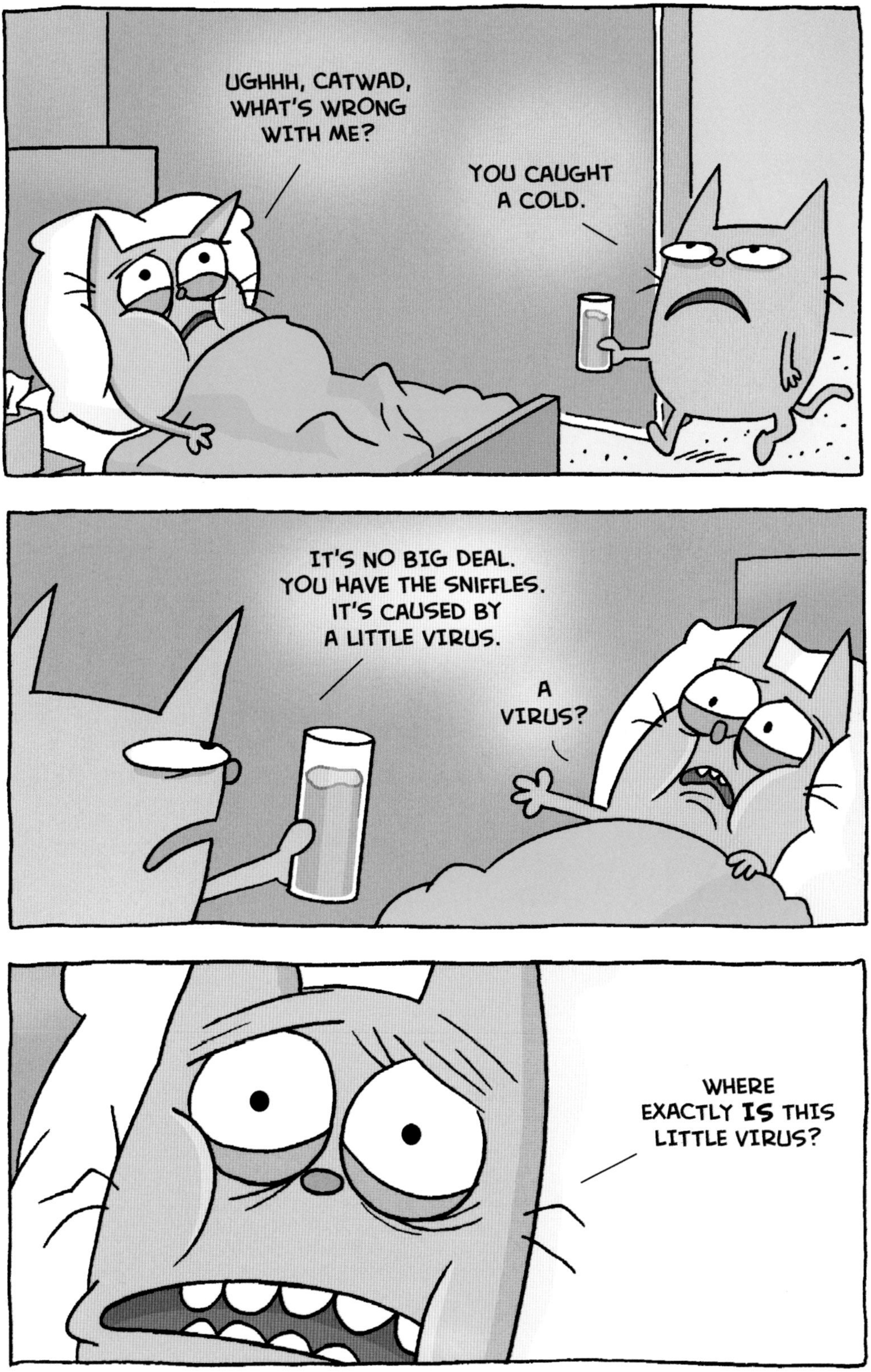
UGHHH, CATWAD, WHAT'S WRONG WITH ME?
YOU CAUGHT A COLD.
IT'S NO BIG DEAL. YOU HAVE THE SNIFFLES. IT'S CAUSED BY A LITTLE VIRUS.
A VIRUS?
WHERE EXACTLY **IS** THIS LITTLE VIRUS?

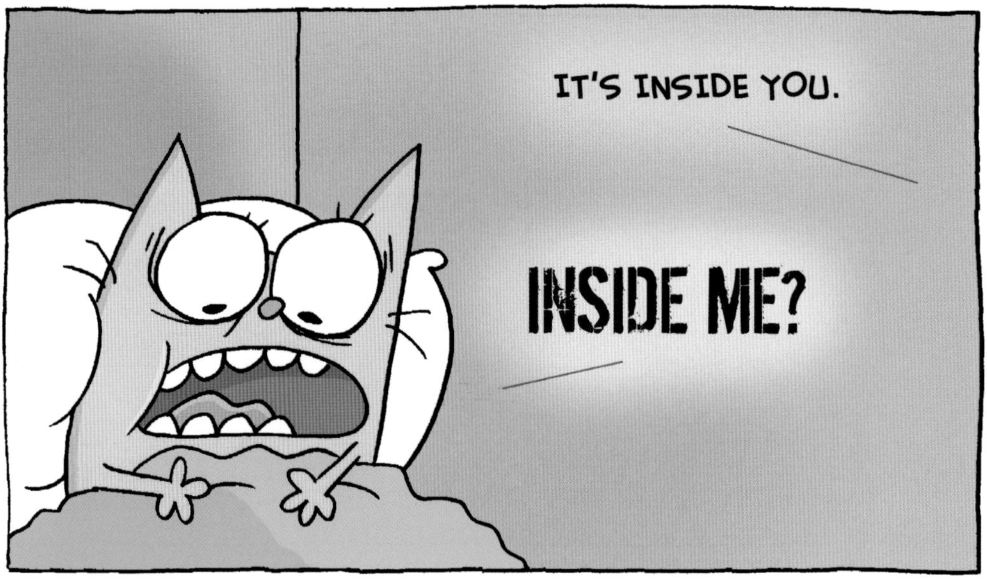
IT'S INSIDE YOU.
INSIDE ME?

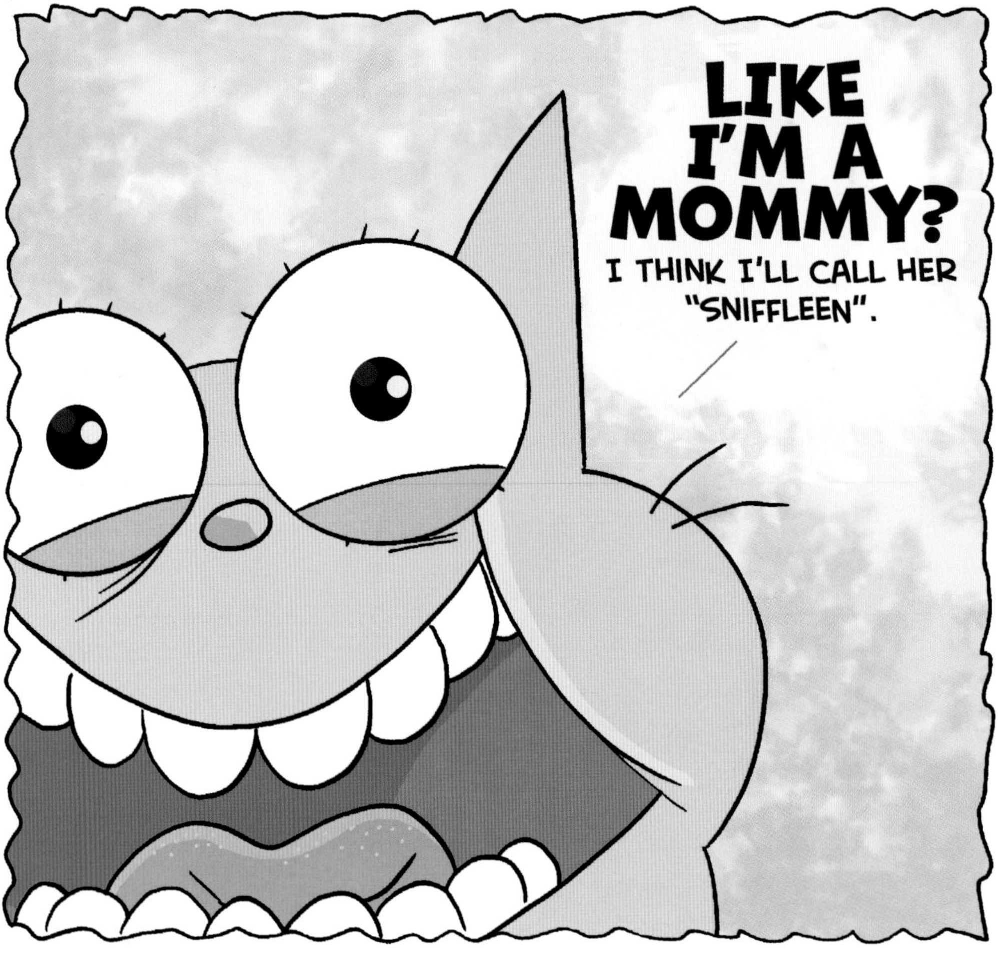
LIKE I'M A MOMMY?
I THINK I'LL CALL HER "SNIFFLEEN".

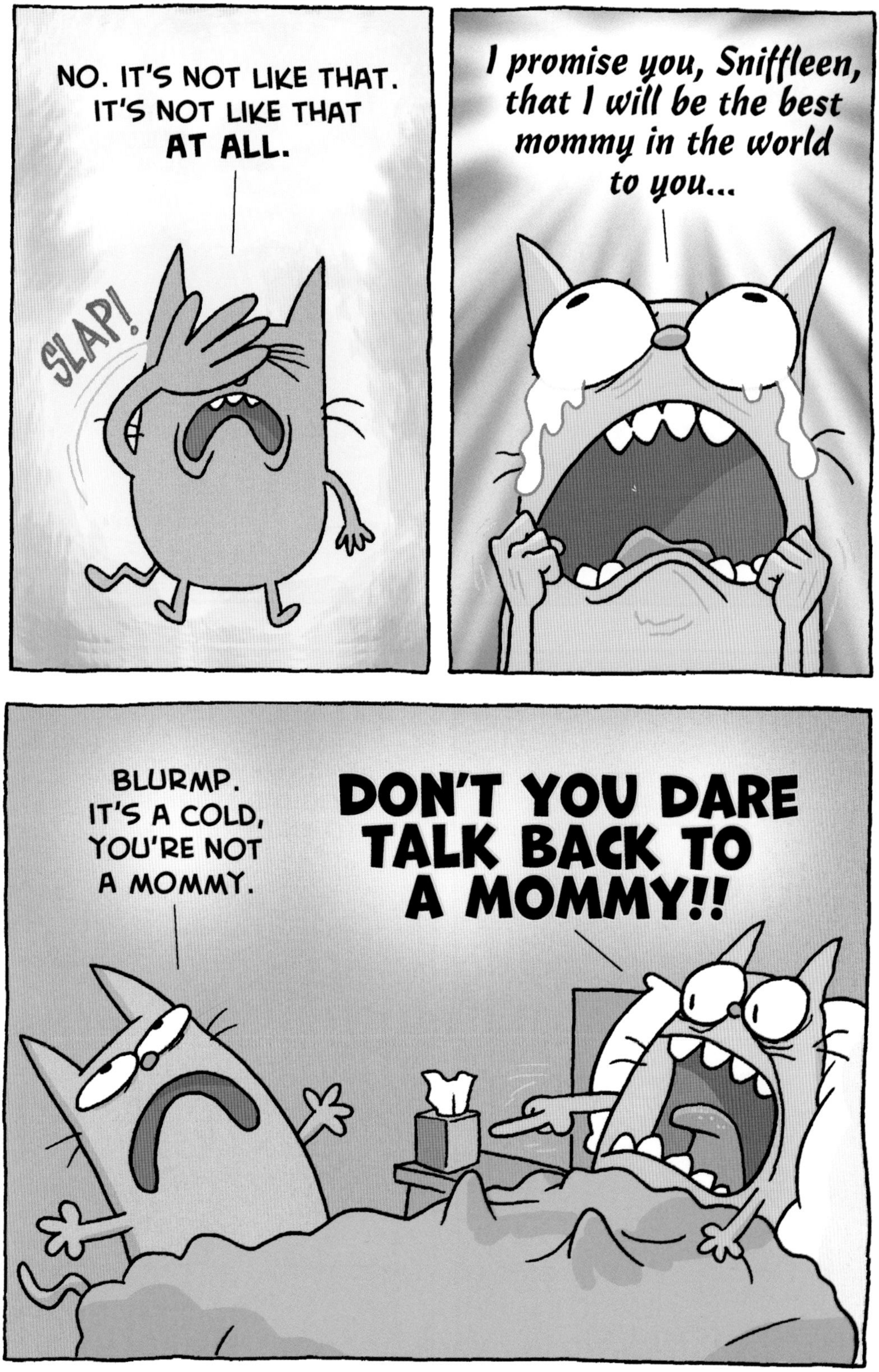
NO. IT'S NOT LIKE THAT. IT'S NOT LIKE THAT AT ALL.
SLAP!
I promise you, Sniffleen, that I will be the best mommy in the world to you...
BLURMP. IT'S A COLD, YOU'RE NOT A MOMMY.
DON'T YOU DARE TALK BACK TO A MOMMY!!

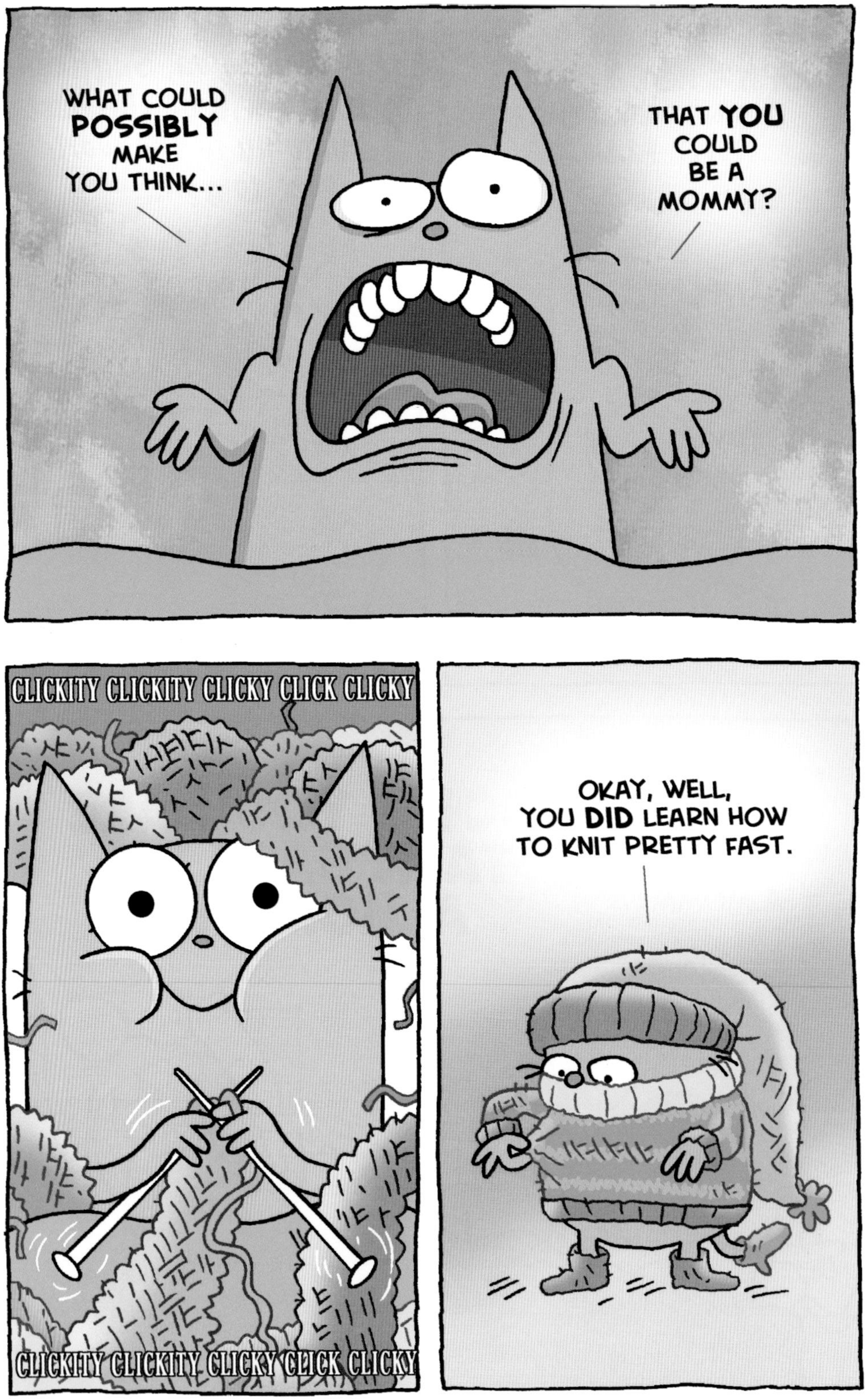
WHAT COULD **POSSIBLY** MAKE YOU THINK...
THAT **YOU** COULD BE A MOMMY?
CLICKITY CLICKITY CLICKY CLICK CLICKY
CLICKITY CLICKITY CLICKY CLICK CLICKY
OKAY, WELL, YOU **DID** LEARN HOW TO KNIT PRETTY FAST.

AND A FEW MORE THINGS...
EVERYTHING HAS TO
BE PERFECTLY CLEAN
FOR BABIES EVEN THOUGH
THEY LIKE TO THROW
UP ON THEMSELVES
AND SIT AROUND IN
DIRTY DIAPERS.

AND WE CAN'T HAVE
ANYTHING SHARP SHE COULD
HURT HERSELF WITH OR
STUFF SHE COULD
ACCIDENTALLY SWALLOW
LIKE GUM OR DYNAMITE.

AND I DON'T WANT HER TO SEE
ANYTHING TOO SCARY, LIKE
ZOMBIE MOVIES OR
MY GRANDMA'S
GIANT UNDERPANTS.

AND ALSO I WANT TO...
MAKE...SURE..THAT...
ZZZZZZZZZZ

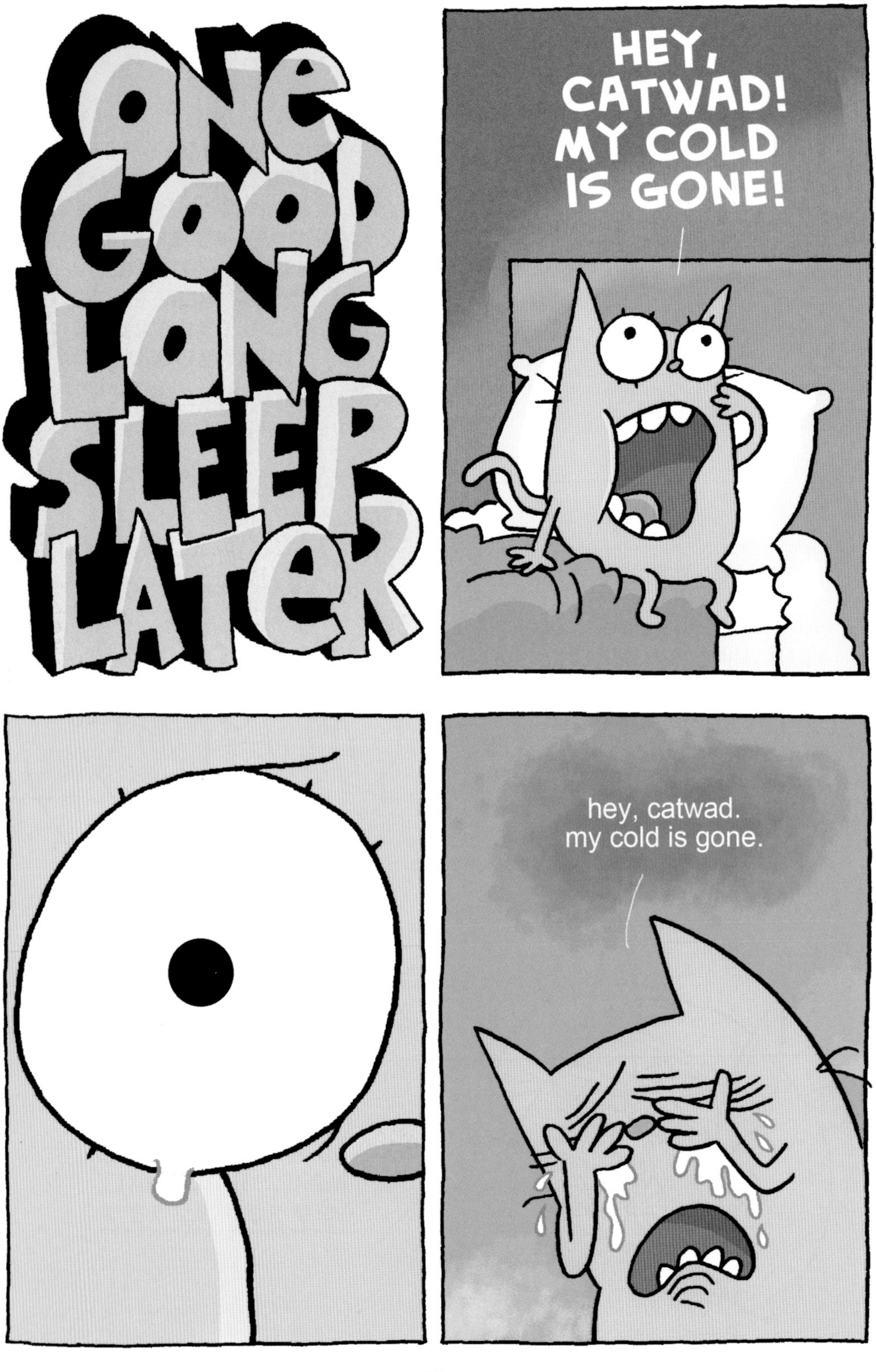
ONE GOOD LONG SLEEP LATER
HEY, CATWAD! MY COLD IS GONE!
hey, catwad. my cold is gone.

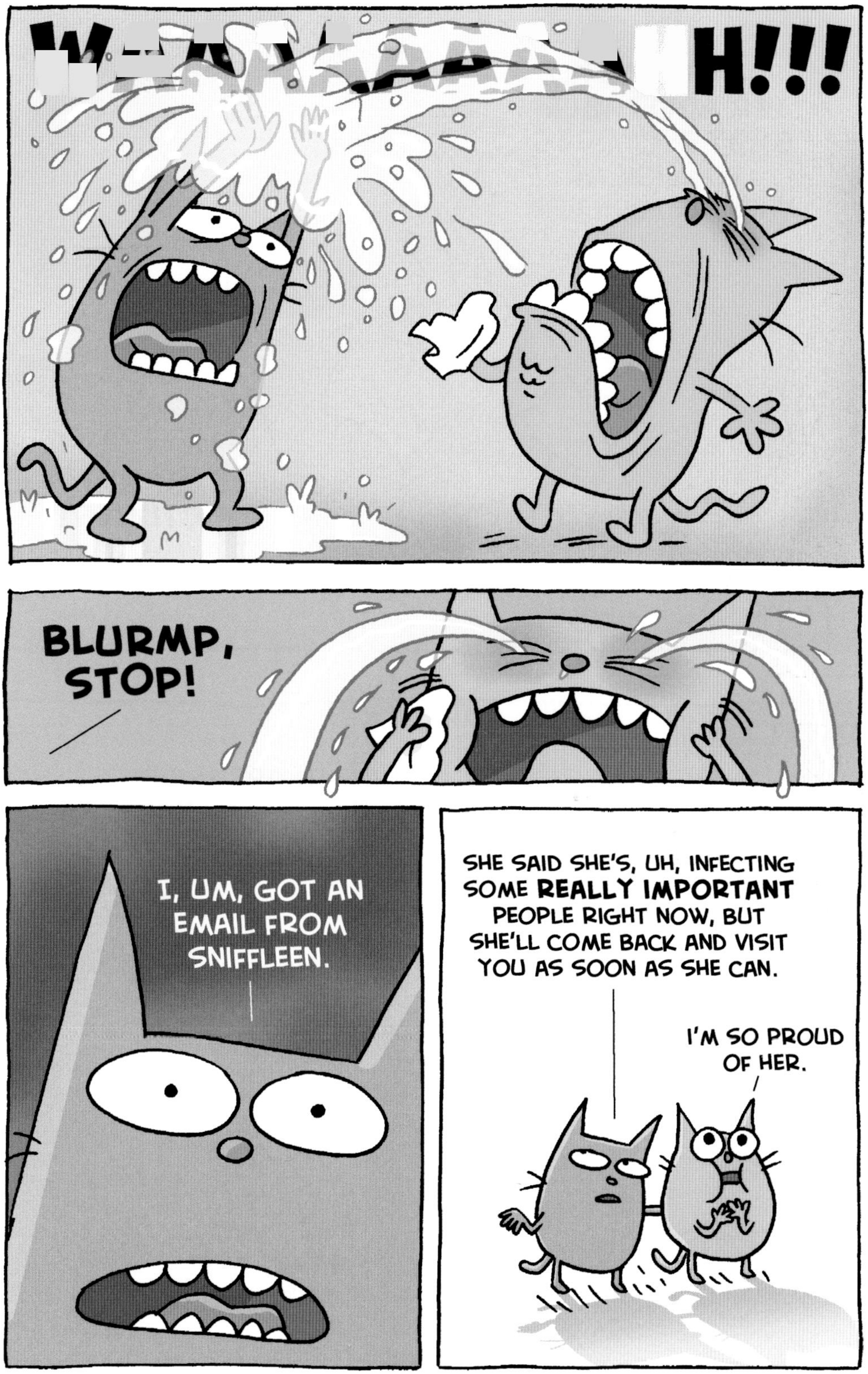
BLURMP, STOP!
I, UM, GOT AN EMAIL FROM SNIFFLEEN.
SHE SAID SHE'S, UH, INFECTING SOME **REALLY IMPORTANT** PEOPLE RIGHT NOW, BUT SHE'LL COME BACK AND VISIT YOU AS SOON AS SHE CAN.
I'M SO PROUD OF HER.

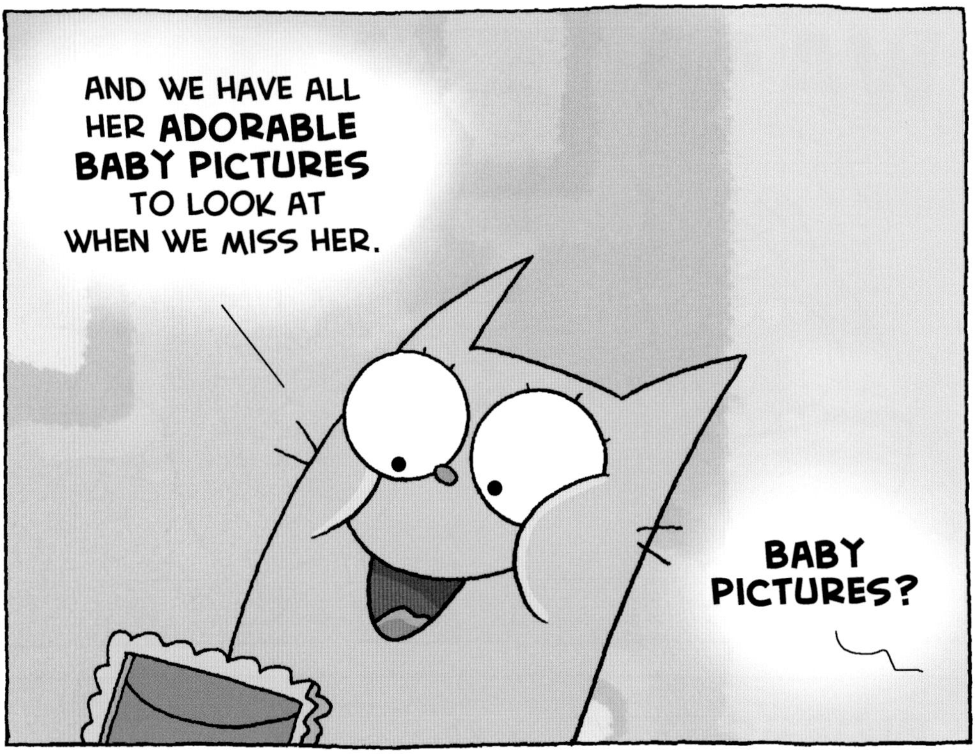
AND WE HAVE ALL HER **ADORABLE BABY PICTURES** TO LOOK AT WHEN WE MISS HER.
BABY PICTURES?

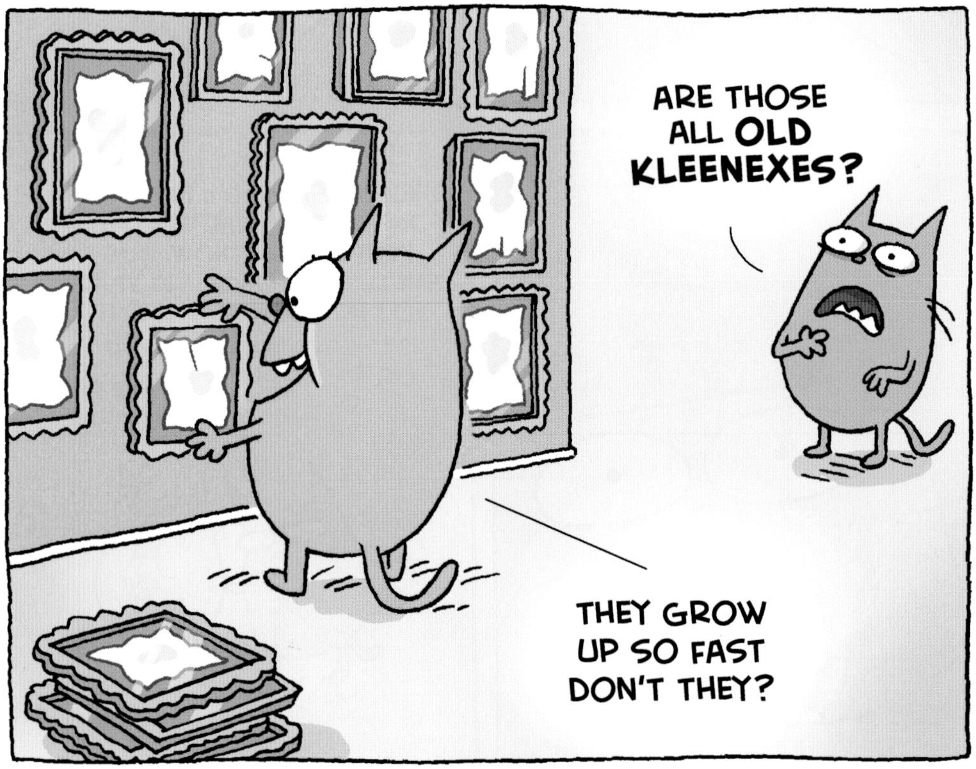
ARE THOSE ALL **OLD KLEENEXES?**
THEY GROW UP SO FAST DON'T THEY?

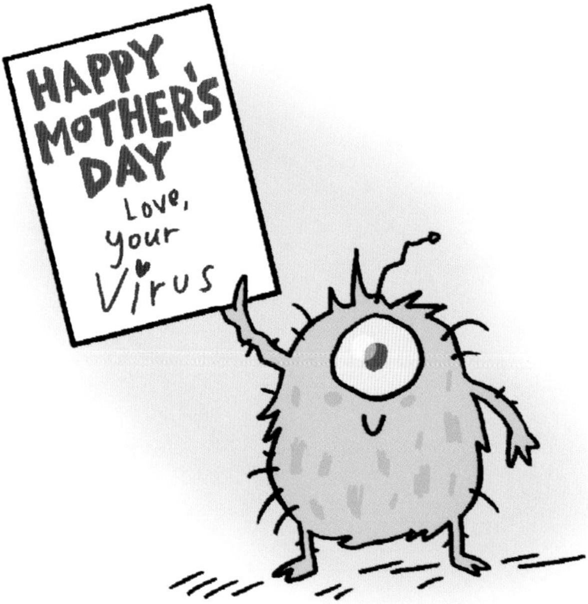
HAPPY MOTHER'S DAY
Love, your Virus

JACK

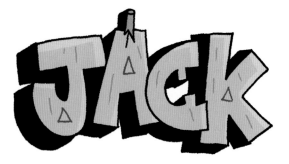

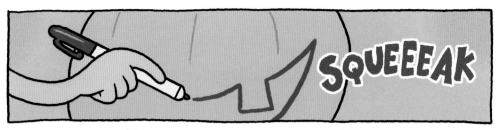

SQUEEEAK

CATWAD! COME HERE AND LOOK AT MY JOLLY **JACK-O-LANTERN**.

LOOK! I DREW A BIG HAPPY FACE TO CUT OUT.

LET'S SEE HOW LONG HE FEELS HAPPY...

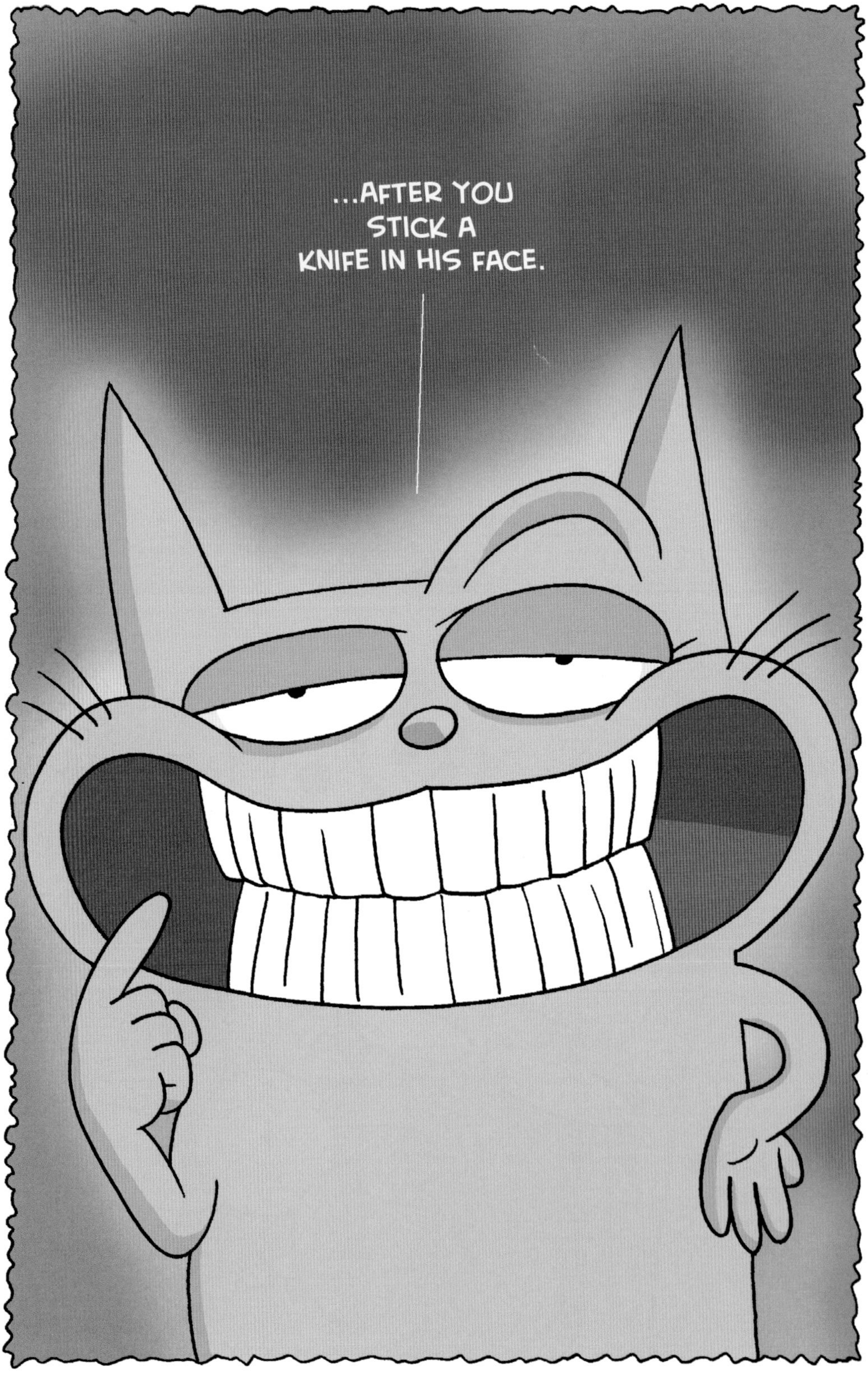
...AFTER YOU STICK A KNIFE IN HIS FACE.

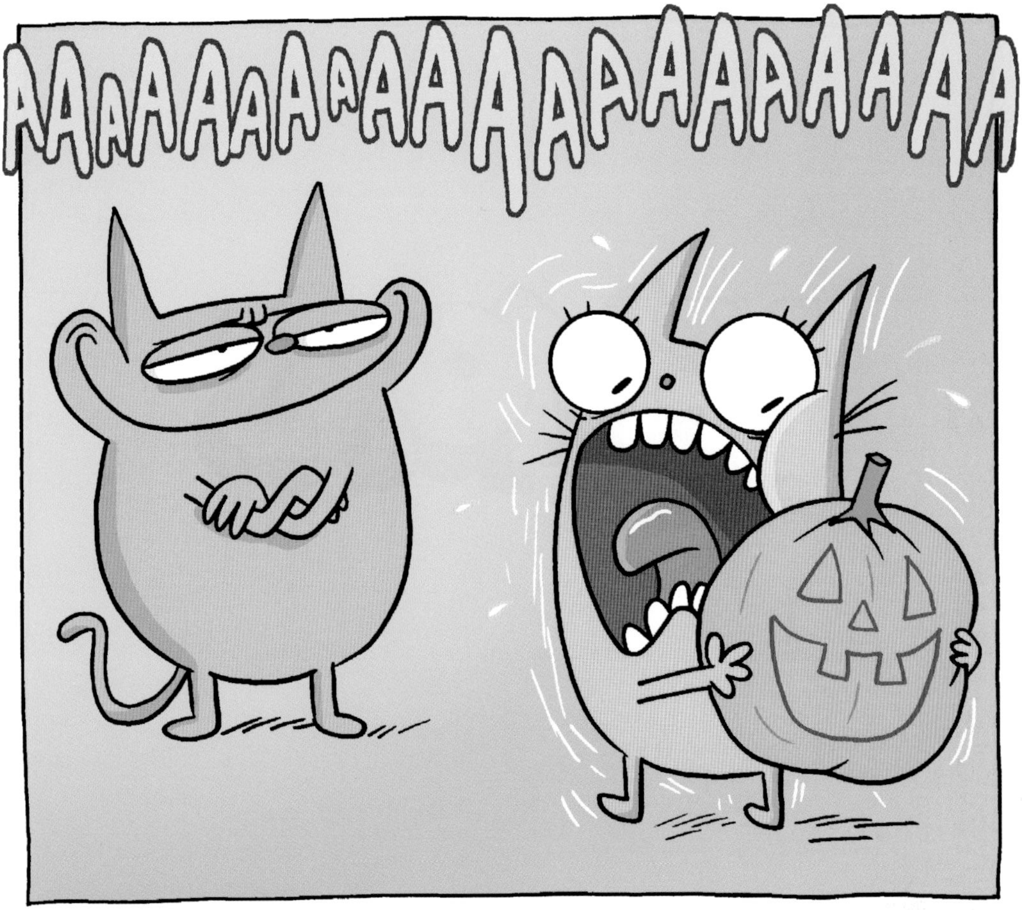
AAAAAAAAAAAAAAAAAA

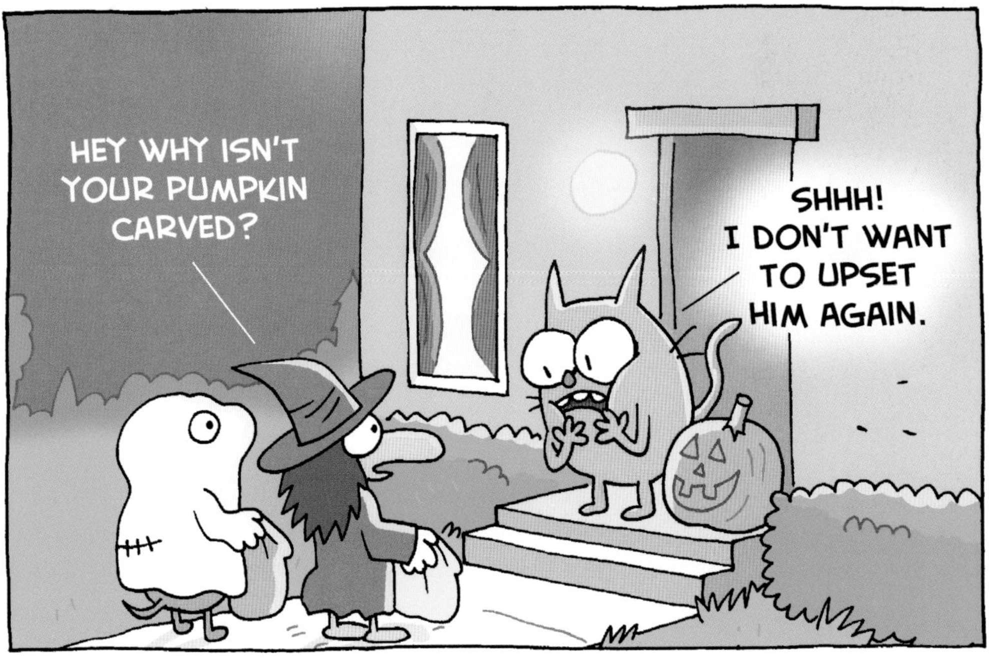
HEY WHY ISN'T YOUR PUMPKIN CARVED?
SHHH! I DON'T WANT TO UPSET HIM AGAIN.

LEMONS

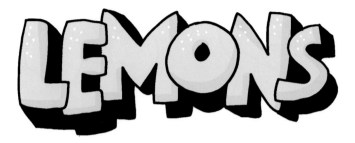

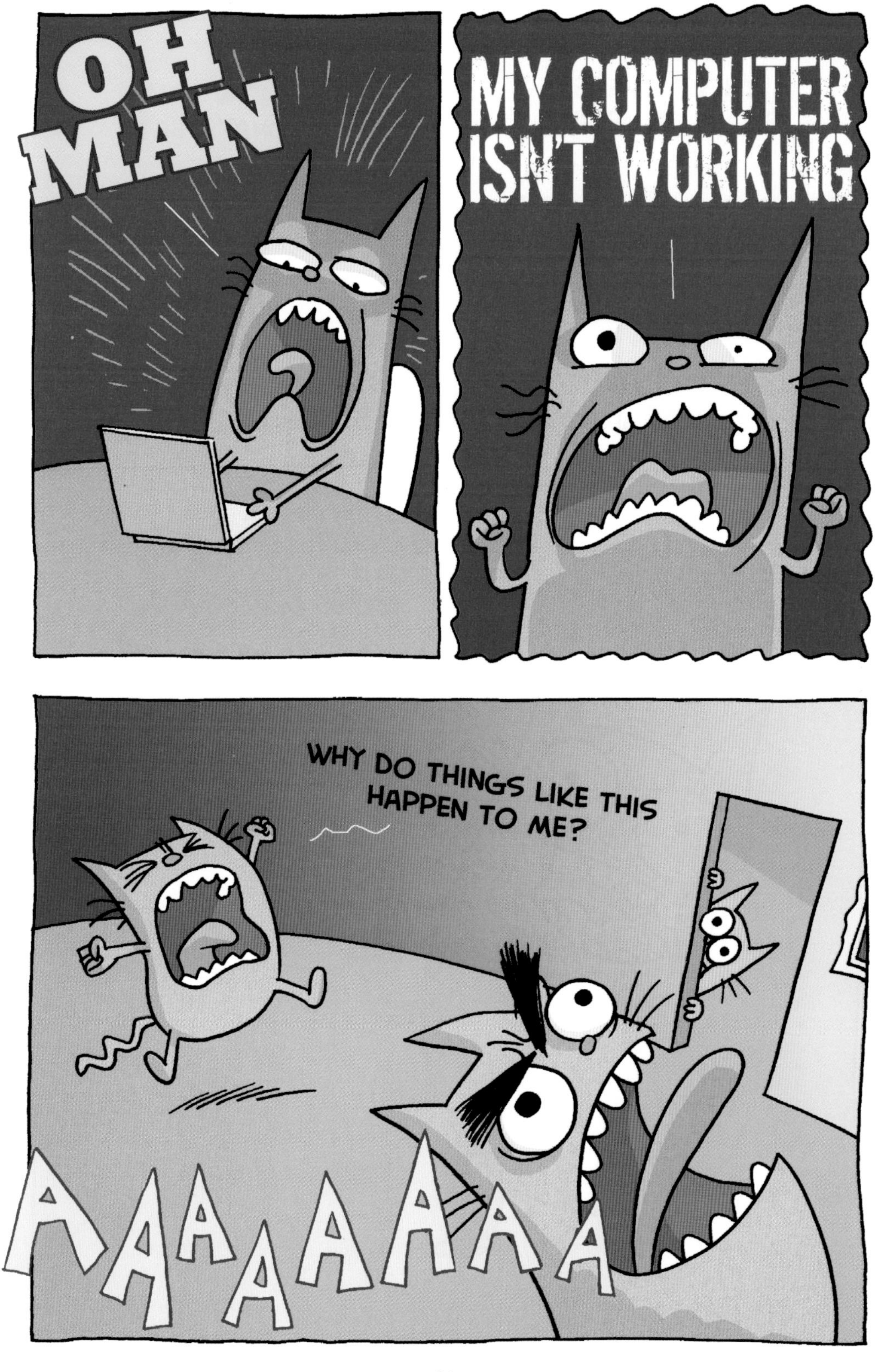
OH MAN
MY COMPUTER ISN'T WORKING
WHY DO THINGS LIKE THIS HAPPEN TO ME?
AAAAAAAA

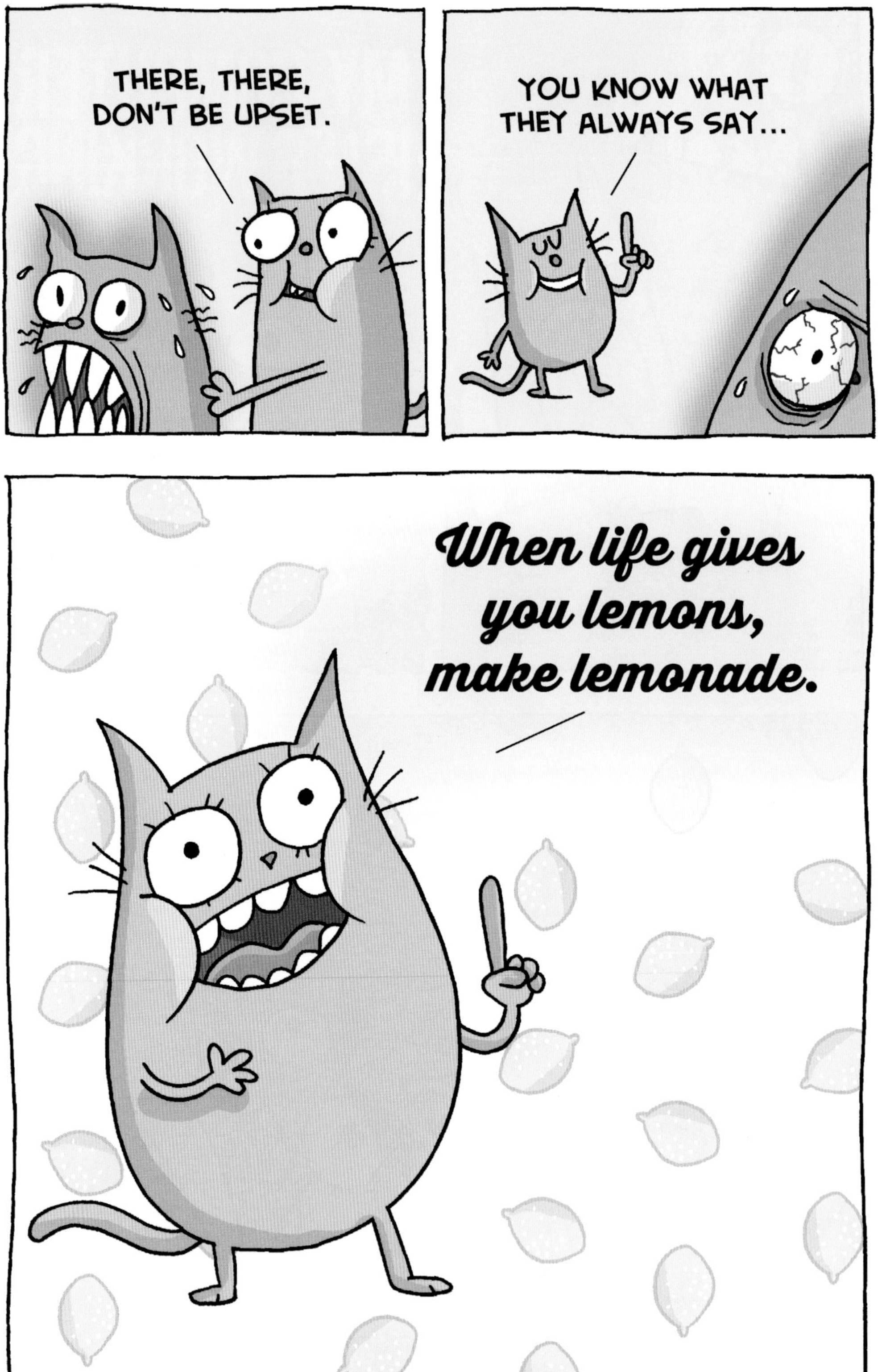
THERE, THERE, DON'T BE UPSET.
YOU KNOW WHAT THEY ALWAYS SAY...
When life gives you lemons, make lemonade.

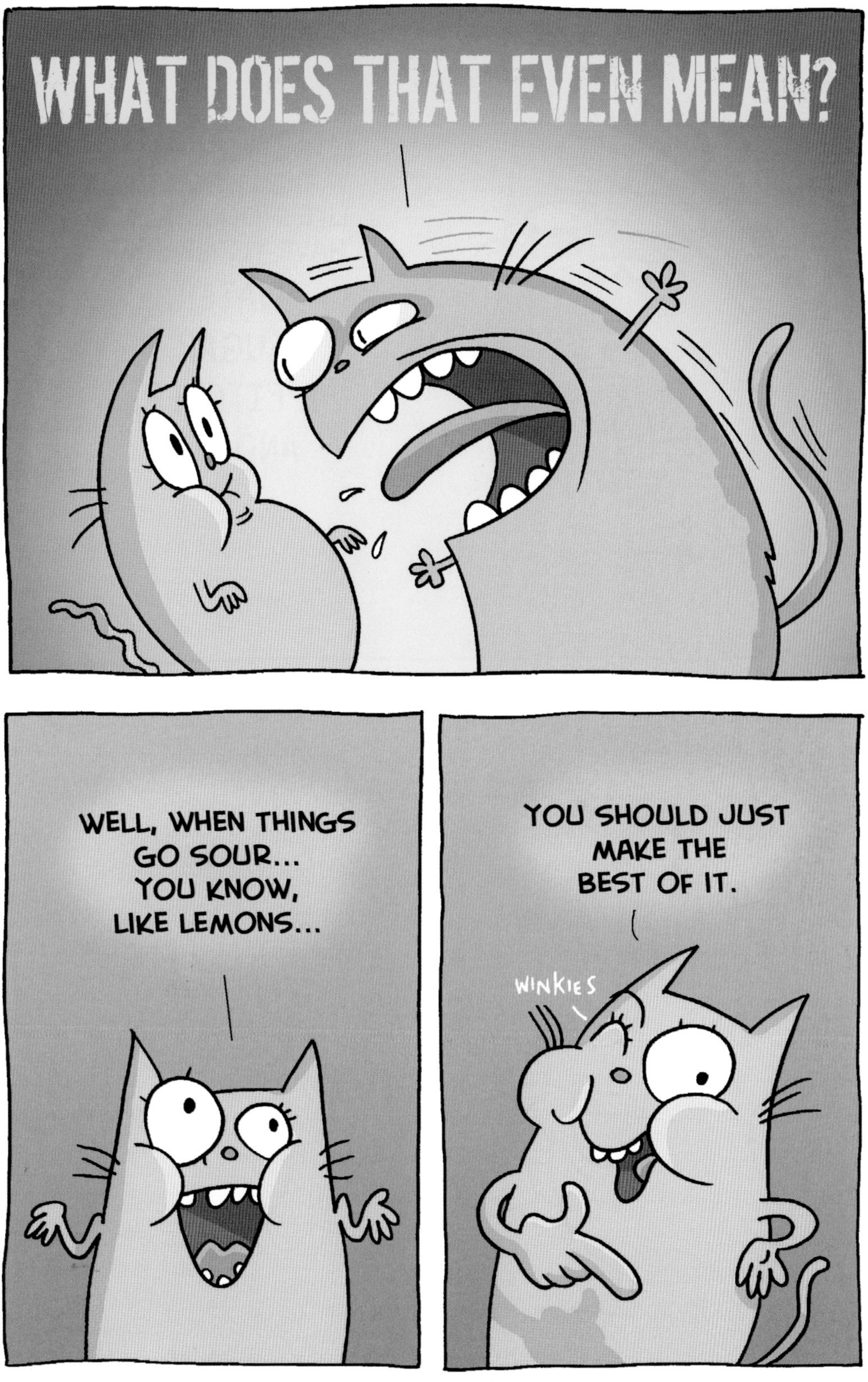
WHAT DOES THAT EVEN MEAN?
WELL, WHEN THINGS GO SOUR... YOU KNOW, LIKE LEMONS...
YOU SHOULD JUST MAKE THE BEST OF IT.
WINKIES

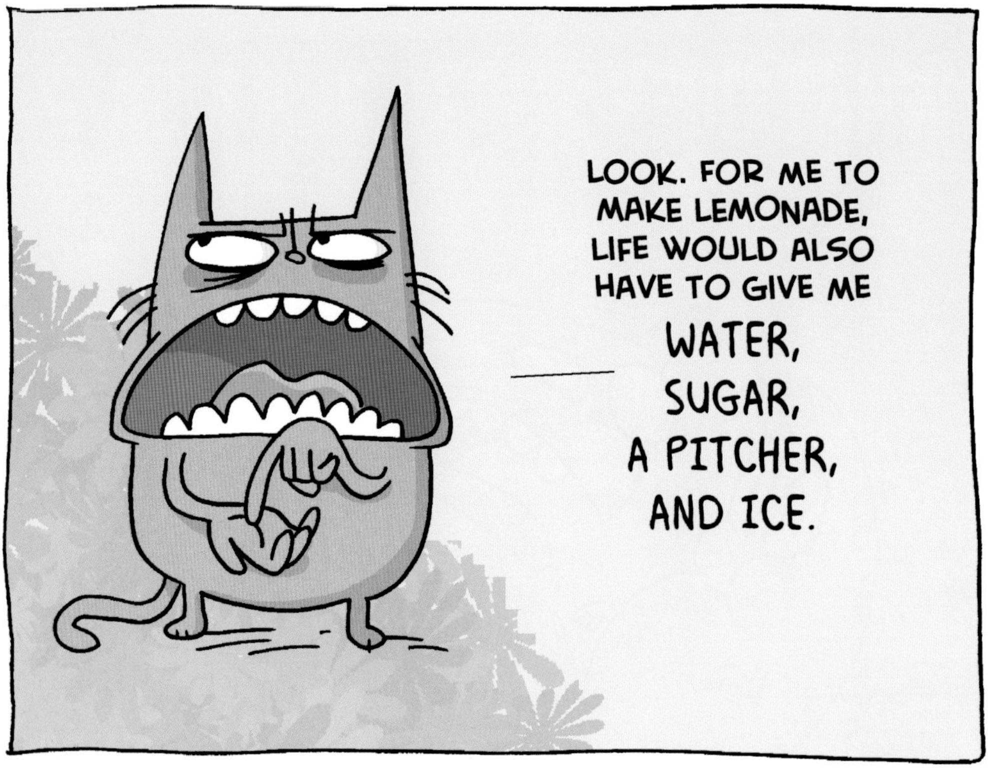
LOOK. FOR ME TO MAKE LEMONADE, LIFE WOULD ALSO HAVE TO GIVE ME WATER, SUGAR, A PITCHER, AND ICE.

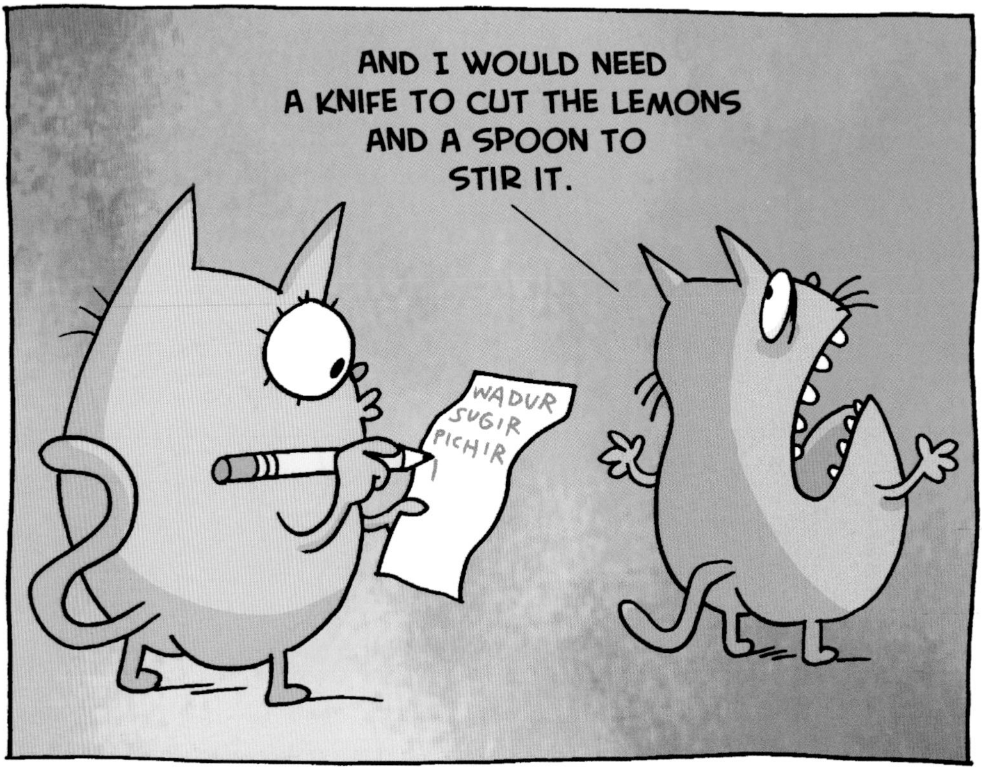
AND I WOULD NEED A KNIFE TO CUT THE LEMONS AND A SPOON TO STIR IT.
WADUR
SUGIR
PICHIR

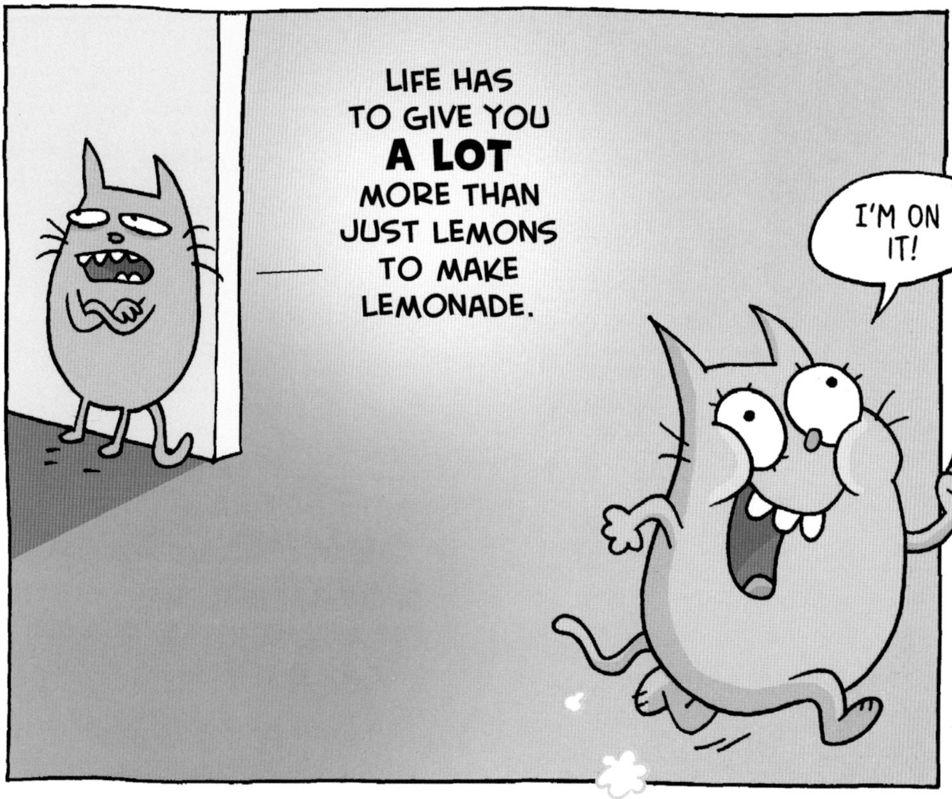
LIFE HAS TO GIVE YOU **A LOT** MORE THAN JUST LEMONS TO MAKE LEMONADE.
I'M ON IT!

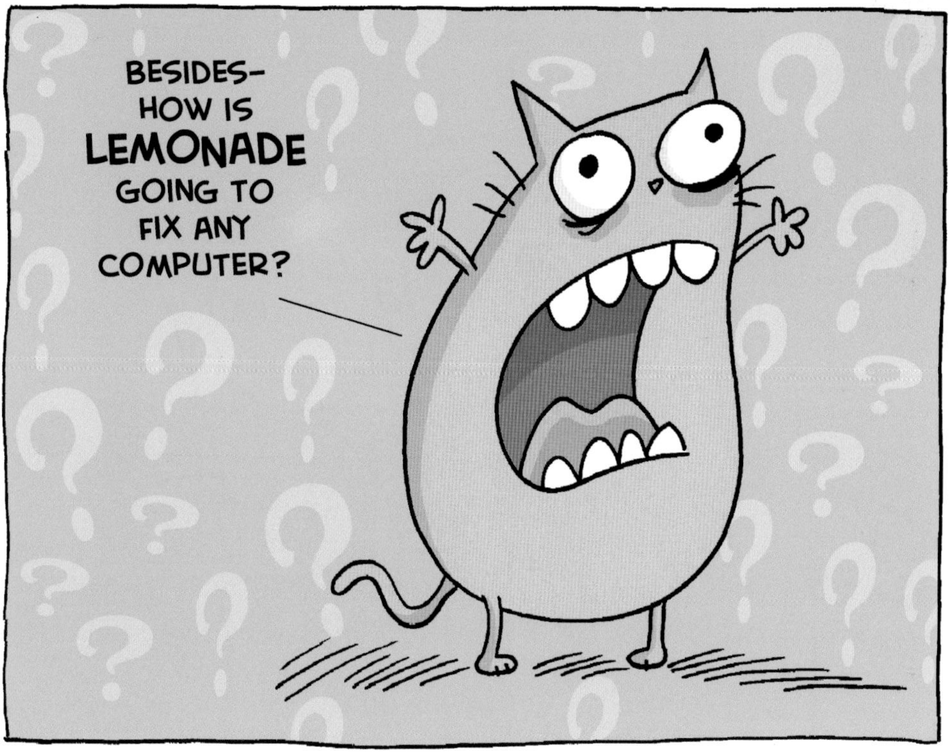
BESIDES– HOW IS **LEMONADE** GOING TO FIX ANY COMPUTER?

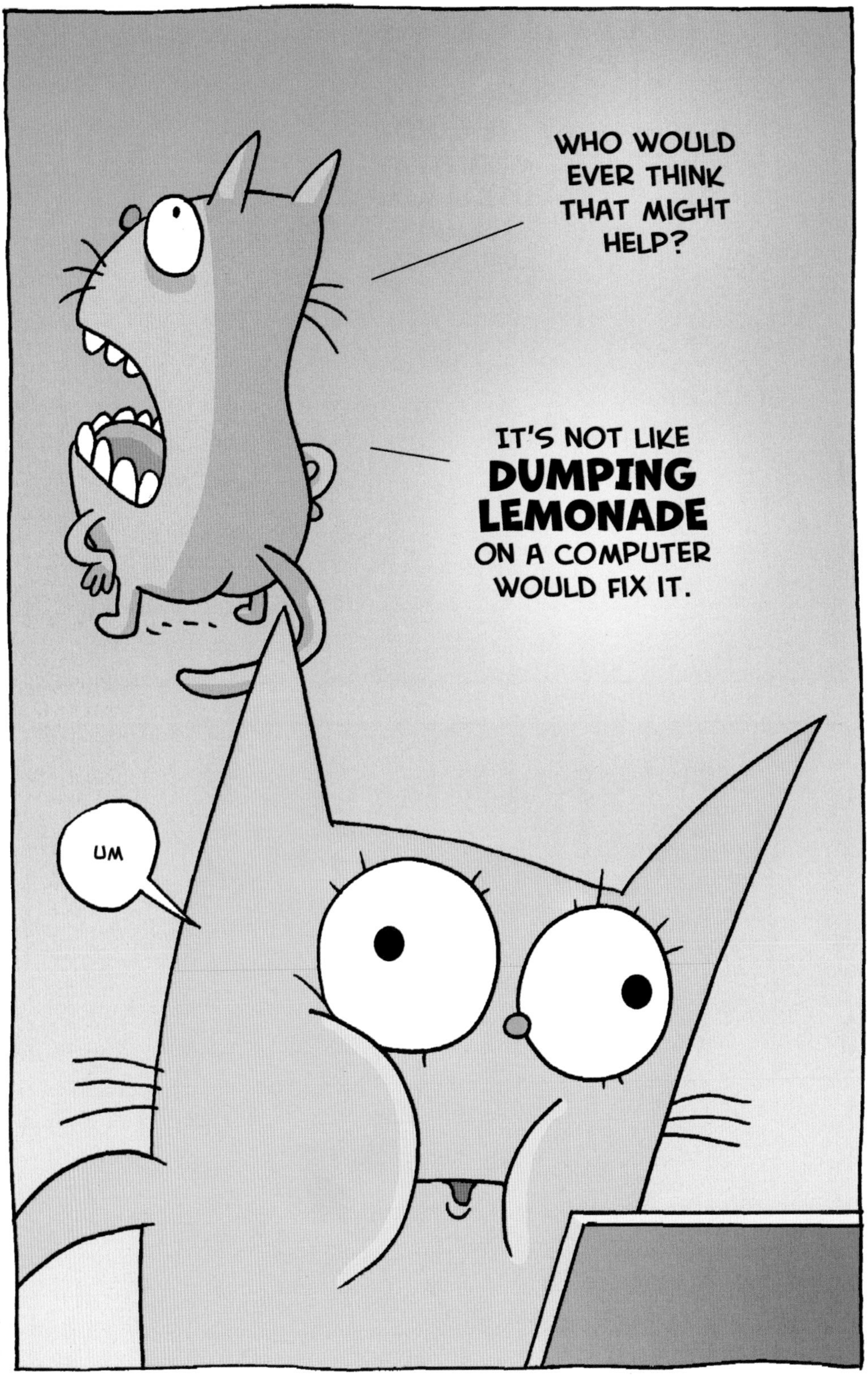
WHO WOULD EVER THINK THAT MIGHT HELP?
IT'S NOT LIKE **DUMPING LEMONADE** ON A COMPUTER WOULD FIX IT.
UM

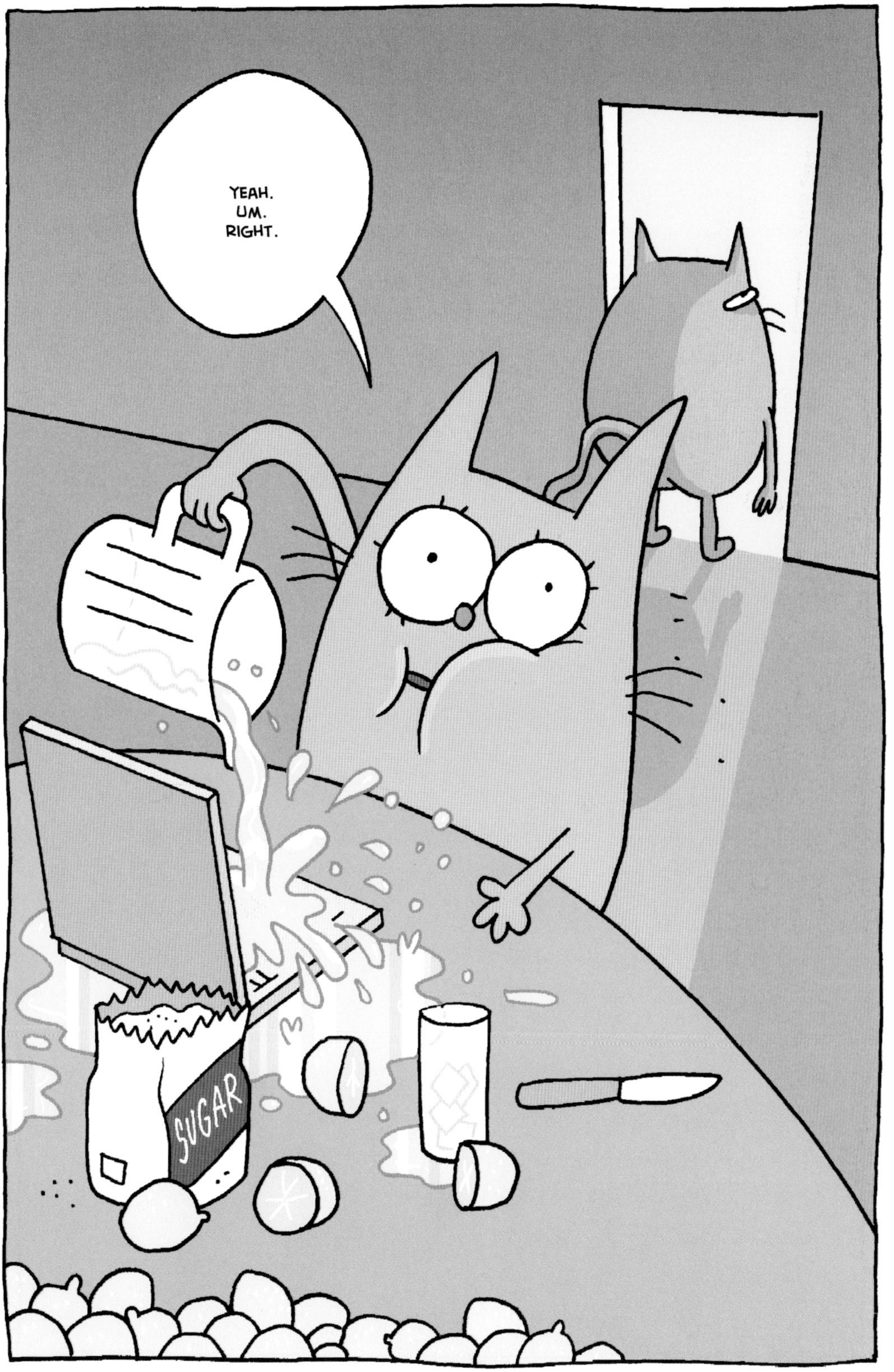
YEAH.
UM.
RIGHT.
SUGAR

SKULL

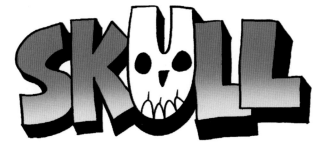

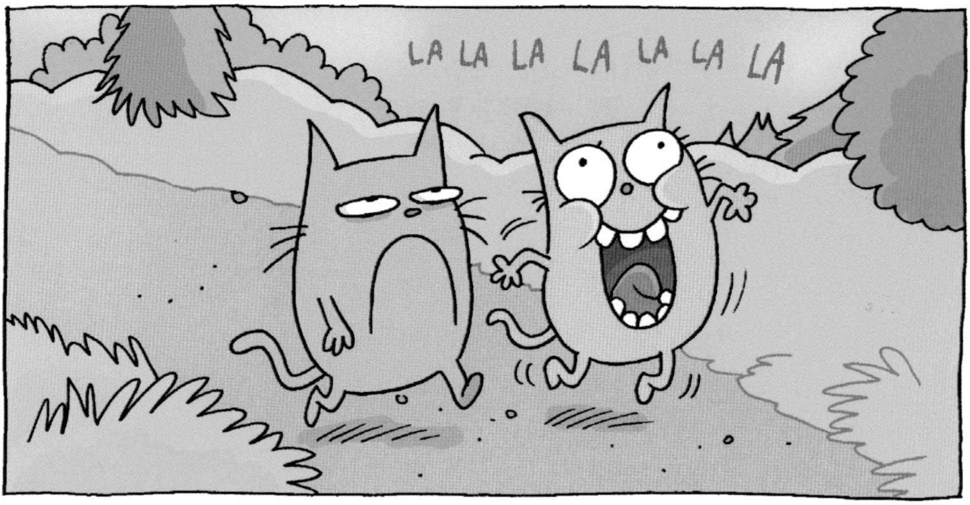
LA LA LA LA LA LA LA

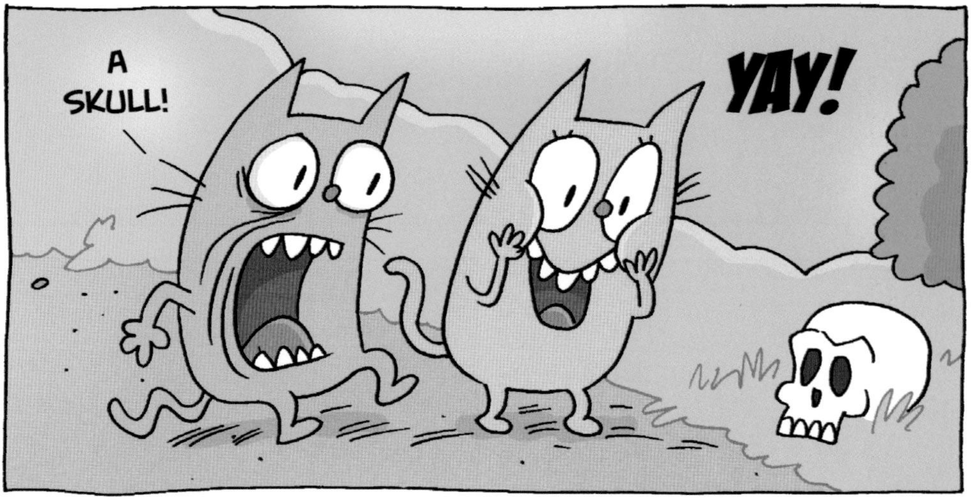
A SKULL!
YAY!

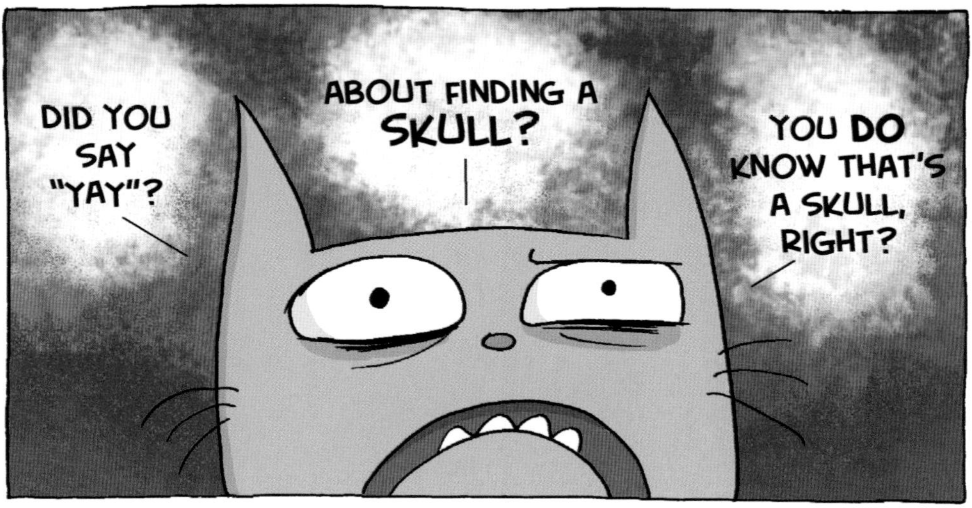
DID YOU SAY "YAY"?
ABOUT FINDING A SKULL?
YOU DO KNOW THAT'S A SKULL, RIGHT?

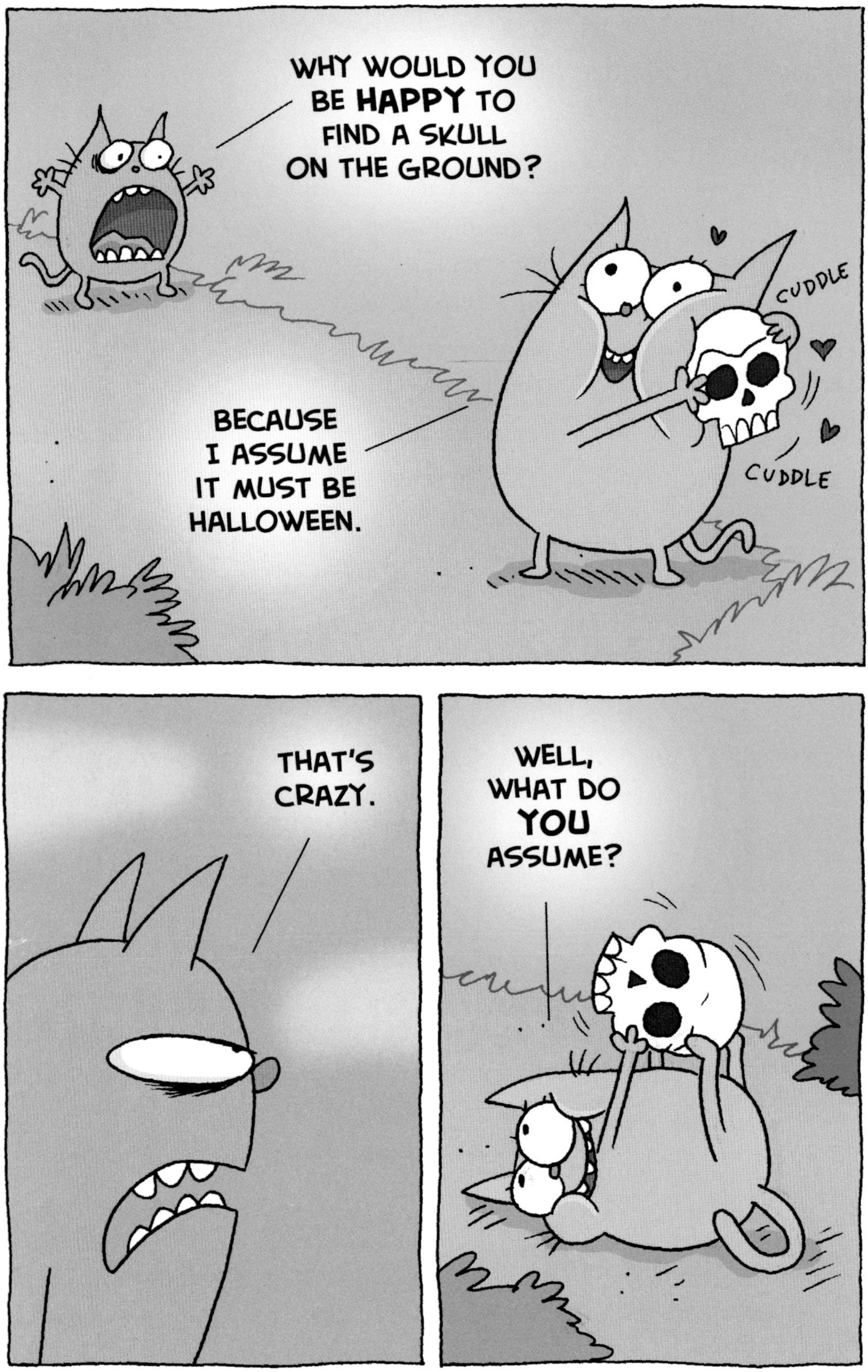
WHY WOULD YOU BE HAPPY TO FIND A SKULL ON THE GROUND?
CUDDLE
CUDDLE
BECAUSE I ASSUME IT MUST BE HALLOWEEN.
THAT'S CRAZY.
WELL, WHAT DO YOU ASSUME?

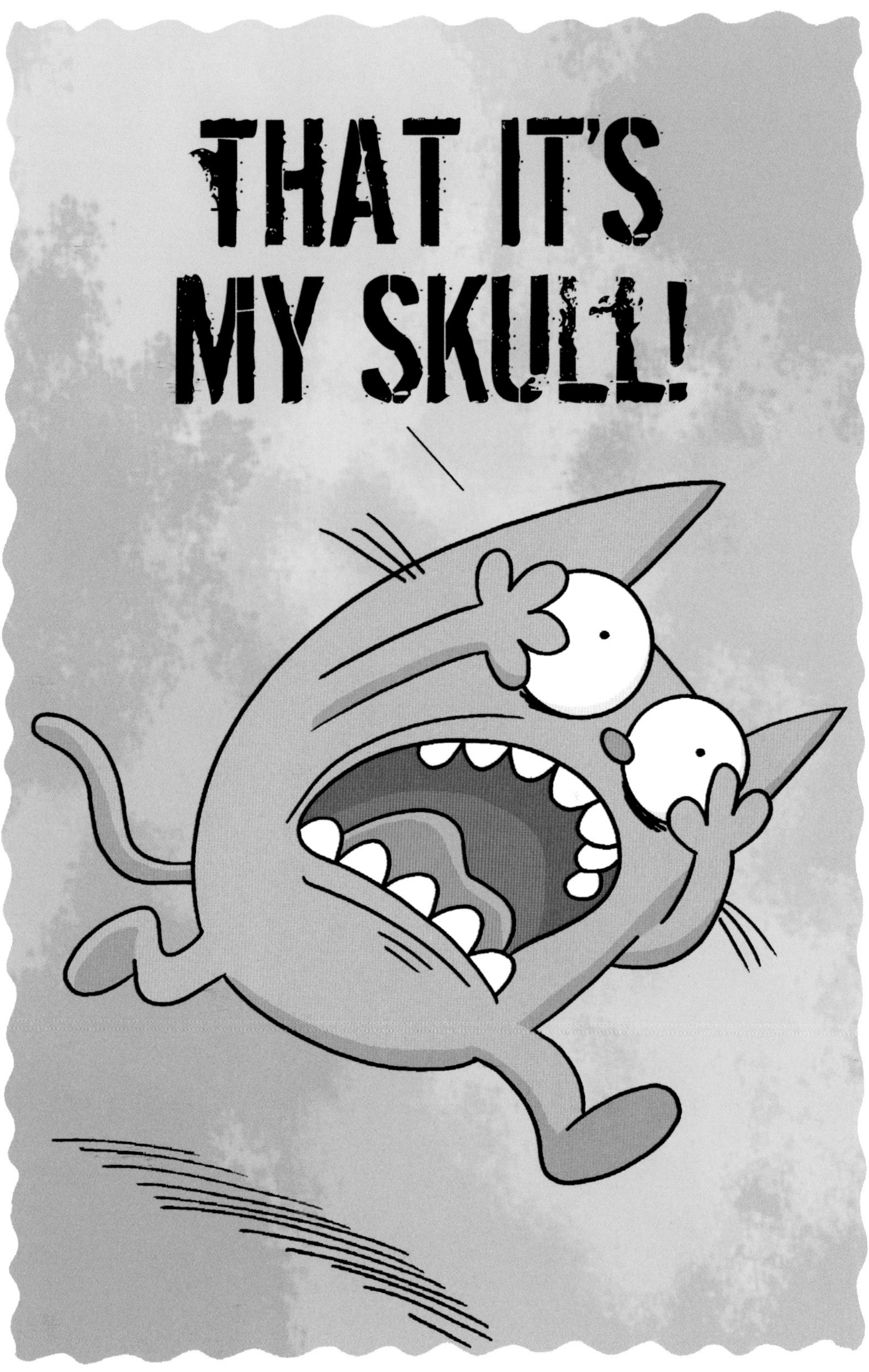
THAT IT'S MY SKULL!

DARE

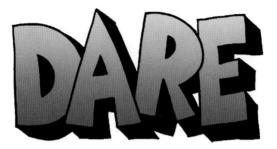

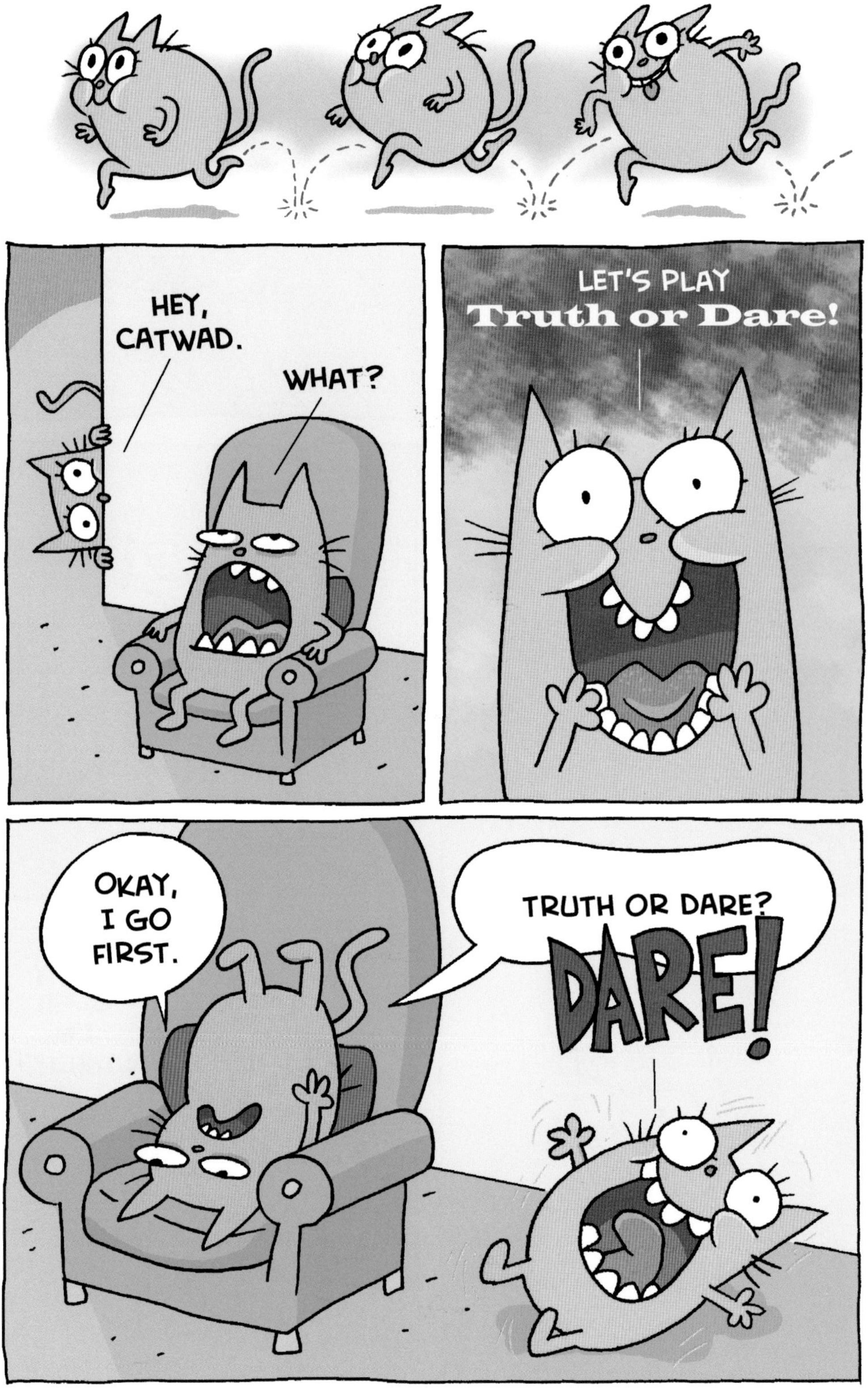
HEY, CATWAD.
WHAT?
LET'S PLAY Truth or Dare!
OKAY, I GO FIRST.
TRUTH OR DARE?
DARE!

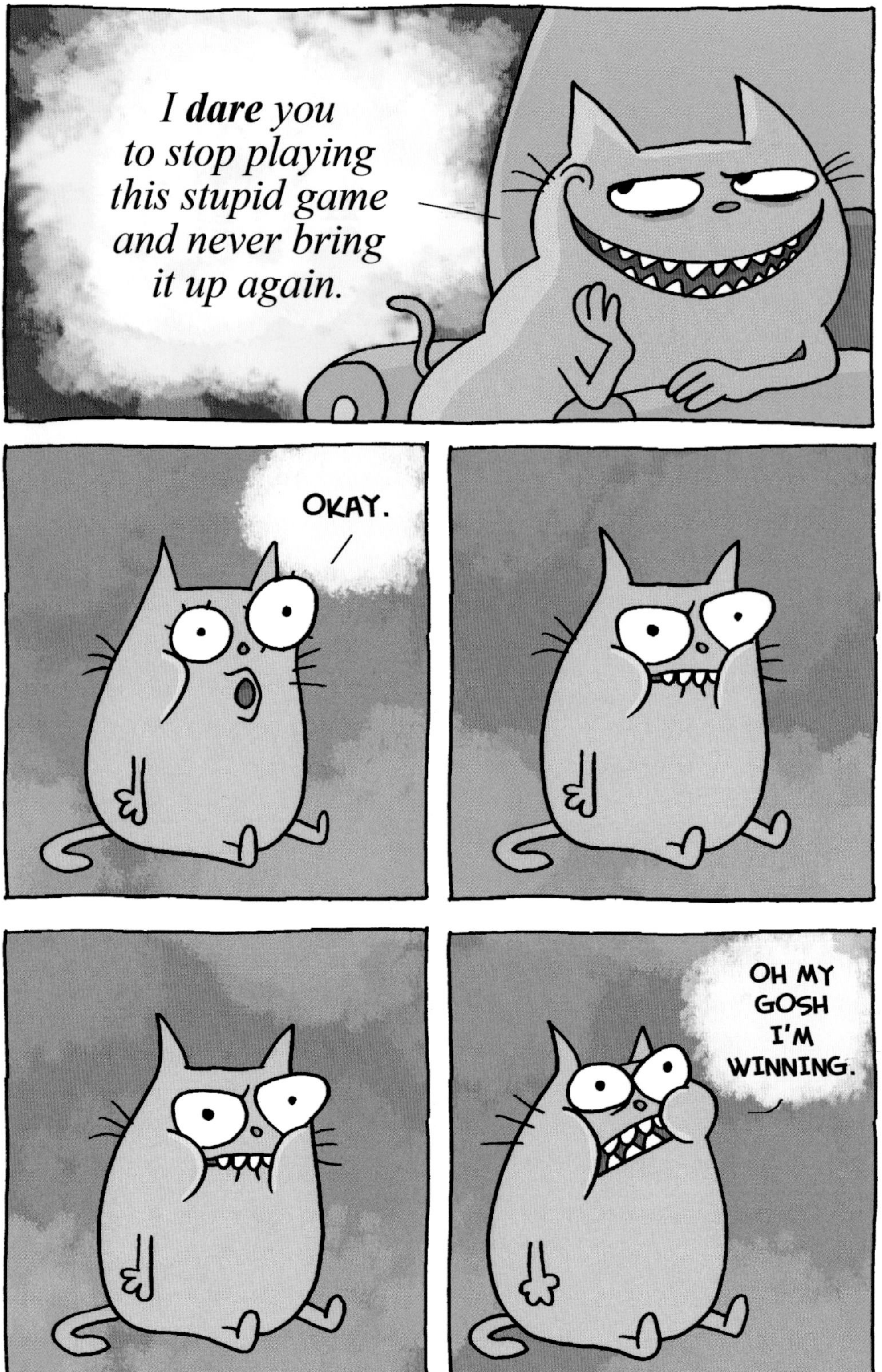
I **dare** you to stop playing this stupid game and never bring it up again.
OKAY.
OH MY GOSH I'M WINNING.

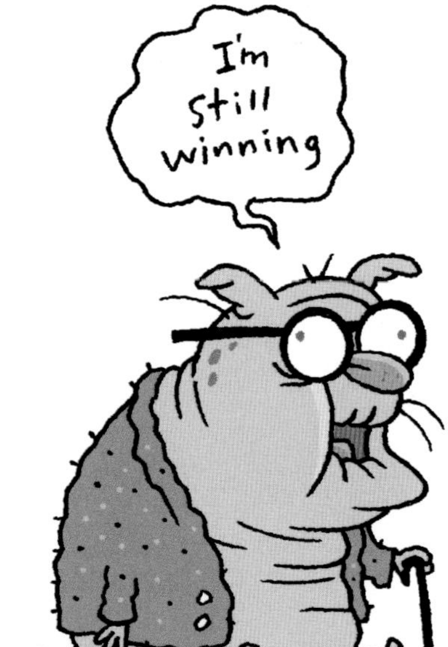
I'm still winning

SMILE

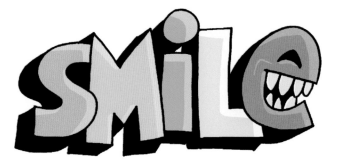

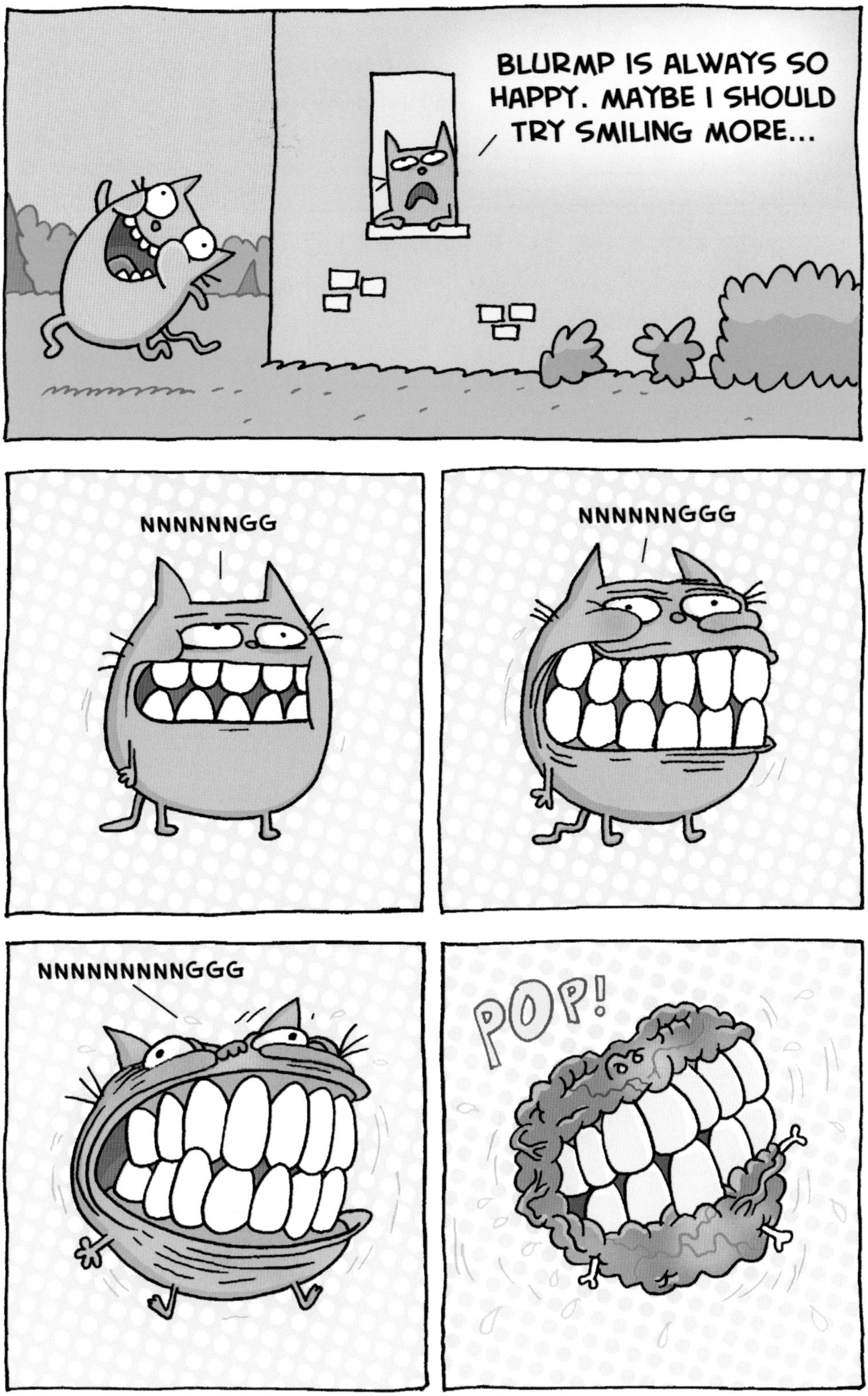
BLURMP IS ALWAYS SO HAPPY. MAYBE I SHOULD TRY SMILING MORE...
NNNNNNGG
NNNNNNGGG
NNNNNNNNNGGG
POP!

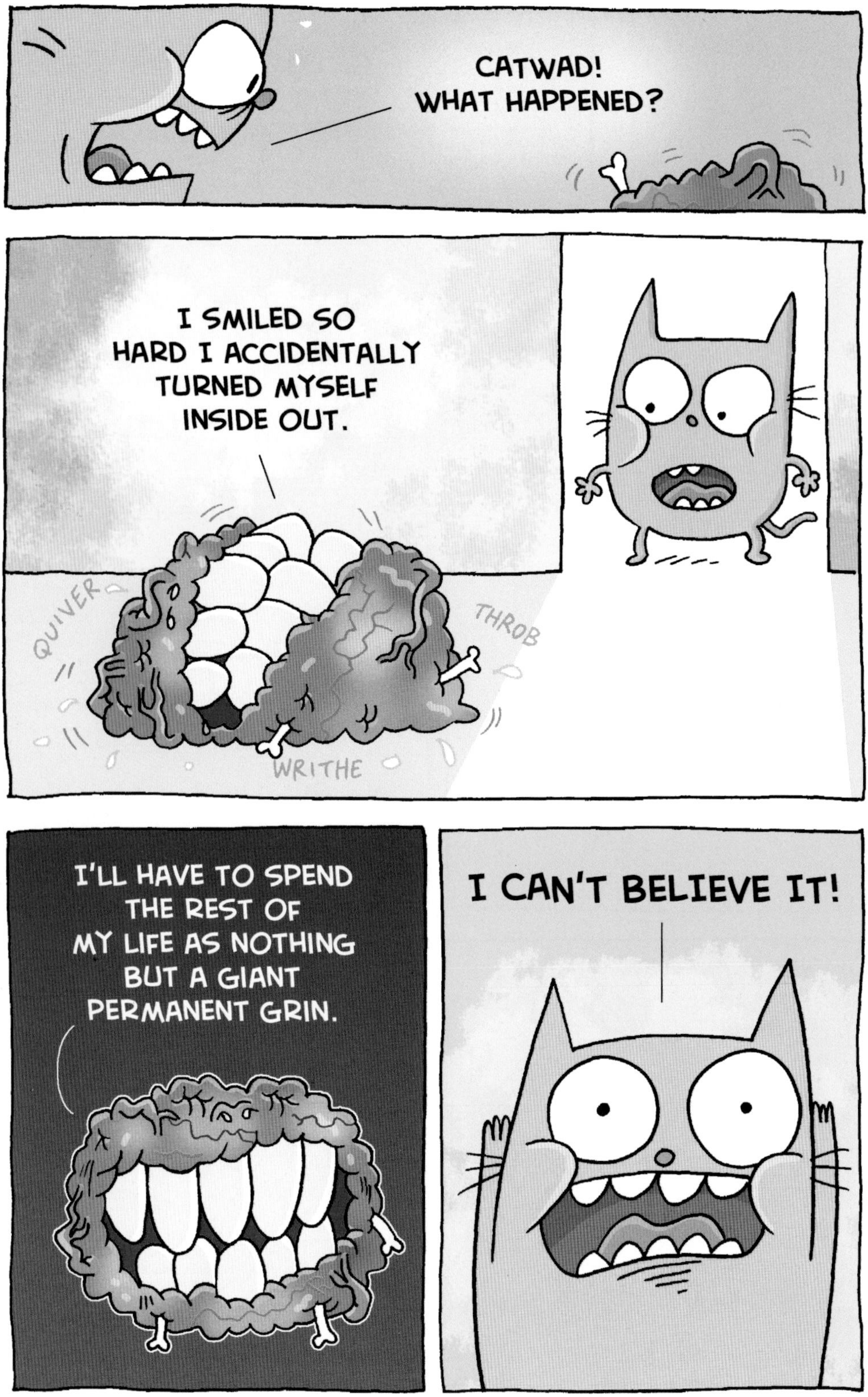
CATWAD!
WHAT HAPPENED?
I SMILED SO HARD I ACCIDENTALLY TURNED MYSELF INSIDE OUT.
QUIVER
THROB
WRITHE
I'LL HAVE TO SPEND THE REST OF MY LIFE AS NOTHING BUT A GIANT PERMANENT GRIN.
I CAN'T BELIEVE IT!

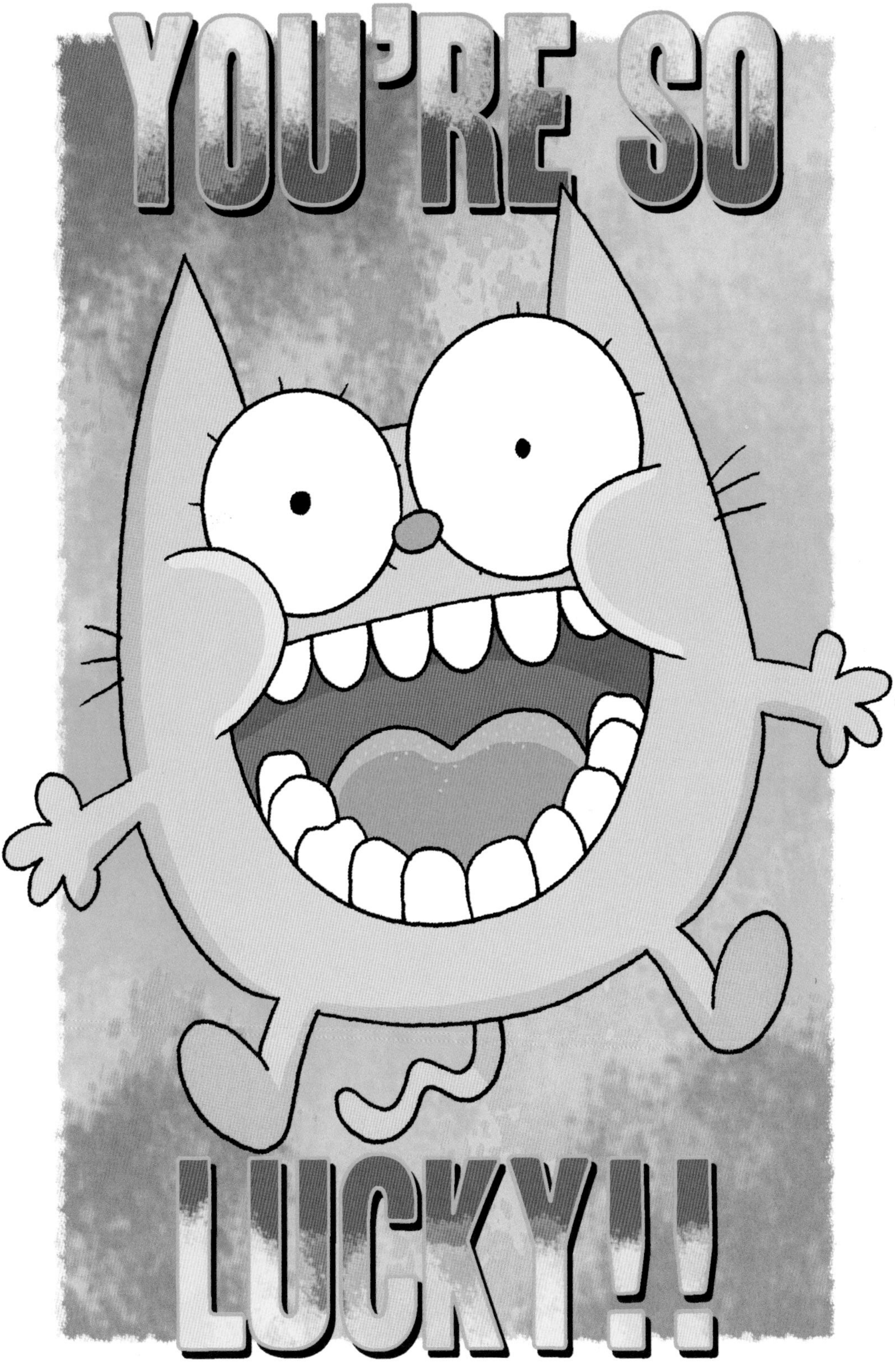
YOU'RE SO
LUCKY!!

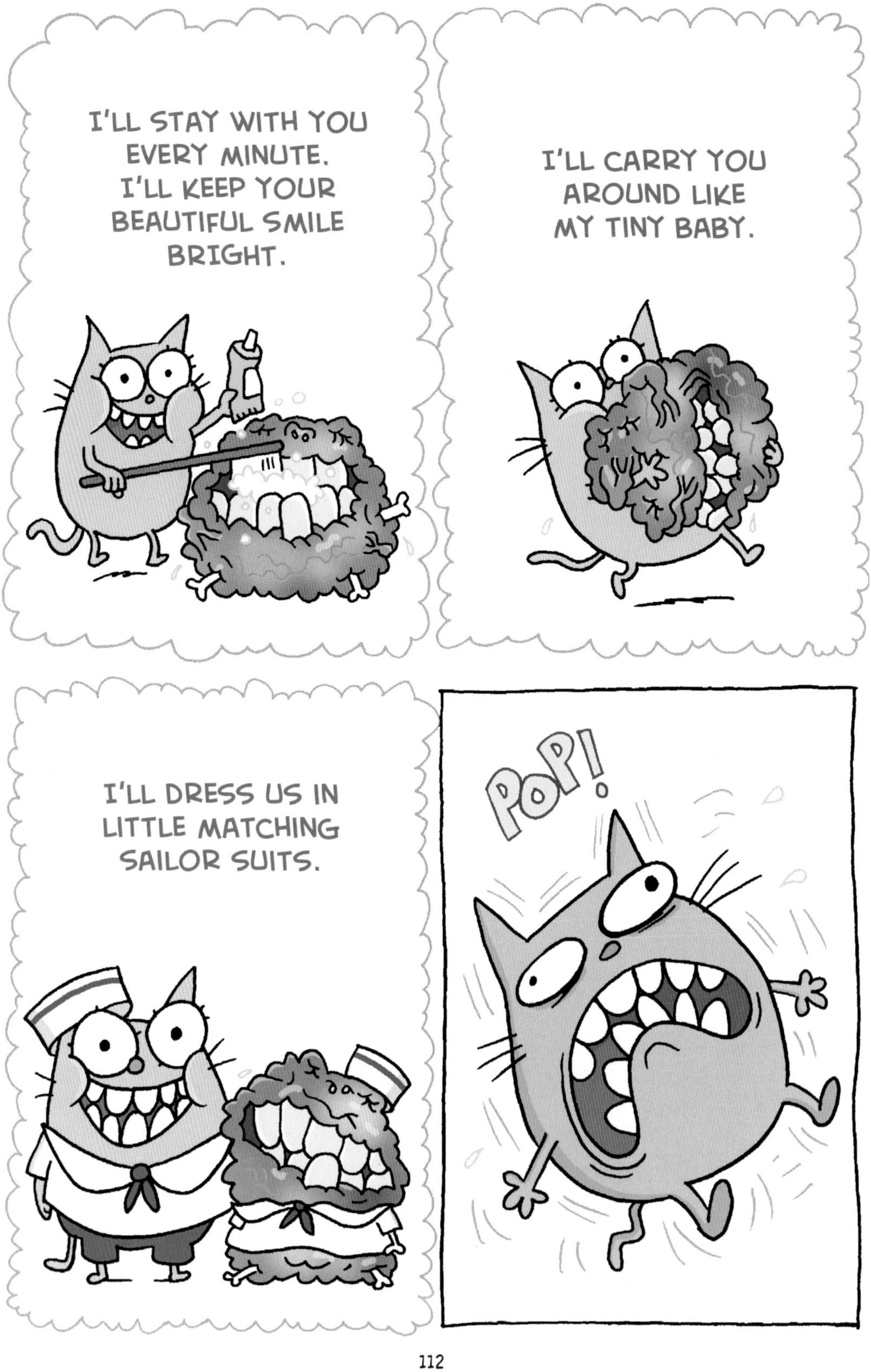
I'LL STAY WITH YOU EVERY MINUTE. I'LL KEEP YOUR BEAUTIFUL SMILE BRIGHT.
I'LL CARRY YOU AROUND LIKE MY TINY BABY.
I'LL DRESS US IN LITTLE MATCHING SAILOR SUITS.
POP!

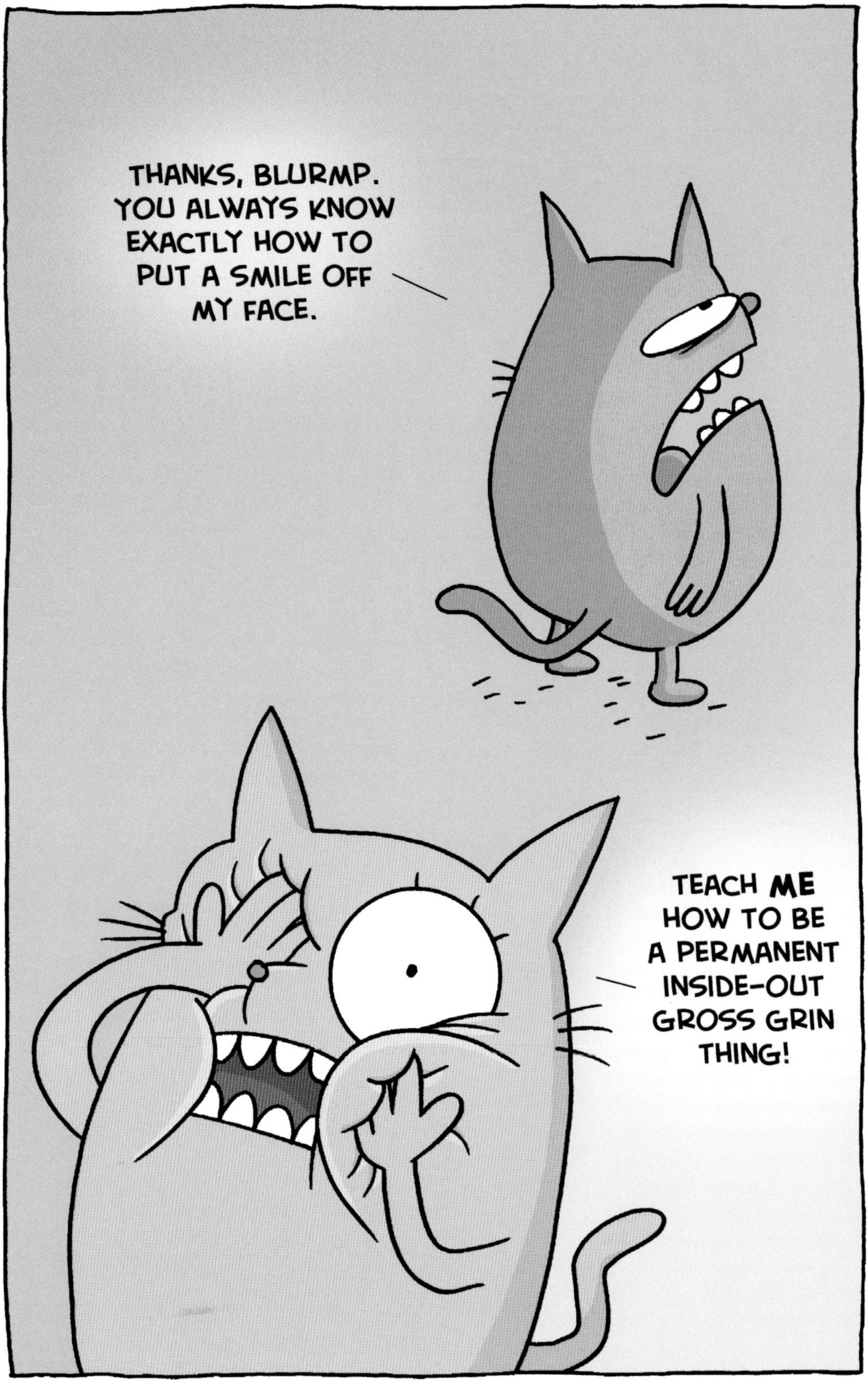
THANKS, BLURMP. YOU ALWAYS KNOW EXACTLY HOW TO PUT A SMILE OFF MY FACE.
TEACH **ME** HOW TO BE A PERMANENT INSIDE-OUT GROSS GRIN THING!

SPECIAL PREVIEW OF
CAT #2
2019!

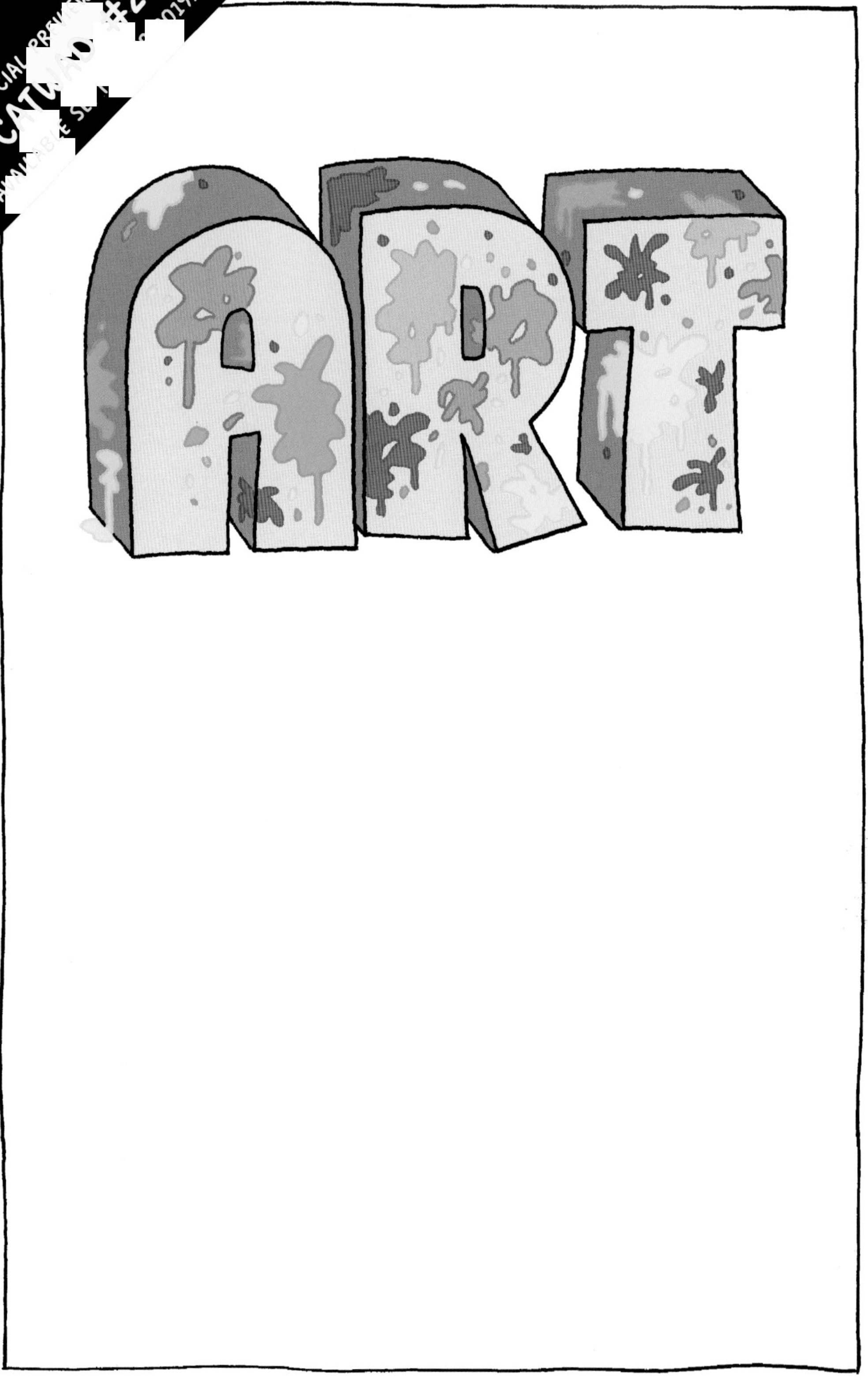
ART

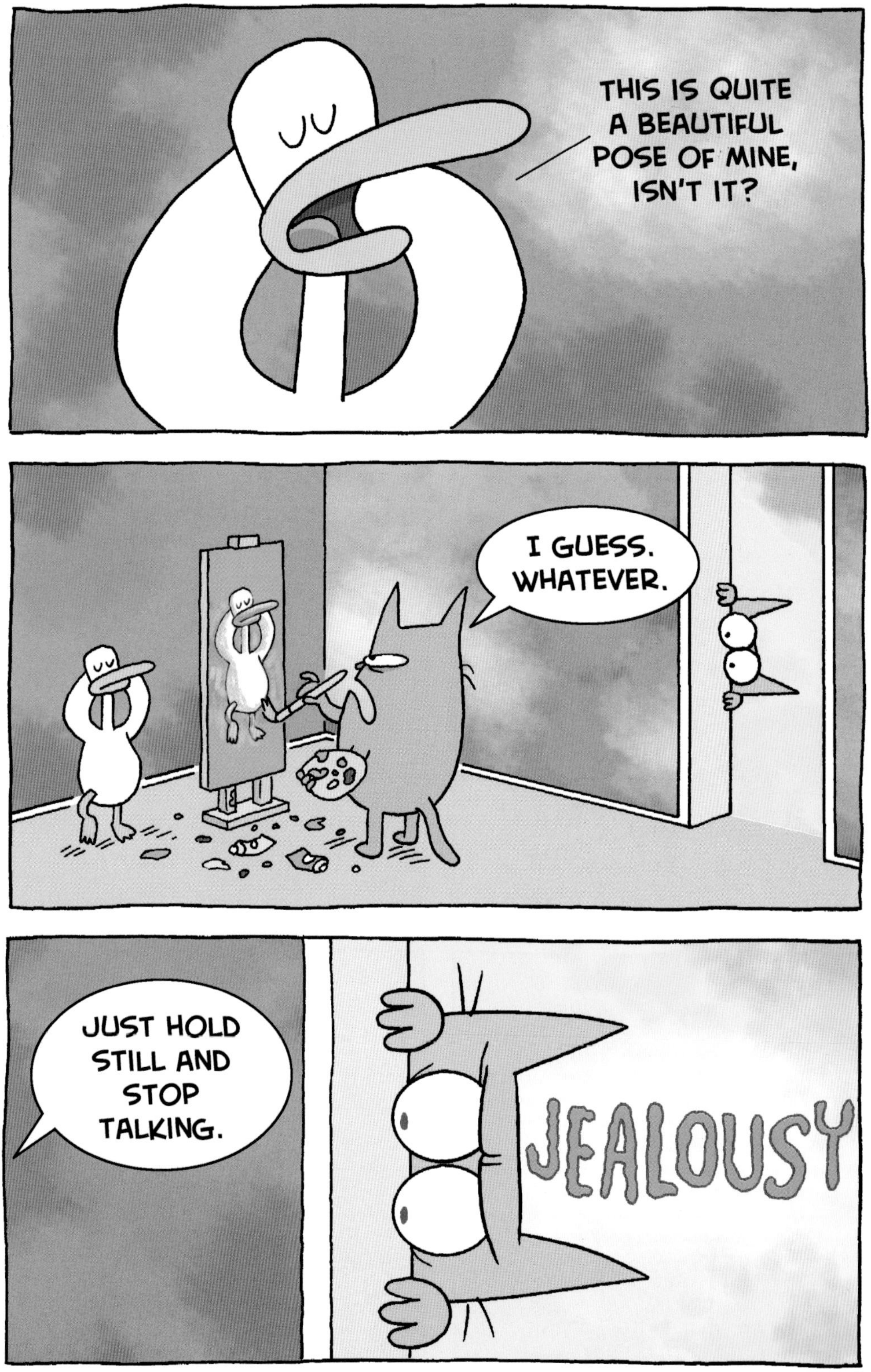
THIS IS QUITE A BEAUTIFUL POSE OF MINE, ISN'T IT?
I GUESS. WHATEVER.
JUST HOLD STILL AND STOP TALKING.
JEALOUSY

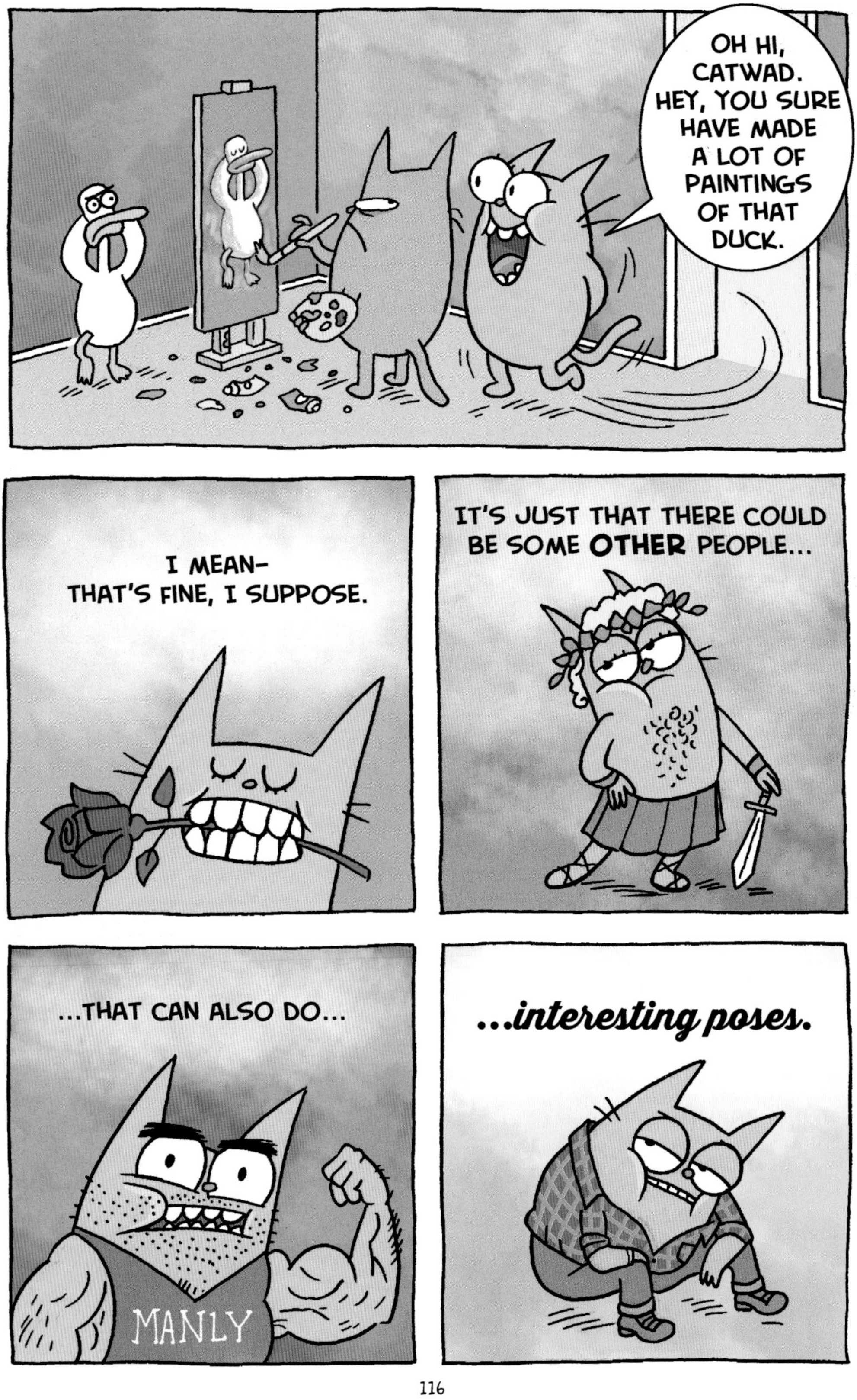
OH HI, CATWAD. HEY, YOU SURE HAVE MADE A LOT OF PAINTINGS OF THAT DUCK.
I MEAN– THAT'S FINE, I SUPPOSE.
IT'S JUST THAT THERE COULD BE SOME **OTHER** PEOPLE...
...THAT CAN ALSO DO...
MANLY
...interesting poses.

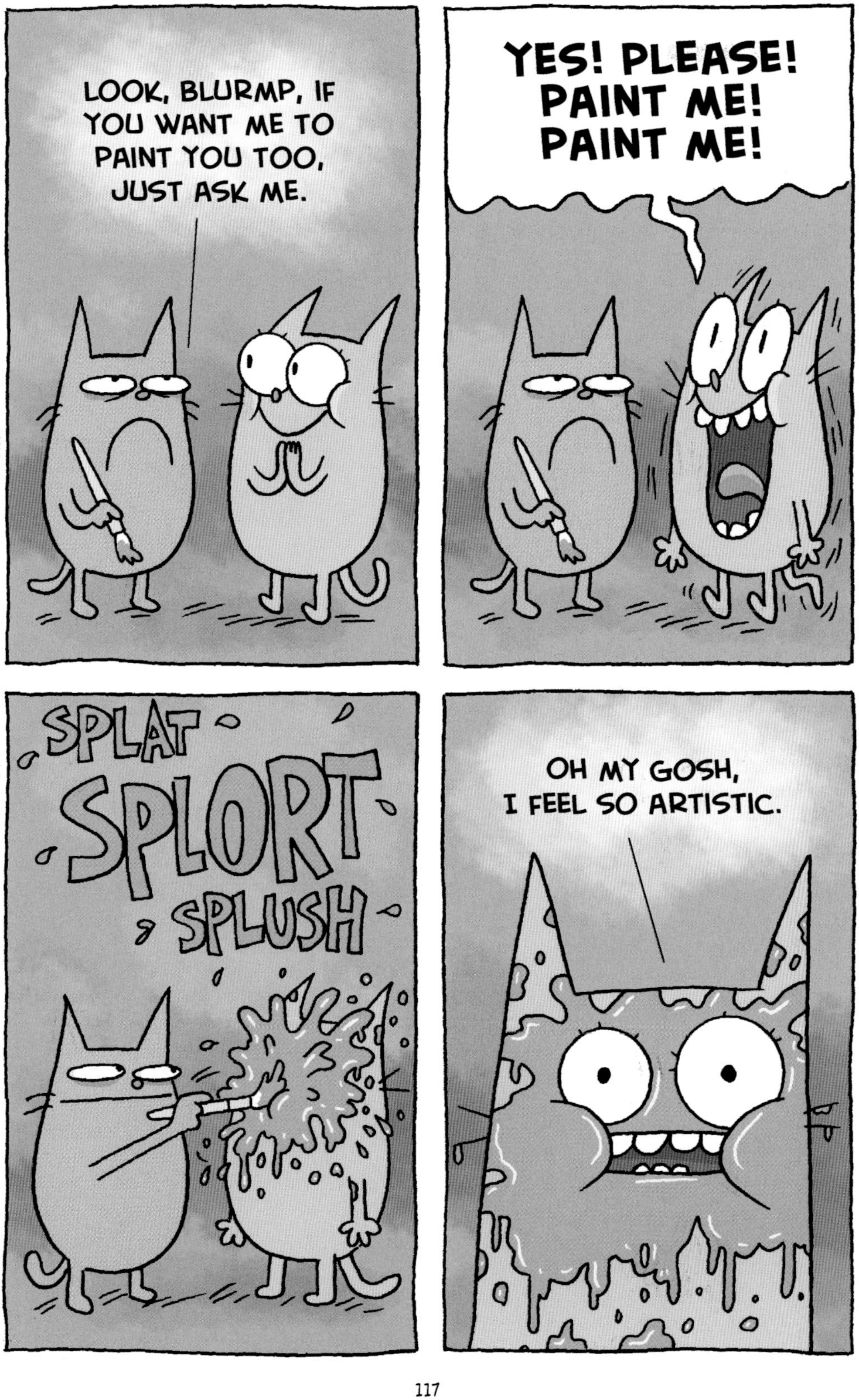
LOOK, BLURMP, IF YOU WANT ME TO PAINT YOU TOO, JUST ASK ME.
YES! PLEASE! PAINT ME! PAINT ME!
SPLAT
SPLORT
SPLUSH
OH MY GOSH, I FEEL SO ARTISTIC.

DUMB

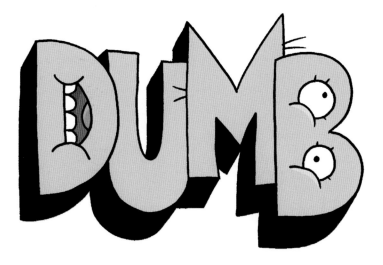

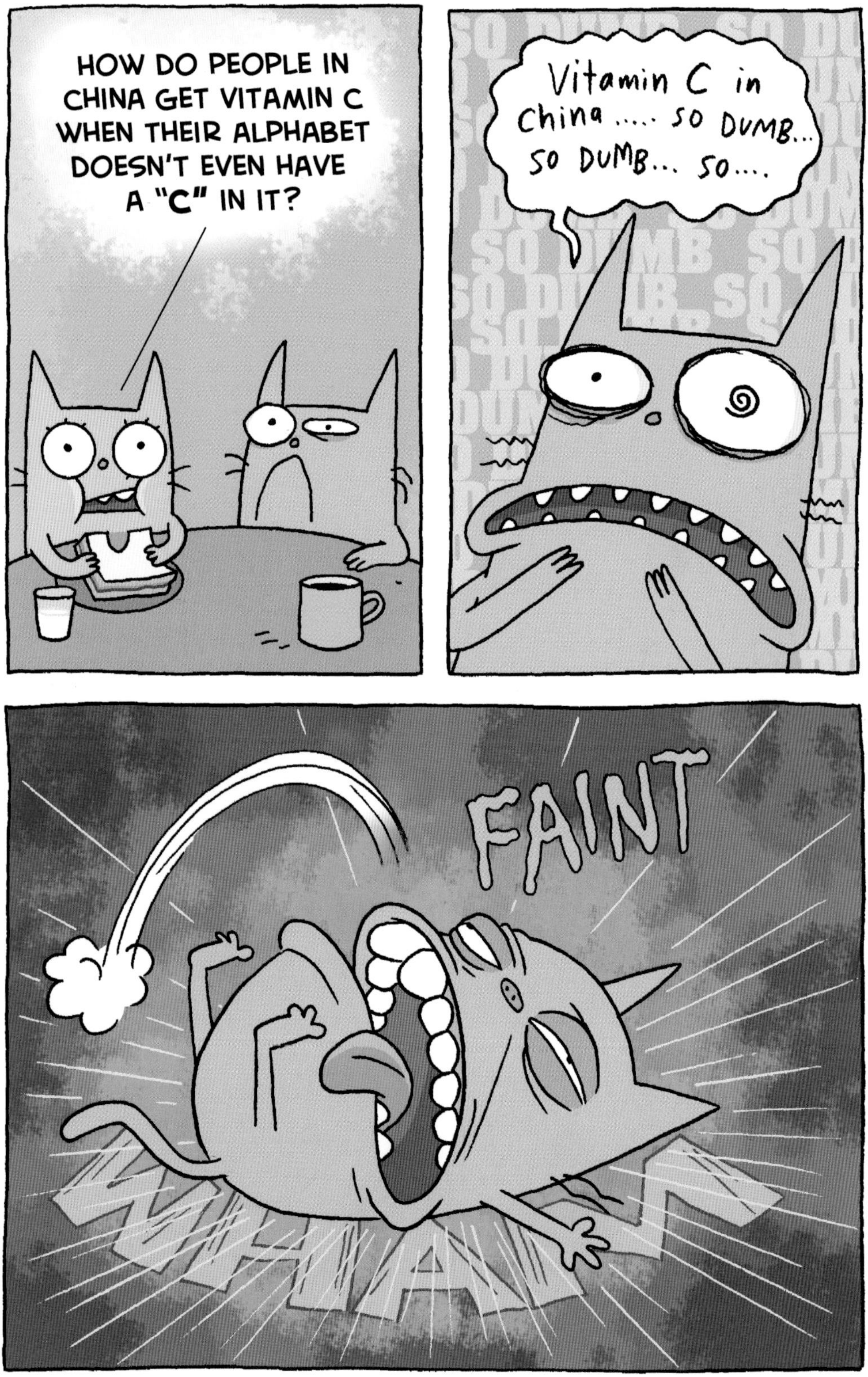
HOW DO PEOPLE IN CHINA GET VITAMIN C WHEN THEIR ALPHABET DOESN'T EVEN HAVE A "C" IN IT?
Vitamin C in China ..... SO DUMB... SO DUMB... SO....
SO DUMB
FAINT

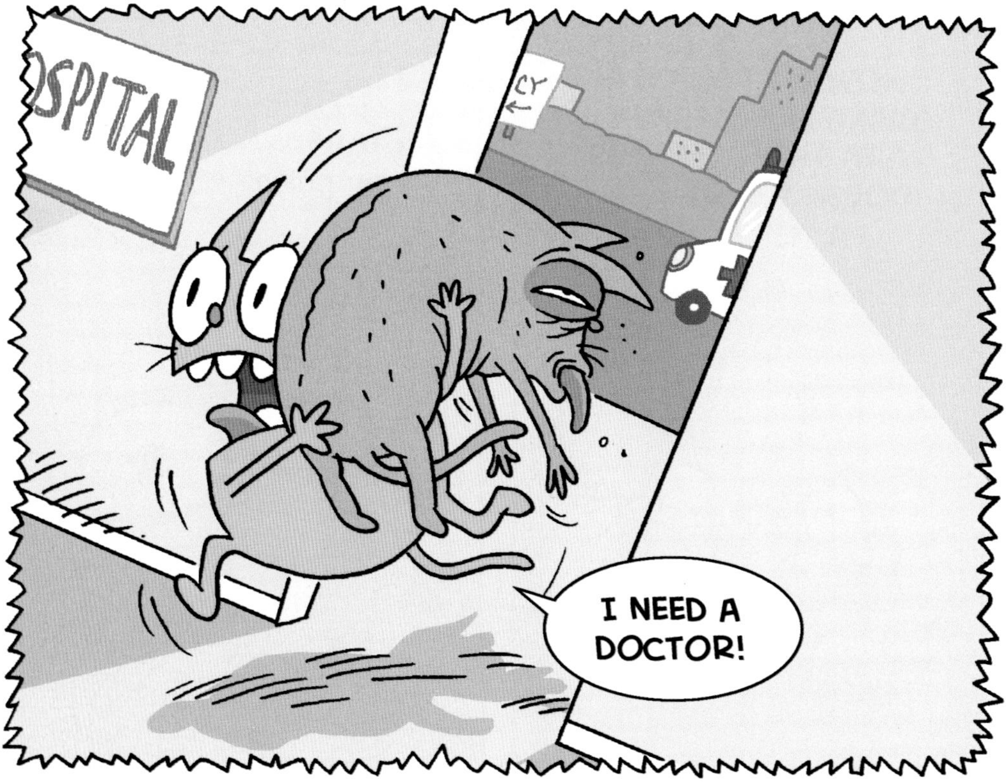
SPITAL
I NEED A DOCTOR!

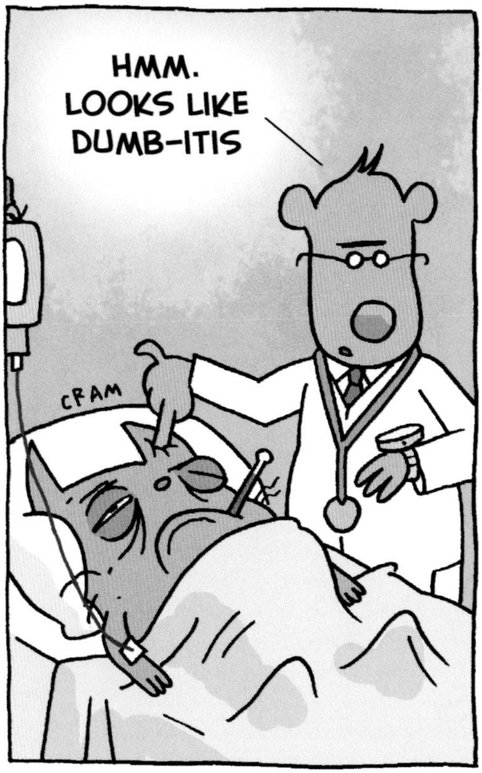
HMM. LOOKS LIKE DUMB-ITIS
CRAM

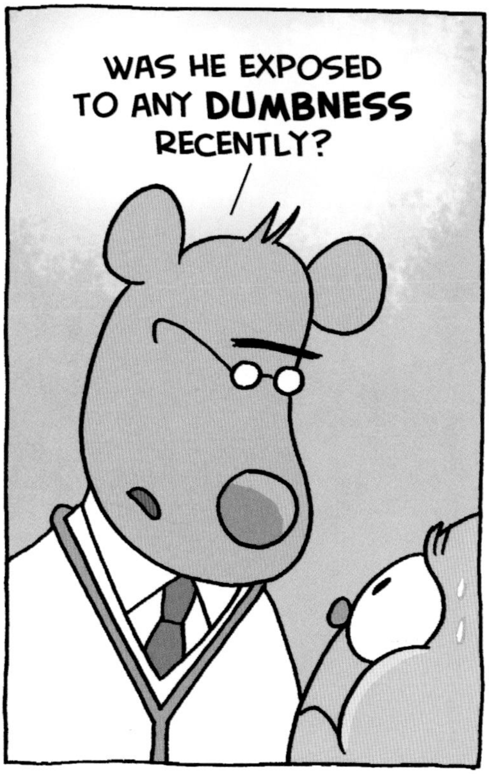
WAS HE EXPOSED TO ANY **DUMBNESS** RECENTLY?

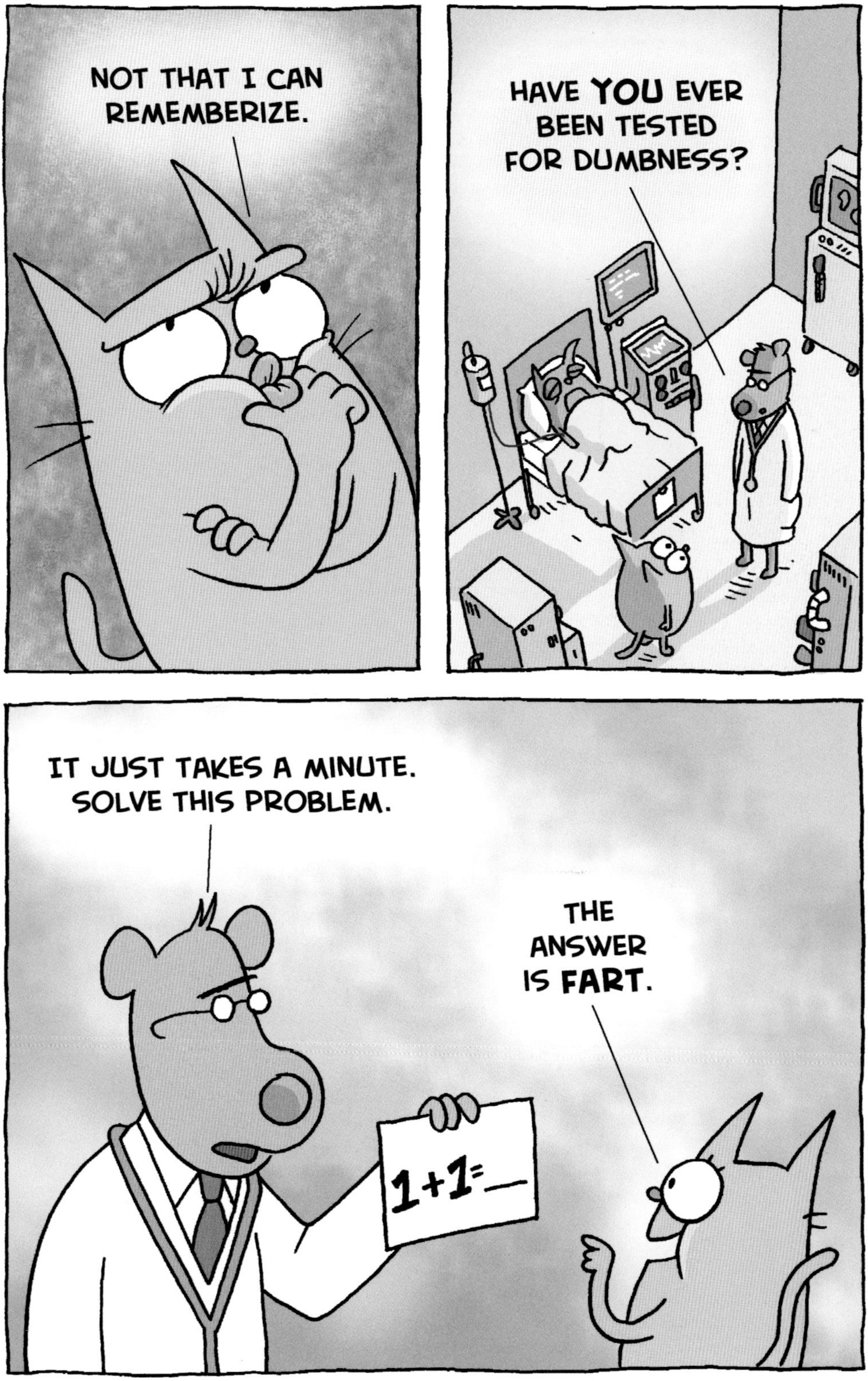
NOT THAT I CAN REMEMBERIZE.
HAVE YOU EVER BEEN TESTED FOR DUMBNESS?
IT JUST TAKES A MINUTE. SOLVE THIS PROBLEM.
1+1=__
THE ANSWER IS FART.

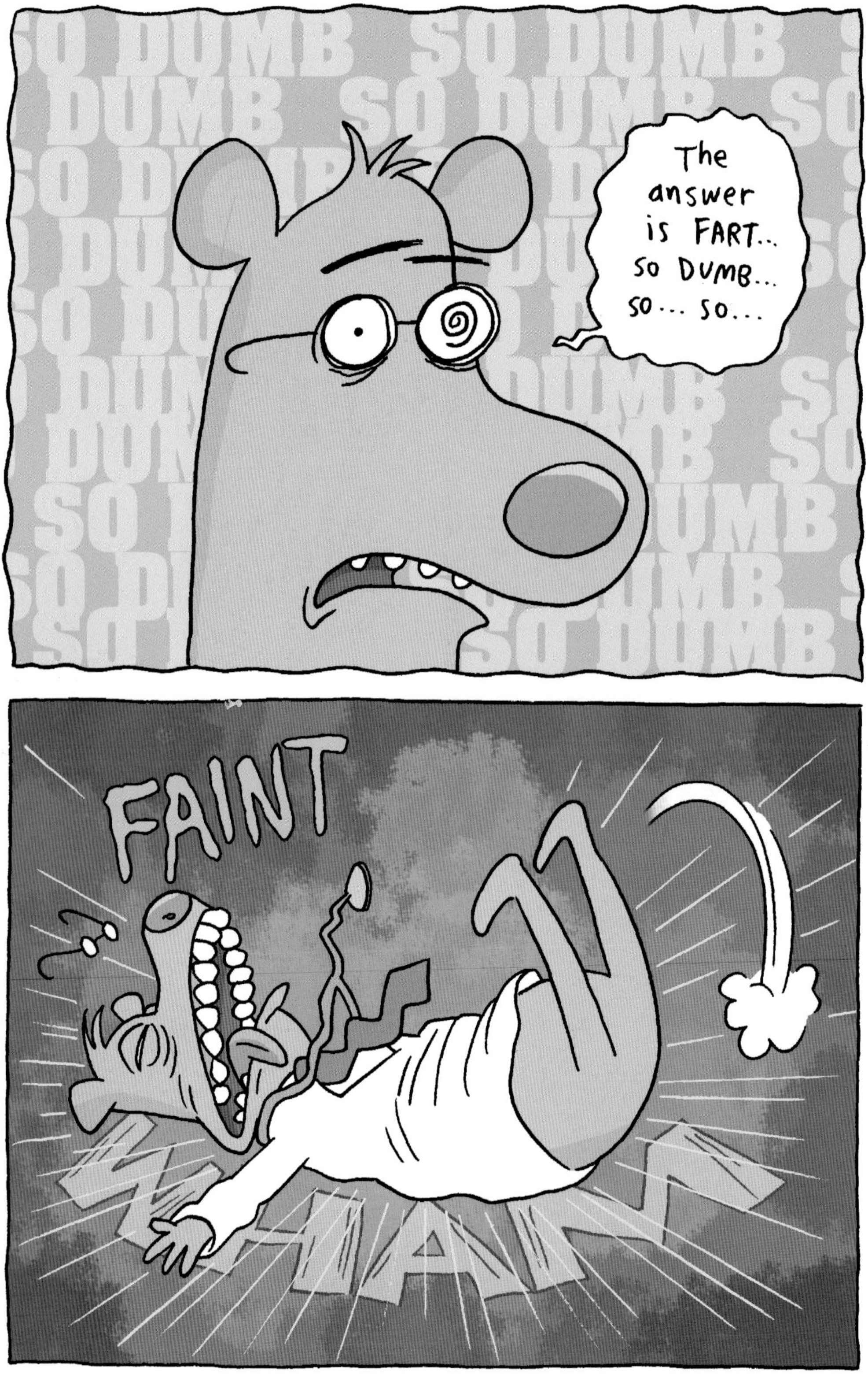
SO DUMB SO DUMB
The answer is FART... so DUMB... so... so...
FAINT
WHAM

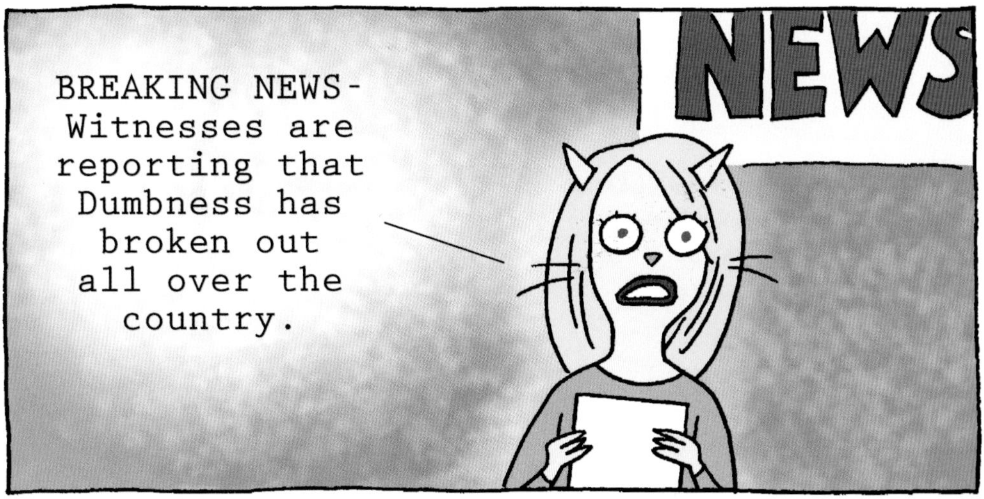
NEWS
BREAKING NEWS- Witnesses are reporting that Dumbness has broken out all over the country.

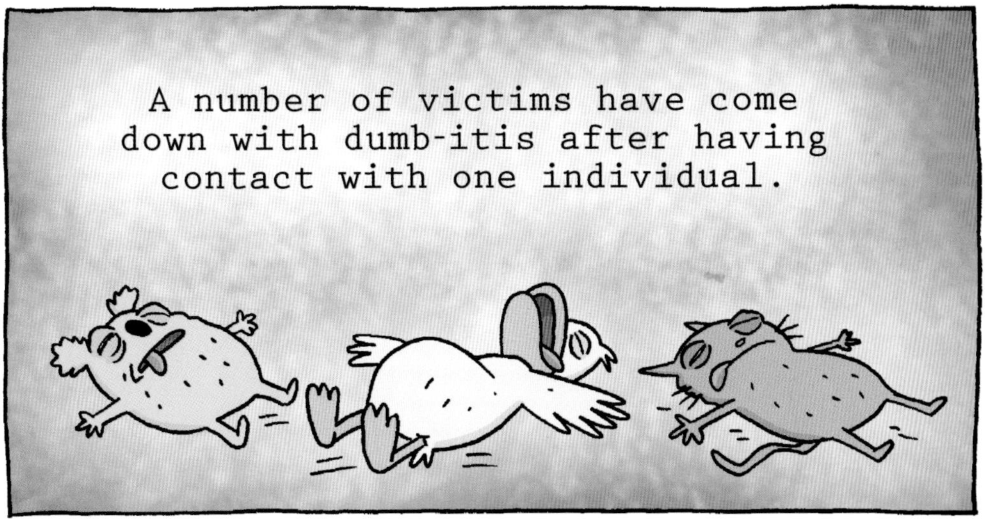
A number of victims have come down with dumb-itis after having contact with one individual.

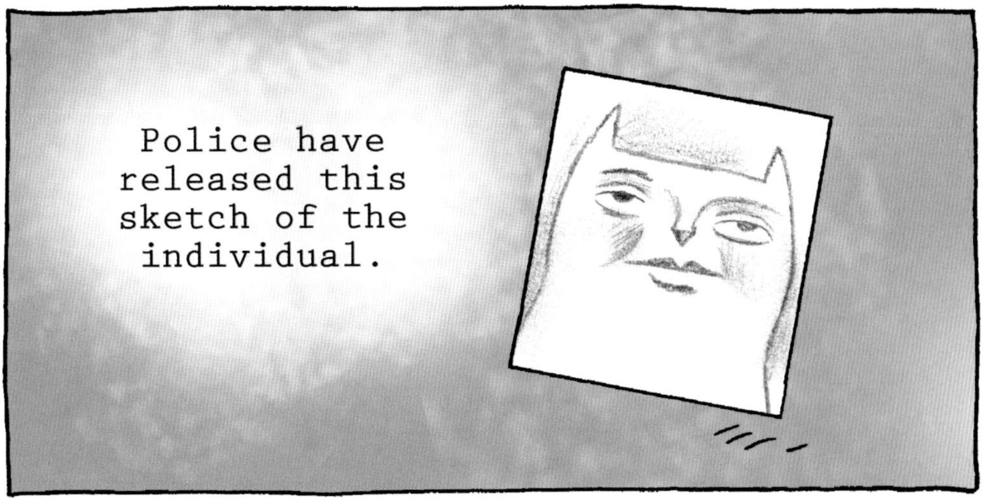
Police have released this sketch of the individual.

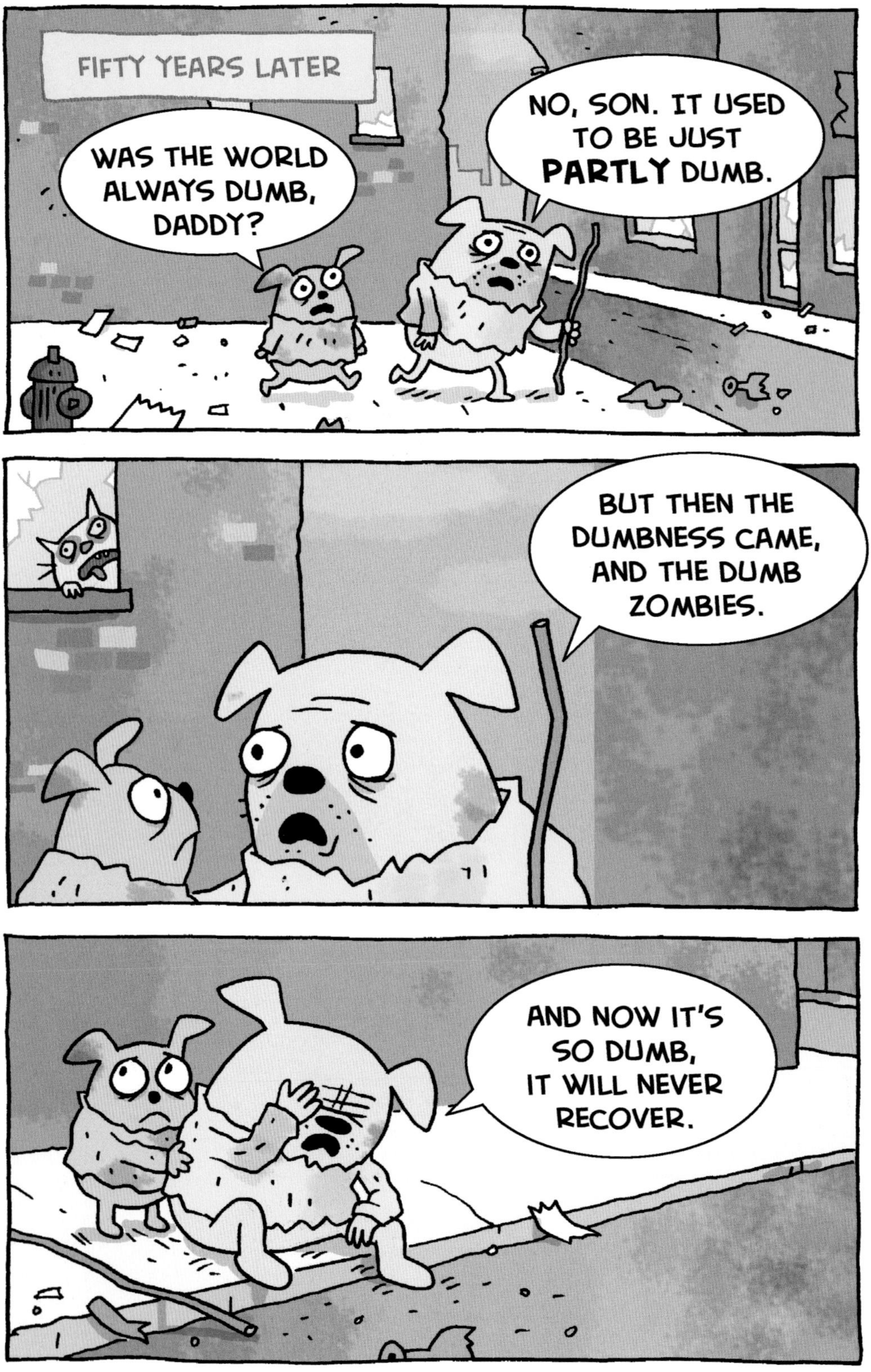
FIFTY YEARS LATER
WAS THE WORLD ALWAYS DUMB, DADDY?
NO, SON. IT USED TO BE JUST **PARTLY** DUMB.
BUT THEN THE DUMBNESS CAME, AND THE DUMB ZOMBIES.
AND NOW IT'S SO DUMB, IT WILL NEVER RECOVER.

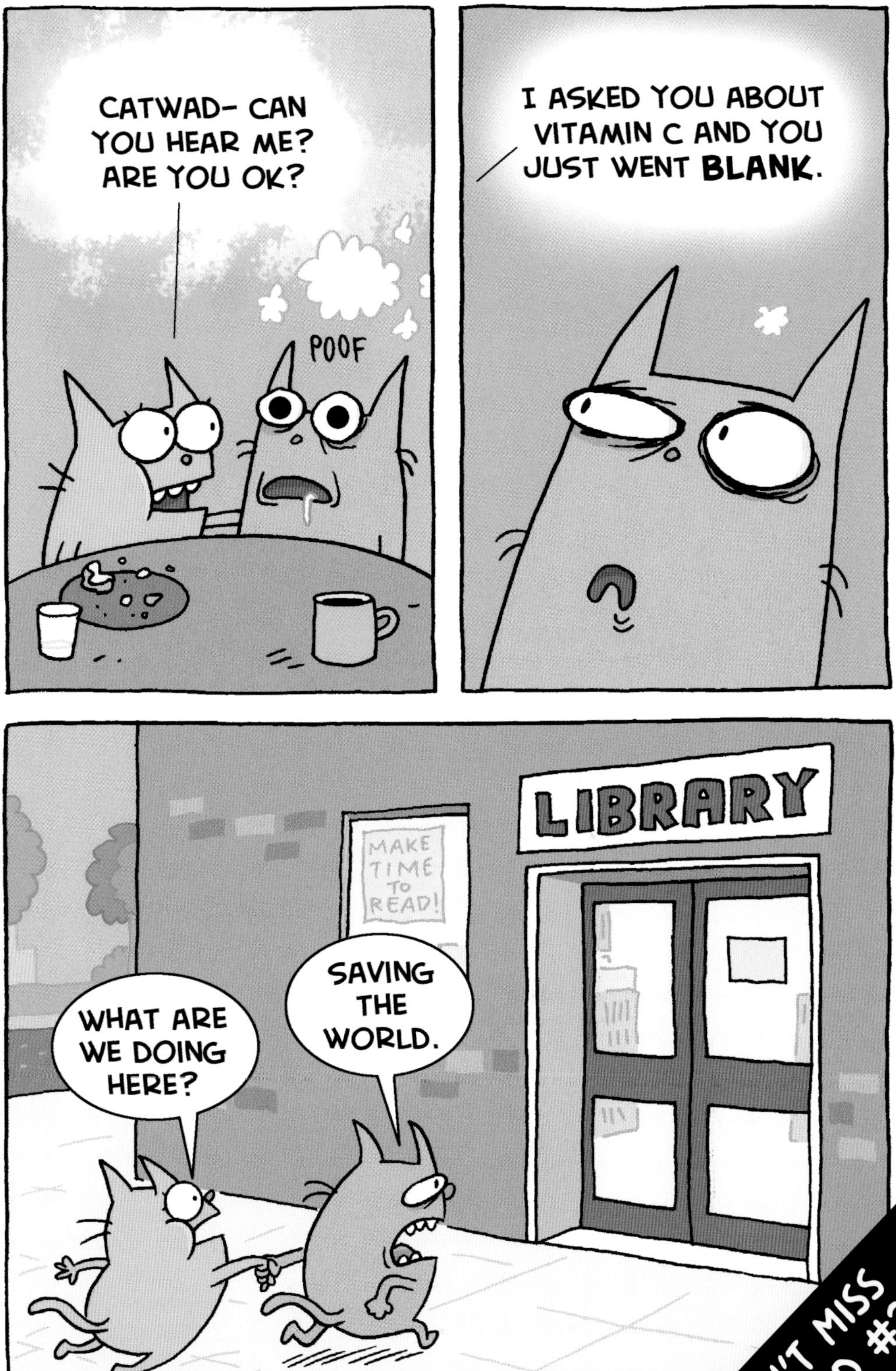
CATWAD- CAN YOU HEAR ME? ARE YOU OK?
POOF
I ASKED YOU ABOUT VITAMIN C AND YOU JUST WENT **BLANK**.
LIBRARY
MAKE TIME TO READ!
WHAT ARE WE DOING HERE?
SAVING THE WORLD.

DON'T MISS CATWAD #2!

BONUS ACTIVITY!
CAN YOU FIND THE TWO IDENTICAL BLURMPS?

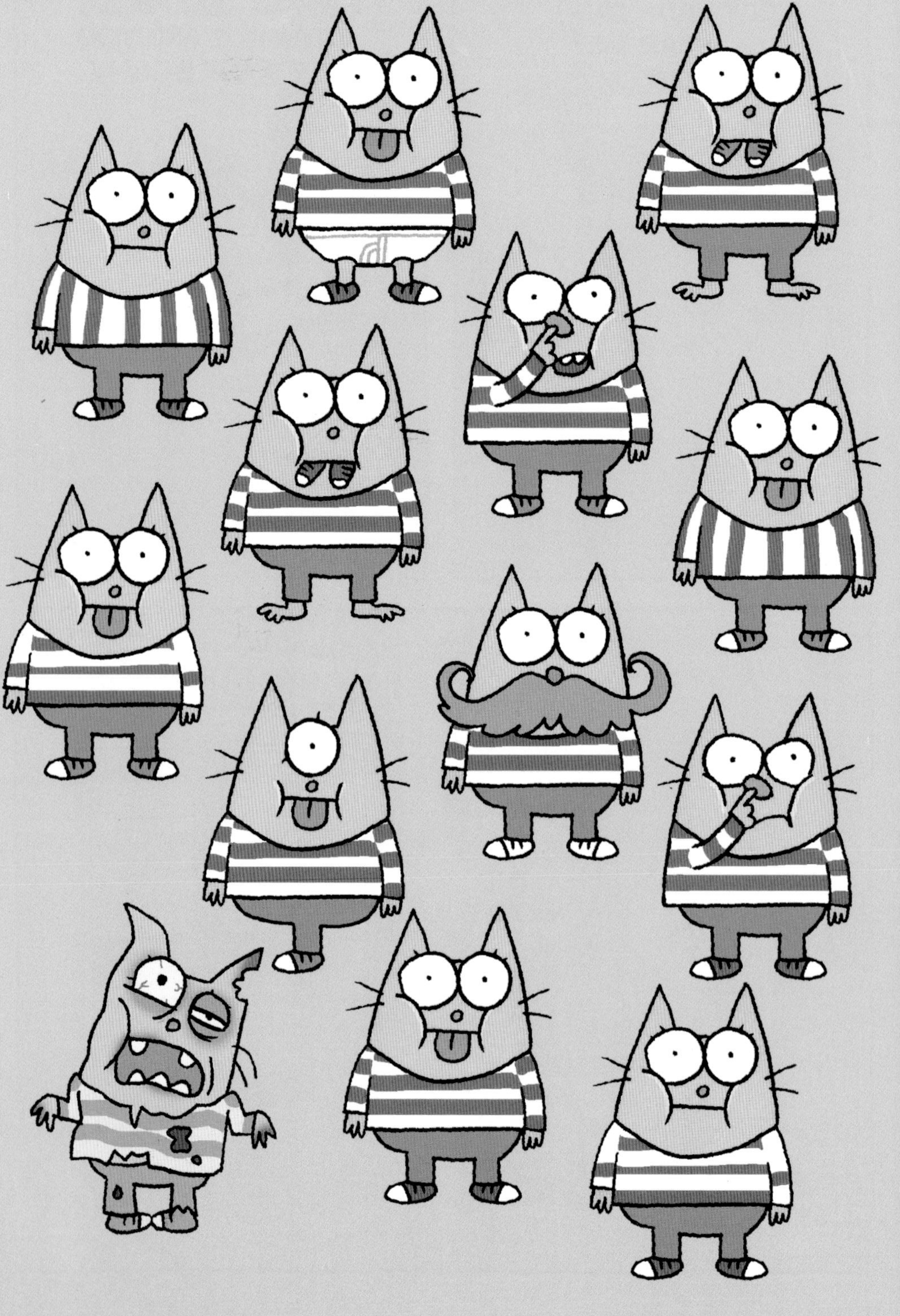

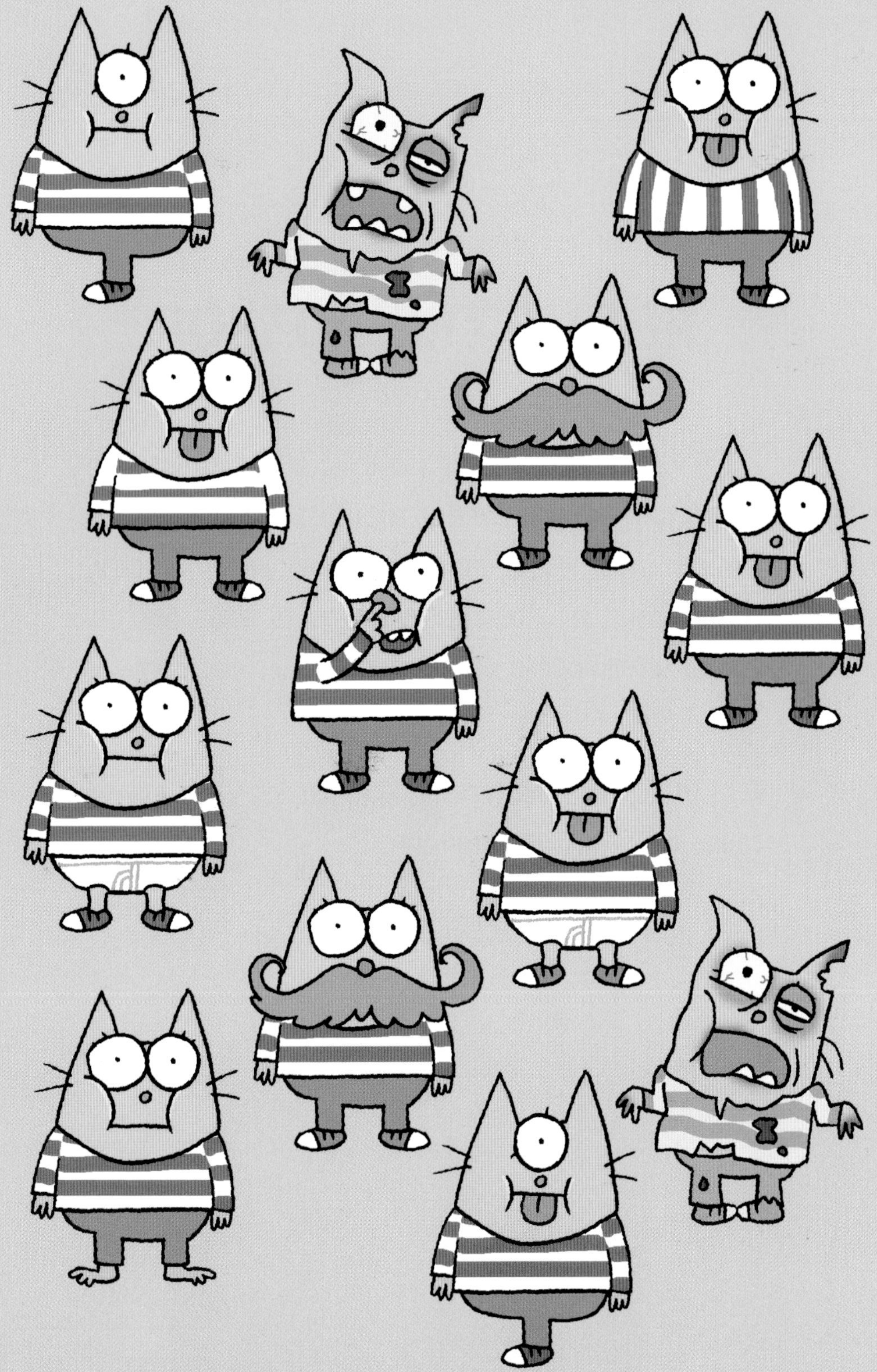

ABOUT THE AUTHOR

JIM BENTON IS AN AWARD-WINNING AUTHOR AND ARTIST. YOU MAY KNOW SOME OF THE OTHER THINGS HE'S MADE, LIKE *IT'S HAPPY BUNNY*, *DEAR DUMB DIARY*, *FRANNY K. STEIN*, *VICTOR SHMUD*, AND MORE. HE'S CREATED A TV SERIES, WRITTEN BOOKS, AND PRODUCED A MOVIE, AND HE'S CATWADDY HALF OF THE TIME AND BLURMPY THE OTHER HALF.

JIM LIVES IN MICHIGAN WITH HIS WIFE AND KIDS AND CAN BE FOUND ONLINE AT JIMBENTON.COM.